OFF THE BOOKS

Lucy Arlington

BERKLEY PRIME CRIME, NEW YORK

BERKLEY
PRIME
CRIME

An imprint of Penguin Random House LLC
375 Hudson Street, New York, New York 10014

OFF THE BOOKS

A Berkley Prime Crime Book / published by arrangement with the author

ISBN: 978-0-425-27667-9

PUBLISHING HISTORY
Berkley Prime Crime mass-market edition / February 2016

PRINTED IN THE UNITED STATES OF AMERICA

10 9 8 7 6 5 4 3 2

Cover art by Julia Green.
Cover design by Lesley Worrell.
Interior text design by Tiffany Estreicher.

Penguin
Random
House

To booksellers everywhere
who dedicate their time
to sharing the magic of a good story.
Thank you.

Chapter 1

I LOVED WINTERTIME IN THE QUAINT HAMLET OF INSPI-
ration Valley, especially when it snowed, which wasn't often.
Our little village, with its neat clapboard cottages and brick-
front businesses, was nestled deep in North Carolina's Balsam
Mountains, which protected us from the moist southern winds
and kept us dry for most of the winter months. But today, snow
was falling in big silver flakes, blanketing the ground like a
loosely crocheted afghan and giving the Valley the magical
appearance of a freshly shaken snow globe.

"Don't worry, everyone. This snow isn't going to damper
our week," my boss, Bentley Burlington-Duke, founder and
president of Novel Idea Literary Agency, declared from the
driver's seat. We were returning to the Valley after picking
up a couple of authors from the airport located in nearby
Dunston. Tomorrow was the opening day of our agency's
weeklong event, Booked for a Wedding, which was to feature
a unique combination of literary and bridal events. "Neither

rain, nor sleet, nor this darn snow will keep our agency from holding every single event this week. We fully intend to make sure the show goes on no matter what. Isn't that right, Lila?" she added, throwing me a resolute look.

I nodded and turned toward the murmur of chuckles Bentley's string of mangled clichés brought from the two authors in the backseat. Bentley was a keenly determined businesswoman. Leave it to her to think she could control everything about this week's schedule, including Mother Nature.

"I can't wait for things to get started," said Jodi Lee, author of *The Billionaire's Bride*. "What a brilliant idea to combine a bridal expo and books." Her compliment brought a murmur of appreciation from Bentley, who loved it when someone recognized, and acknowledged, the brilliance behind her marketing schemes. And brilliant she was. When I joined Novel Idea Literary Agency a couple of years ago, I was intimidated by her authoritative presence. But since then, I'd come to admire her tenacious drive and sharp business instinct, which had helped scores of authors realize their dreams.

"Not me. I'm so nervous," admitted Lynn Werner, my client who was a new author with the firm. "Especially for my presentation. I've never really talked in front of a crowd before, or read my work out loud to anyone."

"You'll be fine," I assured her. "We'll practice a few times before your talk." I'd just signed her the previous summer for her novel, *Murder and Marriage*, which had been retitled *Wed 'til Dead*. I thought the snappy title was the perfect fit for her cleverly written cozy mystery. "Besides," I told her, "everyone's going to love it. I think it'll be a big seller."

"Think?" Bentley bellowed. "Novel Idea only represents successful books. *Wed 'til Dead* will be a bestseller. That's what this week is all about, Lynn. Getting your name out there in front of readers' eyes. That way, when your book does release, you'll have a ready-made audience."

Lynn quickly tucked a strand of brown hair under her stocking cap and let out a nervous sigh. I felt for her. Most authors experienced newbie jitters. It wasn't easy putting your work out there for everyone's judgment. And public appearances were just one more intimidating task for most writers. Mostly because, by nature, authors tended to be introverts. But it was a necessity of the business, especially for an unknown author like Lynn. She needed to build name recognition before her novel was released this spring.

"Oh, don't worry about a thing," Jodi said, waving her mittened hand through the air. "You'll get used to public speaking. Besides, book readers are some of the friendliest people around. You're going to have a blast this week."

I smiled appreciatively. Her kind words seemed to put Lynn at ease. Jodi, a bestselling romantic suspense author, was represented by my coworker, Flora Merriweather. Flora had sung her praises: "She's the easiest client ever, always so positive and upbeat, easy to work with . . ." Now I could see what Flora meant. I'd only just met Jodi, but I already liked her sunny attitude. Even her choice in outerwear, a cheery pink puffy jacket topped off with pom-pom toboggan in fuchsia with purple snowflakes, was bright and cheerful.

"We've booked you both rooms at the Magnolia Bed and Breakfast," I said, steering the conversation in a different direction. "I think you'll both be comfortable there. It's a lovely old Victorian on the edge of the village and the owner is such a gracious hostess."

"That sounds wonderful," Lynn replied. "I don't remember it being open when I lived in the area."

Bentley glanced in the rearview mirror. "When was that again?"

"It's been about five years since I moved to the coast. I actually used to live in Dunston. I haven't been back since I left."

Bentley nodded, carefully maneuvering the vehicle over the snowy pavement as we turned onto Sweet Pea Road. "In that case, the Magnolia probably wasn't open when you were here. Cora Scott—that's the owner—only opened a couple of years ago after several years of remodeling. She put a substantial amount of money into it, too, but I think she's making a good return on her investment. The place is constantly booked."

"Is that it?" Jodi asked, pointing to a tall domed turret peeking above the trees. She followed up her question with a long "Awww" as we rounded the corner and pulled up to what we locals sometimes referred to as "The Grand Lady."

"I can see where it gets its name," Lynn commented, staring out at the pink and white exterior of the home. "It reminds me of the blossoms on the magnolia tree in my mother's backyard. Such a gorgeous pink color. It's exquisite."

My thoughts traveled across the same lines, and I realized how lucky the town was that Cora had swooped in and rescued the place. In the 1970s, during the Illumination Valley days, when our town was a haven for nonconformists and freethinkers, the historic Victorian was occupied by a group who let the place fall into disrepair. Then, after a couple of decades as a multi-rental unit, it was left abandoned for several years. Luckily, Cora came onto the scene and painstakingly restored its original glory with three stories of repaired white spindle work, freshly painted gables and turrets, and new carved pillars on the expansive front porch. And that was just the outside!

We'd just started unloading luggage when the front door popped open and Cora Scott came bustling outside to greet us.

"Welcome, welcome!" she called out, making her way down the small walk that connected the side carport to her front door. "I'm so glad you made it okay. Especially with this dreadful weather. How were the roads?" But before we could reply, she turned to our guests. "Let me help you with your bags. You two must be the authors I've heard so much about."

"Excuse me," I said, apologizing for my bad manners. "Cora, this is Lynn Werner and Jodi Lee. Ladies, this is Cora Scott, your charming hostess for the week."

Cora's deep brown eyes gleamed warmly as she shook their hands. A sturdily built woman, Cora had strong features that would have looked harsh on anyone else, but her sweet personality softened her face and made everyone around her feel instantly at ease. "Come in, come in," she said, motioning for us to follow her toward the house. "I've got a pot of tea on. Just the thing to warm you."

Once inside, she hung our coats in the front hall closet. Then she directed Bentley and me to the kitchen while she led the authors around the corner to where a small elevator was located. Cora had possessed the foresight to install it during renovations, knowing that two flights of stairs might not be easy for her guests to manage, especially with luggage.

I'd been in the Magnolia Bed and Breakfast a handful of times, but the magnificence of its intricate woodwork and ornate furnishings never ceased to impress me. Admittedly, though, there was a certain heaviness to it all that made me glad for the simpler lines of my sunny cottage on Walden Woods Circle. Still, as I followed Bentley's determined footsteps toward the kitchen at the back of the house, it was hard to resist the urge to stop and ponder the magnificent details of the antique book stand that held the guest registry or the skilled needlepoint design on a nearby Rococo armchair.

"Pam!" Bentley gushed as soon as we entered the kitchen.

A thin, dark-haired woman rose from the kitchen seating area and grasped Bentley's outstretched hands. They exchanged a series of cheeky air kisses and traded comments on how great each looked. Bentley adored Pamela Fox. Her popular erotic series, The Reluctant Brides of Babylon, had hit the top ten of the *New York Times* bestsellers list last year, which succeeded in propelling Pam to the top of Bentley's list also.

We settled into the padded seating built into an octagon area formed by the large turret that ran up the back side of the house. The nook was surrounded by windows framed in pretty yellow and blue fleur-de-lis valances that matched the padding on the built-in benches. To me, this was the best feature of the home: a bright, sunny spot for guests to lounge with a cup of coffee. Much more comfortable than the adjacent formal dining area with its dark oak table and thick Oriental rug of burgundy and forest green.

"I hope you slept well last night," Bentley said to Pam, serving herself from the antique tea set arranged in the middle of the table. I skipped the tea but snagged a roll.

"Everything has been just wonderful," Pam said, cringing at the sound of hammering coming from the opposite side of the kitchen. "Except for that."

"What is that?" Bentley asked, twisting her head to locate the source.

Pam covered her ears lightly. "Apparently the owner is having some shelving put up in the pantry. She mentioned it yesterday when I checked in; I just never expected it to start so early in the morning."

I glanced at my watch. It was nearly ten o'clock here, but Pam arrived yesterday from California, which meant it was really only seven o'clock her time. Poor thing. I leaned in and raised my voice over the pounding. "The last of the authors just arrived," I told her. "They're getting settled but should be down in a minute. We wanted to make sure you're introduced before we leave. But someone will be back around twelve thirty to pick you up for today's meeting." Bentley had set an organizational meeting for one o'clock at the James Joyce Pub. There would be over a dozen authors participating in the week's events, so organizing and keeping track of everyone was going to be a challenge.

"I'm looking forward to meeting everyone," Pam practically shouted. The noise coming from the pantry seemed to be growing louder. "There's only a few of us here; where are the others staying?"

"At Bertram's Hotel," Bentley replied, her lips tight with annoyance. "It's not as nice as this place, but it certainly might be quieter. Maybe we should consider moving you there."

As if in response, the hammering suddenly ceased. Pam tipped back her head and chuckled. "Bertram's Hotel? Like in the Agatha Christie book? No thanks! If I remember correctly, things didn't go all that well for the guests at Bertram's. So, I think I'll stay here. At least we know there won't be any dead bodies." She pointed toward the pantry. "Unless Mr. Hammer Happy wakes me up again at some ungodly hour tomorrow."

We all laughed. Just then Cora came into the kitchen with Lynn and Jodi on her heels. "Make yourselves comfortable, ladies. I'll get some fresh tea." She started rifling through the kitchen cabinets as Bentley made a round of introductions. Just as I'd hoped, the ladies seemed to get along well, instantly settling into a comfortable conversation about their hometowns and the books they liked to read. Vicky Crump, our ever-efficient office manager, had asked my opinion when she was setting up accommodations for everyone. During renovations, Cora had combined two of the bedrooms into a large living suite for herself, leaving three spacious en suite rooms to rent to guests, so I'd specifically asked that these three authors be placed together. I wanted Lynn to have the experience of being around more seasoned authors. It looked like I'd chosen the right mentors for her.

"I'll have you know," Cora started, setting the teakettle to boil on the stove, "I plan on attending all the events this week, even the wine tasting." She let out a little giggle as she uncapped a glass jar and started measuring loose tea into a diffuser. "Good thing I got my tickets when I did; I hear all the events sold out."

Bentley rubbed her hands together and smiled. "That's right. Undoubtedly it will be another successful venture for our agency."

To some, Bentley came off as overconfident, brash even, but in my mind, she'd earned the right to pat herself on the back. Before Bentley arrived, the town's businesses had all but dried up during a hard-hitting recession. When she relocated her literary agency from New York to our humble village, it sparked renewed interest in the area. Soon all the businesses jumped on the bandwagon, changing the town's name to Inspiration Valley and adopting literary-themed names for many of the small shops. Now our agency's events drew crowds from all over the country.

Just then the racket started up again, pulling me from my thoughts. "Oh my goodness," Cora said. "I didn't realize just how much noise this project would make. Let me ask him to take a little break while we enjoy some tea."

"No more for us," Bentley said, standing and glancing at her watch. "We've got to get over to the Arts Center and make sure things are on track there." We were holding most of the events at the Marlette Robbins Center for Fine Arts, a large facility recently built on the edge of town.

Cora nodded, but still headed off, I assumed to talk to

the Hammer Man. I stood and pushed in my chair, resisting the urge to grab another roll for the road, and started following Bentley toward the door. At the last minute, she turned back to the table of authors and donned her business face. "Please know that every single agent at Novel Idea is here to assist you in any way—"

A metallic jingling sound interrupted the start of her spiel. We turned to see Cora leading a handsome middle-aged man our way. He was clad in jeans and a fitted T-shirt and wore a leather tool belt strapped around his waist. As he approached, his friendly smile faded and his eyes narrowed. I turned to see the object of his sudden switch in attitude and saw Lynn staring back with a wide-eyed expression. "Chuck?" she said, a slight tremble to her lower lip.

"Hello, Lynn. It's been a while."

My head ping-ponged between the two of them. This must be someone Lynn knew from when she lived in the area, but judging from the look on her face, she certainly wasn't happy to see the guy.

"Oh, so you two already know each other," Cora gushed. "Everyone else, this is Chuck Richards. Chuck's helping me redo the butler's pantry. It's one of those projects I never got to when I renovated the rest of the kitchen." She swept her hand around the room's antique white cabinetry, granite counters, and state-of-the-art appliances with pride. Who could blame her? She'd done a marvelous job updating, while still maintaining much of the original integrity of the room. Her expression suddenly sobered. "But I am so sorry for the timing. I just hate it that everyone has to endure the noisiness. But Chuck was supposed to have started a couple of days before you all arrived. And"—she offered an apologetic shrug to us while tipping her head at him—"he promised the project wouldn't take more than a day, two tops."

Chuck shook his head. "I never promise. I estimate. And my previous job took longer than expected. And, actually, it's looking like yours will now take two or three days." He raised his palms upward. "Sorry, ladies, but you'll just have to put up with the noise a little longer."

Bentley eyed him pointedly. "I tell you what . . . uh, Chuck. The authors will be out this afternoon at a meeting, so you can make all the noise you want then. But it just won't do to have them constantly disturbed by this racket for the next couple of days. They'll need to be well rested and on top of their game for all the events. You could work out a schedule over, say, the next four days around their events so that—"

"I don't really have time to work out a schedule around your events," Chuck said, folding his arms across his chest and leveling his gaze on Bentley. "I've got other jobs this week and I'm trying to wrap things up because I've got a trip planned." He sighed. "And last week, I took on a contract to do maintenance for the Arts Center. I'm a busy man."

Bentley cast a furtive look Cora's way. "Can't this project wait for a while?"

Chuck shifted and gave her a hard glare. I knew Bentley was just being . . . well, Bentley. She knew no boundaries when it came to making things right for her authors and probably didn't realize how officious her comments were sounding. Or, maybe she did. It would be just like Bentley to think she could change the handyman's and Cora's schedules to better suit her authors.

Cora answered with a shake of her head. "I'm afraid I'm booked solid for the next two months. I wouldn't know when to get it done."

Bentley drew in her breath and took a step forward. As quickly as I could, I stepped in and grabbed hold of her arm, while glancing at my watch. "You wanted to stop by the Arts

Center to check on the other agents' progress before heading over to the pub for the meeting, right?" It would be prudent to get her out of there before she said something even more offensive. I gently coaxed her away from Chuck before she could even switch gears to answer me. "Thank you for the tea, Cora. No need to see us out. We can manage just fine." I cast a waning smile at Chuck as we passed by on our way to the front hall closet to retrieve our coats.

Bundled up and back outside again, Bentley turned to me. "Why'd you usher me out like that, Lila? I had something more I wanted to say to that arrogant jerk in there."

No doubt. But telling her that she couldn't boss around someone else's hired help would only aggravate the situation. So instead I said, "With this snow and all, I know you didn't want to be late to the Arts Center, right?"

Bentley stood a little straighter. "Absolutely."

"Then we'd better get a move on."

"I guess you're right," Bentley relented. "Besides, if a little extra noise is the only problem we have this week, then we'll be in good shape."

Chapter 2

BY ONE O'CLOCK THAT AFTERNOON WE WERE GATHERED in the James Joyce Pub, a cozy, wood-paneled bar and grill located just down the street from the agency. The other agents and I often came here for business lunches, finding it easier to hash out contract details or divvy up assignments for upcoming author events over a pitcher of ale and a hearty bowl of Irish stew.

Today, I was seated at a table with my friend and fellow agent Flora Merriweather, who was raving about the shepherd's pie. "You should really try this, Lila. The crust is just so flaky, and the meat . . ." She took a quick bite and rolled her eyes. "*Mmm . . .* so tender."

Next to her, Jodi nodded in agreement. "It is divine. Does everyone in this town cook this well? The rolls Cora served with tea this morning were out of this world."

"I'd say," agreed Pam. "If I keep eating like this, I'm not going to fit into my jeans by the end of the week."

I squinted at her slim figure and sighed, wondering if she seriously ever had to worry about her weight. "I believe Cora orders those from the Sixpence Bakery. Nell, the owner, makes wonderful baked goods. But Cora is a good cook in her own right; she's . . ." My voice trailed off as I noticed that Lynn was only picking at her food. She'd hardly said a word since we'd arrived. "Is your food okay, Lynn?"

Her head popped up. "What?" Then, noticing that everyone was staring, she sighed and put down her fork. "I'm sorry to be such a downer. I have something on my mind, that's all."

I wanted to ask if that something, or rather someone, was the handyman whom she'd seemed to recognize earlier that morning, but Bentley's voice interrupted. "Excuse me. If I can have your attention, please. Welcome, authors, to Inspiration Valley and to Novel Idea's exclusive event, Booked for a Wedding. I'm proud to announce that, thanks to my hard-working agents, this week's events are completely sold out!"

A round of applause erupted across the room. Bentley glanced over the rims of her bejeweled reading glasses and signaled toward our sports and screenplay agent, Zach Cohen, who stood and scooped up a thick stack of papers. "I'm sending around an itinerary of this week's events," Bentley continued. "Please take note of your assignments."

I smiled and accepted my copy of the itinerary from Zach and glanced over the schedule. The sheer number of vendor booths and events scheduled for this week was dizzying. Thank goodness, the other agents and I had been able to convince Bentley to bring in an expert organization to help us coordinate this venture. Not that convincing Bentley was an easy task. True to her nature, she'd wanted the agency to take on the entire expo alone, but after a lot of arguing, and a threatened mutiny, Bentley wised up and hired Southern Belles

Bridal Company, a professional wedding exposition group out of Raleigh. Their people brought with them their own nationally based exhibitors and a professional setup team to help transform the Marlette Robbins Center into a professional venue. However, the best part of the package was the ability to add our own local flavor to the event. In addition to the plethora of national vendors and keynote speakers, Southern Belles Bridal sent one of their reps, Ms. Lambert, to act as a local liaison for our own business community.

As if on cue, the pub's door swung open and Ms. Lambert rushed in on a wintery blast of cold air, brushing snow from the faux-fur trim of her maxi coat. She shot Bentley an apologetic look and immediately headed for an empty chair at the head table. Jude Hudson, our agent representing thrillers and quite the lady thriller himself, immediately stood and pulled out her chair.

Bentley cleared her throat and continued, "Tomorrow is opening day and will commence with a meet and greet reception. There will be vendor booths set up throughout the Arts Center. We'll also have a table near the entrance stocked with your books for customers to purchase. Each one of you will have your own table, which our agents have already set up with everything you'll need to sign books as well as plenty of promotional materials to hand out to prospective readers. Remember, people, this is your chance to connect with your readers and sell your books." She paused for a second to shuffle papers. "In the queue for tomorrow's schedule is a reading from renowned author and local psychologist Dr. Sloan Meyers. She'll be reading from her blockbuster hit, *Strong Women: Strong Marriages*."

Everyone began clapping, their eyes drawn to the table where Dr. Meyers sat with Franklin Stafford, our nonfiction agent. He had several authors to keep track of this week, including a popular author of wedding craft books and a woman who'd written a top seller about budget-friendly weddings.

Bentley adjusted her glasses and continued, "Then, on Tuesday night, the main attraction will be our display of unique wedding cake creations from both local and statewide bakers."

"Yes, that's right." All eyes turned to Ms. Lambert, who'd stood and was now addressing the room in her sweet southern drawl. "And everyone in attendance will have a chance to taste these marvelous creations, too."

Bentley took a couple of steps forward, removed her readers, and leveled her gaze on the woman. "Thank you, Ms. Lambert," she said tightly. "Everyone, this is Ms. Trudy Lambert. She's the local coordinator from Southern Belles Bridal Company. Her organization is responsible for the wonderful setup you'll see later at the Marlette Robbins Center for Fine Arts." Bentley paused politely while everyone clapped for Ms. Lambert. "And right before the cake display and tasting"—she nodded toward the coordinator, who took the hint and sat back down—"patrons will be treated to a reading from one of our newest clients, Lynn Werner." Bentley pointed our way. "Ms. Werner is a promising writer of cozy mysteries. We thought her reading would appropriately accompany Tuesday's cake theme, since the murder victim in her mystery was found facedown in a wedding cake."

A chorus of spirited laughter broke across the room along with an enthusiastic round of clapping. Poor Lynn, not used to so much attention, shrank back in her chair, her face flushing. But she didn't have to endure the scrutiny for long, because a series of sharp yaps and high-pitched whimpers sounded from the other side of the pub's front door. Zach hurried over to investigate, opening the door and allowing a little brown and white dog to dart inside.

"Zach!" Bentley started to admonish, but stopped when the dog came to her side and pawed at her legs, whimpering and shivering. I held my breath, thinking surely Bentley would be upset that the pooch was pawing her designer trousers, but instead my usually fastidious boss bent over and rubbed her hand between the dog's fluffy ears. "Well, who do we have here?" she cooed. And then, "Oh my goodness, you're so cold. You poor thing." I watched in amazement as she squatted down lower, repositioned her readers on her nose, and leaned in to examine the dog's ID tag. "Olive. What a cute name."

Olive? That sounded familiar. Then I remembered that I'd seen this dog last summer at the pet shop down the street. Of course, it was just a puppy then, but how many Cavalier King Charles spaniels named Olive could there be in this town?

"Lila!" Bentley called out. "Go find this cutie pie's owner. This sweet little thing shouldn't be out in this snowy weather. We'll keep her here until you get back."

Cutie pie? Sweet little thing? That was a shocker. Bentley never used endearments. Who'd have thought our can't-keep-a-houseplant-watered, all-business boss would ever have a soft spot for animals? And a dog inside a restaurant? I wasn't sure how that was going to go over with the James Joyce Pub people. I shot a furtive glance at Flora, but she simply shrugged and offered to have the waitress keep my plate warm for me. So I slipped back into my coat and headed out in search of the dog's owner.

MY BREATH CAME out in sharp white bursts as I made my way up and down High Street, searching for anyone who might have lost a dog. I wasn't having much luck. Determined, though, I continued walking, passing by Sherlock Holmes Realty and the Sixpence Bakery. When I reached the corner, I decided to cut through the town's small center park, pausing for a second to admire the Nine Muses fountain. Even though the water had been drained in anticipation of colder weather, the fountain, with its nine beautiful goddesses, was still awe-inspiring. Today, the goddesses seemed to have dressed for the weather, the snow making it appear like they were wearing white shawls and fluffy caps.

Then, as I gazed in wonderment, the sun peeked out from behind a cloud, causing the snow to sparkle like diamonds. Like magic, their shawls and caps were transformed into dazzling sequined attire, fit for a wedding party. I couldn't help but let my mind wander to visions of my own dazzling yet-to-be-chosen wedding gown—maybe I'd find the perfect one this week! Along with my work duties, I hoped to get a lot of personal wedding planning done with my best friend and our local barista, Makayla. To our delight, we'd both become engaged just last summer. Which made planning our weddings double the fun.

On an impulse, I opened my cell and called my fiancé, Detective Sean Griffiths. I apologized for calling him at work, but he said he was glad to take a break from his paperwork. He was immediately concerned whether I was calling because of still feeling blue. Ever since Christmas break ended and my son, Trey, had headed back to UNC Wilmington, I'd been a bit in the dumps. "If you're thinking about Trey, don't worry, Lila. I'm sure he's doing fine. Besides, it'll be spring break before you know it and then he'll be back and eating you out of house and home."

I laughed. So true. Trey had recently developed an interest in cooking, and his new hobby had taken its toll on my food budget. "Actually," I said, "Bentley's got us all hopping

enough that I haven't had time to worry as much about Trey."
Then I told Sean about my hunt for the wayward dog's owner,
and he suggested calling the pet store, where I'd seen what I
thought might be the same puppy last summer. If it was the
same dog, they might have records on the buyer.

But I didn't need to call. I glanced across the street and
noticed the lights were on at All Creatures, Feathered and
Furry. The store wasn't usually open on Sundays, but it looked
like the owner, Matt, might be in doing a little extra work.

"Hello, Matt?" I called out, entering through the shop's
main door. The place appeared to be empty. "Matt?"

Somewhere in the back of the store I heard a soft swishing
noise. I made my way down the cat toy aisle, my eyes catching here and there on new little treats I'd love to buy for Eliot,
an orphaned cat our office manager, Vicky, had introduced to
the agency last summer. "Matt?" I called out again. "It's Lila."

"I'm back here," he answered.

I finally found him in the back corner of the store near the
puppy and kitty area. He was stooped over sweeping up water
and broken glass. Pieces of splintered wood and sea coral lit-
tered the floor around him. "Oh no! What happened?"

He stopped sweeping and glared up at me. My stomach
gave a little lurch. With his larger-than-a-linebacker size, Matt
was an imposing figure under any circumstances, but I'd never
seen him look angry before. It was more than a little intimidating. "I'll tell you what happened. That menacing little mutt
killed half my fish. Look at all this damage! Do you know
how much this setup cost me?"

"Olive?" I asked, my eyes roaming to what must have
been a very large saltwater aquarium. It looked like the
stand had been tipped over. "You think Olive did this?"

"Well, what should I think? I'd just come by to check on
a few things and when I opened the door that dog shot out

of here like a bat out of hell. Come over here," he said, leading me to the area where he kept puppies. "Look at this."

I'd always liked the way Matt set up his shop. He housed
only a few animals at a time, all of them "last chance" animals brought in from shelters across the state. He kept the
dogs in a large, open pen where they could trot around and
play together. "I've only got one cat and two other dogs right
now. They've been going home with me in the evenings and
on the weekends, but Olive . . ." His voice trailed off as he
shook his head and pointed down at the doorframe, which
looked like it'd been attacked by a shark. "That darn dog's
chewed it to the point where I can't even get the door to shut
anymore. That dog's such a pain in the—"

"I'm sorry, Matt. This looks like a huge mess. It's hard
to believe that one little dog could do this much damage."

He shook his head. "You don't even know the half of it.
You should see what she did to our house last time I took
her home. My wife is still upset about it. You know, I'm glad
that dog is gone. For all I care, she can fend for herself out
there on the streets!"

I had to keep from laughing at the absurdity of this statement. When I first met Matt I was taken aback, alarmed even,
by his imposing physical stature, immediately thinking of
Lennie Small, Steinbeck's lumbering character in *Of Mice
and Men*. Not a good thing, since Lennie often killed the
animals in his care. But as I'd come to know Matt, especially
the uncanny rapport he had with the animals in his store, I'd
begun to think of him more like Lofting's Dr. Dolittle. Admittedly, I sometimes caught myself wondering if Matt actually
did possess a secret ability to talk to animals. But one thing
I knew for sure: He cared. He cared for every animal he ever
came across, and Olive was no exception.

"Oh, is that so?" I bantered back. "Are you sure you don't care about what's happened to her?"

He suddenly looked concerned. "Why? Do you know where she is?"

I nodded.

"Where?"

"Thought you didn't care."

He shuffled a bit, the corners of his lips tugging into a little grin. "It's just that it's hard telling what type of trouble she might get into. I'd hate for her to bother anyone else."

"In that case, you should probably know that she's at the pub."

His eyes popped open. "At the pub? You mean outside the pub, right?"

"Nope. Inside."

"Oh for cryin' out loud!" He threw up his hands and headed straight for the door, pausing only to grab his jacket off the front counter. "I swear, this dog is going to be the death of me," he mumbled.

I bit my lip to keep from laughing and followed, struggling to keep up with his long-legged pace as we made our way back to the pub. When we got there, the authors were out on the curb, loading into the large SUVs Bentley had rented for the week to shuttle them around town. A man on a mission, Matt elbowed his way through the crowd and into the pub with me on his heels.

To my surprise, Bentley was still there, sitting in a chair with the dog on her lap. Franklin and Flora were there, too, both of them fawning over Olive. "There you are, Olive," Matt said, reaching down for the dog.

Bentley pulled Olive a little closer. "Aren't you the man who owns the pet store?"

I stepped forward. "Matt, this is Ms. Bentley Burlington-Duke, owner of Novel Idea Literary Agency. Bentley, Matt Reynolds." I introduced Flora and Franklin, too, while I reached down and scratched between willing ears. "It seems Olive escaped from the store earlier. Matt's been looking everywhere for her."

Matt shot me an appreciative look and reached again for the dog. "I can take her now. Thank you for keeping her safe, Ms. Duke."

"Bentley, please." My boss smiled warmly at Matt but made no move to hand the dog over.

Matt dropped his hands and shuffled awkwardly. Flora and I exchanged a surprised look. This was the calmest we'd seen Bentley in almost a month. Even though we'd brought in a professional service to facilitate the wedding portion of Booked for a Wedding, there was still a lot of ground to cover just preparing for and managing the authors and their tasks. Not to mention that Bentley and Ms. Lambert, the coordinator from Southern Belles Bridal Company . . . Well, let's just say there were one too many lionesses in the den. All this, plus the unexpected snow, made for a lot of stress. But watching Bentley now, nestling the sweet little fluff ball of a dog, you'd think she didn't have a care in the world.

"You know," Franklin, our nonfiction expert, said, "just last year, I signed on the most wonderful author. He wrote this book about how dogs improve our lives." He adjusted the cashmere scarf tied around his neck. Franklin was the most senior agent at Novel Idea and a true southern gentleman at heart. I noticed that his normally fluffy gray hair was tamer than usual and his matching mustache neatly trimmed. He must have made a trip to the barber in preparation for this week's events. "Just a marvelous book," he continued. "And if I remember correctly, he'd cited many professionals who claim that owning a dog reduces stress. Even helps lower blood pressure."

"That's right," Bentley concurred. "I remember that book. What was its title again?"

"*Get a New Leash on Life*," Franklin said, tipping his chin up slightly. "A bestseller, of course."

"Of course," Bentley resounded.

"I completely agree with that theory," Matt stated. "Except when it comes to Olive. You see, Olive is a handful, I'm afraid."

"A handful?" Bentley narrowed her eyes. "What do you mean? She seems perfect to me."

"She usually does. It's only after you get to know her that her true personality shines through. In fact, she's been returned twice now."

"Returned?" Bentley clutched Olive little tighter. "Whatever for?"

I eyed the pup, thinking about the chewed doorframe and the demolished fish tank. I knew why. Despite her sweet face and innocent brown eyes, this adorable little spaniel was a tornado of destruction.

Then I heard Bentley saying, "I think I'll volunteer to be her foster mommy this week. I've been under a lot of stress lately, and if what Franklin says is true, this little pup will be good for me."

Matt drew in a deep breath. "You might want to reconsider. Olive's not at all the typical Cavalier King Charles spaniel. She's needy, demands a lot of attention, and barks and whines when she doesn't get her way."

Bentley held the dog at arm's length and stared into her deep brown eyes. "Well, I can see why she would. She knows she's too adorable to be ignored or not get her way, don't you think?"

No one answered. Flora and I looked at each other, both of us no doubt thinking the same thing: It seemed that Olive and Bentley had a lot in common.

Chapter 3

AS SOON AS I OPENED THE TRUCK'S DOOR MONDAY morning, I was affronted by a blast of heat and about a hundred decibels of Patsy Cline's soulful voice. "Loud enough, Mama?" I asked, shoving aside a couple of full grocery bags and climbing into the passenger side of her 1970s turquoise pickup truck.

"What's that, darlin'?" she shouted.

I reached over, turned down the radio, and settled back into the seat with a sigh. "Nothing. Good morning, Mama."

"Good mornin', sug. Beautiful outside, isn't it? Looks like someone shook a white bedsheet over the world."

I smiled, thinking she'd just come up with the perfect analogy. "I don't think I ever remember it snowing this much in the Valley." The tires crunched over the packed road as we pulled away from the curb. I waved at my neighbor, Mrs. Bailey, who was outside sweeping snow off her front steps.

"Thanks again for the ride, Mama. I wasn't sure how the Vespa would handle on these roads."

"Don't mention it. Needed a few things from the store anyhow."

I glanced into one of the paper bags from our local grocery store, How Green Was My Valley. "Looks like you're cooking for a crowd. Are you having a party or something?"

She chuckled tightly, her eyes darting my way for a second. "A party? Why, no, sugar." Another chuckle. "I'm just workin' on a few recipes, that's all." She chuckled a little more, which was one too many chuckles. I narrowed my eyes, wondering what was going on, but thought better than to ask. As busy as my schedule was this week, it might be better not to know.

She tapped a container on the seat. "Made a little too much banana bread yesterday. Thought you and the other agents might need some extra fuel to start your busy week."

I snatched up the container and thanked her. Mama made the most amazing banana bread in the world. In fact, "amazing" was the word people used to describe everything about my mother, including her special gift. "Do you have a busy workday planned?" Mama, or the Amazing Althea as most people called her, earned her living as a psychic advisor, specializing in tarot cards and palm readings.

"Reckon I will. That's not my prediction, mind you. I'm just goin' on what Flora told me."

"Flora?" What was she talking about?

"That friend of yours from the agency."

I drew in a deep breath and exhaled slowly. "I know who Flora is. What does she have to do with your work today?"

The back tire slid a little as Mama downshifted and made a turn onto one of the snow-packed side streets. "She didn't tell you? I'm working at the expo all week."

"You're what?"

"I'll be helpin' one of the authors, Pam somethin' or another. Flora said her books have a fortune-teller in them. Said that's why the books are so popular. Seems Pam's readers are fascinated with people like me. People with the gift." She lifted her head slightly. "Anyway, Flora thought it would be interestin' if I sat at Pam's table and offered readings to folks, kind of like I was the fortune-teller in the books."

"Have you ever read one of Pam Fox's books?"

Mama shook her head. "Can't say that I have. But they must be good. She's a bestseller, right?"

"Uh-huh." I pressed my lips together, trying not to crack a smile. Yes, Pam was a bestseller, but I wasn't sure it was the fortune-teller that kept people turning the pages as much as the hot romance. Nonetheless, I had to admit, Flora was a genius. Bringing to life one of Pam's characters? Well, that was simply brilliant. Readers were going to be drawn to Pam's table like flies to honey. Although I wasn't sure I liked the idea of my mother being put on display in such a manner. "You're not going to be wearing a costume, are you?" Hopefully Flora hadn't decided to dress her up like a snake charmer.

"A costume? Why would I need a costume?"

Thank goodness. "You don't. You're perfect just the way you are," I said, glancing across the seat. Underneath her long parka and fur-lined boots, I knew she was more than likely wearing her normal attire: an ankle-length skirt well suited to her tall figure, paired with a flowing blouse in a rich hue of either purple or gold—majestic colors, according to Mama. Today she'd taken extra care to tie her long silver hair back in a braid and accent her wrists and fingers with turquoise jewelry.

She adjusted the knob for the defroster and said, "Startin' a new life with someone can be unsettlin' for a lot of people.

Maybe something I tell one of the brides might bring a little comfort for them or keep them from makin' a terrible mistake."

I sat a little straighter. "A mistake? What do you mean?" But I knew what she meant. I thought back to my own wedding, when Mama came rushing in at the last moment, a tarot card in hand and a dire warning on her lips. "Don't marry him, sugar," she'd warned. "He's going to break your heart. It's right here in the cards."

"You can't do that, Mama. Even if you get a bad reading off someone, you can't tell them not to get married. That's not what this week's all about. It's supposed to be a positive experience for the attendees."

"Well, I can't very well let them go off and make the mistake of a lifetime, now, can I? It's my duty, after all—the burden that I carry for havin' the gift." She sighed dramatically. "Anyway, I'm just the messenger. It's really the cards that hold the answers."

I rolled my eyes and wondered if Flora knew what she'd signed up for when she asked Mama to *act* the part of a fortune-teller. She probably thought that was all there was to my mother's gift: acting. Not that I blamed Flora. As much as I hated to admit it, I often found myself torn between being skeptical of my mama's gift and in awe of her uncannily accurate predictions.

I rubbed at the knot forming on the back of my neck. Fortunately, we were pulling onto High Street and the agency was just ahead. "Just drop me at the door," I told her. "And thanks for the ride."

Mama carefully maneuvered through the back lot and alongside the stairs that led up to the agency. She put the truck in gear and turned my way. "Say, darlin', do you have a few minutes?"

I glanced at my watch and then longingly toward the back door of Espresso Yourself, the local coffee shop located just below our agency. I'd hoped to have enough time to pop in, say hello to the owner and my best friend, Makayla, and grab a caramel latte to start my busy day. I sighed. "Sure, Mama. What is it?"

She hesitated. "Oh, nothin' that can't wait, I suppose. You go along now. I'll be seein' you this afternoon at the Arts Center."

I leaned across the seat, gave her a quick peck on the cheek, and grabbed my banana bread, which was going to go great with my coffee. "Love you, Mama," I said, sliding out the door.

ABOUT FIFTEEN MINUTES later, I settled behind my desk with a caramel latte and a slice of Mama's banana bread. I only had a couple of hours to get some real work done before our normal Monday morning status meeting.

I flipped on my computer. While it warmed up, I eyed with mixed emotions a pile of queries Vicky had placed on my desk. While it appeared to be nothing more than a stack of papers, I knew each query held the hopes and dreams of its creator. Authors poured their hearts into their stories, hoping to one day see their work published. I'd love to be able to make that dream come true for every author; unfortunately only the best-written queries would make it to the next level.

The first few were rejections, one so badly written I had to wonder why it made the cut in the first place. I set it aside, meaning to ask Vicky about it later. Usually she was more thorough when vetting queries, but maybe there was something she saw in this one that I'd missed. The next few were well written, just not what the market was calling for at the moment.

I kept sorting, making piles on my desk, until I came to a query
that caught my eye.

Dear Ms. Wilkins,

*Prominent flapper and unrestrained party girl Zelda
Gray is a regular at the Forty-Sixth Street Speakeasy.
After all, the raucous club secreted away above Luigi's
Ristorante is simply the bee's knees. The jazz is lively,
the illicit booze flows freely, and the patrons party like
there's no tomorrow. Which there isn't for vaudeville
singer Doris Shaw, who's found in the back room blud-
geoned to death with a bottle of bootlegged whiskey.
Unfortunately, witnesses claim they saw Zelda and
Doris arguing just moments before Doris is discovered
murdered. Zelda soon finds that being the main suspect
in a murder case is a sobering situation. Will she be
able to ditch her glad rags and get down to business in
time to prove her own innocence? Or will her next party
be in the pokey?*

My 78,000-word completed novel, Death of the
Dame, *will provide a roaring good read for mystery
fans. I earned a BA in history from Northwestern Uni-
versity and worked as a staff writer for . . .*

This one really made me sit up and take notice. First of
all, while it was short and succinct, it still gave me a good
feel for the author's voice. It also had a great hook. Thanks
to a resurging interest in *The Great Gatsby*, everything
1920s was big right now, so this theme might really pique
readers' interest. I set it aside, planning to contact the author
and ask for the first couple of chapters. Hopefully, the manuscript would live up to this promising query.

After finishing the rest of the queries, I started in on a stack of royalty statements, reviewing each and double-checking the statements against the checks being paid out to authors. Since my client list had grown, this task was becoming more time consuming. Not that I minded. More clients meant more money for the agency. And I was glad to pull my weight.

I'd just turned back to my computer when Eliot, our feline office mascot, wandered into my office and jumped onto my desk. "Why, hello there, handsome," I said, scratching the cream-colored tuft of hair under his chin until he purred. "Have you come to help me read my emails?" Then I laughed as he answered by rubbing his face against the edge of my computer monitor before plopping on top of a pile of papers.

The first email to catch my attention was from an editor for a series I'd signed last summer. The initial submission, a cozy mystery about a woman who designed doggie apparel, had a great plot but lacked direction. I did, however, like the author's writing so I'd offered to represent her. Then we'd worked together the rest of the summer, rewriting the book to emphasize more of the pet angle and brainstorm synopses for two more possible books in the series. The end result was dubbed the Trendy Tails Mysteries and was snatched in the first round of submission for a three-book deal.

Now it looked like the cover art was done for the first book. Excitedly, I clicked on the email and opened the attachment. "Yes!" I said, delighted with the image that filled my screen. I was glad to see that the artist chose to feature both the poodle and the corgi on the front cover, each in a cute doggie sweater. Certainly readers would be drawn in by such a wonderful depiction. I sent the editor a quick note telling her how much I liked the artwork and then forwarded the cover to the author. I knew she'd love it, too.

After clicking send, I stood, stretched a little, and then walked over to my office window and rubbed a circle on the pane. While quaint-looking, the older six-over-six window frosted over at the first sign of cold weather, blocking my view of High Street and all the goings-on outside the office. But today I pressed my nose against the clear spot and let my eyes feast on the bucolic scene before me. Snow had gathered in the crevices of the brick-front buildings and on the boughs of the evergreens, making the entire town look like a white-frosted gingerbread village. Against the all-white backdrop, brightly clad townspeople moved about, adding a dash of color to an otherwise monochromatic scene.

As my eye wandered up the walk, I spied my client Lynn in front of the Constant Reader. She was staring at the store's front window, which I knew contained many of our clients' books. The owner, Jay, who also happened to be one of our very own authors, was always supportive of the agency's efforts and had created a special display to showcase the authors participating in this week's expo. I wondered if Lynn was dreaming of the day she'd see her own book in a book-store window. The thought made me smile. A talented author like Lynn deserved the opportunity to have her work in readers' hands.

I was about to turn back to my own work when suddenly Lynn spun away from the window and started walking quickly down the sidewalk. Surprised by her sudden change in demeanor, I pressed against the window and stared after her. Halfway down the walk, Chuck Richards, the handyman I'd met yesterday at the Magnolia Bed and Breakfast, caught up to her. Almost immediately something exchanged between the two of them. A sort of heated anger bordering on abhorrence that could only exist between two people on intimate terms.

The emotion between them was so strong it was almost palpable even from where I was standing. Chuck was towering over her, his face twisted into an angry scowl as his arms gestured wildly. Who was this man? Her brother? An ex-boyfriend, perhaps? Then something changed. Lynn transformed right in front of my eyes, morphing from angry to defensive to withdrawn. She seemed to shrink into herself until her arms were wrapped around her midsection and her head hung down. Still Chuck hovered over her, his mouth forming angry, maybe hurtful, words, before he let go with one more wild gesture that caused Lynn to noticeably flinch.

"Lila. It's ten o'clock."

Turning, I found Vicky peering through the cracked door, Eliot rubbing against her ankles.

"Everything okay?" she asked.

I turned back to the window, rubbed away the newly generated frost, and glanced back down at the street. Both Lynn and Chuck were already gone. "I don't know," I answered, turning back to Vicky. "I'm worried about one of the authors."

"Which one?"

"My client, Lynn Werner," I started, but before I could explain more, I heard the sound of the office's main door opening.

"It's Bentley," Vicky said. Then she did a double take. "Oh, for Pete's sake. She brought a dog with her." Eliot stopped rubbing, his ears shooting straight upward before they started twitching. Then his back formed into an arch with spiked fur and tail jerking.

"Vicky!" Bentley bellowed from the reception area. "Please put Eliot in the break room. He's upsetting Olive."

"Olive?" Vicky echoed incredulously. Since Vicky hadn't attended yesterday's meeting at the James Joyce Pub, she'd missed Olive's grand entrance. Obviously, no one had filled her in on Bentley's newest acquisition. Now she was looking to me for an explanation, but I hated to be the bearer of bad news. And any rival for Eliot's coveted agency mascot position would certainly be bad news to Vicky. So I simply shrugged and turned away, busying myself with gathering files and paperwork I'd need for the status meeting. Behind me, I heard the scurried clicking of claws against the hardwood floors, then a loud hiss and a sharp doggie yelp, followed by Bentley's own form of barking: "Ms. Crump, get that cat into the break room now!"

I squeezed my eyes shut and took a deep breath. It looked like we were all in for a very long week.

Chapter 4

ENTERING THROUGH THE DOUBLE DOORS OF THE MAR-
lette Robbins Center for the Arts, I felt a mixture of emotions,
including pride that I'd had even a small, albeit roundabout,
part in creating this fine facility. The Arts Center, built on the
edge of town, now stood as a cornerstone to our community
activities, providing space and resources for artists of all
kinds. Although it was funded by the estate of a wonderfully
talented author named Marlette Robbins and existed only
because of his premature death, I knew in my heart that Marlette would be proud for two reasons. First, this building represented a lasting physical legacy of his love of this
community. And second, because his book, *The Alexandria
Society*, given wide acclaim after it was published posthu-
mously, had so skillfully touched the hearts of thousands.

But this wasn't the time to dwell on the past—we had new
authors to introduce to the world of publishing and to the
hearts of readers. So I focused instead on the remarkable

scene before me, which instantly filled my spirit with the joy
of my dream job as a literary agent. Our agency had worked
with Ms. Lambert's crew on and off last week to help transform the Arts Center into what we hoped would be both a
magical and informative expo for the brides who would be
in attendance this week. Now that I saw it all put together, I
couldn't help but smile at all we'd accomplished. Time and
time again, the creative energy and talents of our literary team
amazed me. I felt so fortunate to be a part of it all.

We'd strived to put a creative spin on the usual trade show
format used at many expos. Instead of using just the main
presentation hall, we'd lined the corridor with vendor booths
and even used a few of the smaller rooms to accommodate
displays. The Dragonfly Room, usually used for dance class,
would feature different venues throughout the week. Today,
it had been transformed into a romantic dining room show-
casing floral arrangements and gorgeous ideas for reception
tablescapes. The Textile Workshop Room housed displays of
bridal gowns, bridesmaid dresses, tuxes, and every sort of
wedding attire imaginable, while the smaller classrooms such
as the Potter's Room and Picasso's Studio were converted into
intimate spaces set with tables and seating areas where brides
could take a quiet break and enjoy a glass of champagne while
organizing their notes and wedding plans. However, what was
by far our best idea was the setup of the Arts Center's east
wing, which had an extensive commercial kitchen at one end.
The classrooms in this area would allow guests to visit wine
tasting booths, sample appetizers, and choose their favorite
dishes for their own reception menus.

After checking my coat, I started meandering down the
main corridor, stopping to admire a display of invitations.
I tossed a quick wave to Flora and Franklin, who were a
couple of booths down, chatting next to a display of dried

flower arrangements. My hand glided over the invitation samples and came to rest on a stack of handmade papers. I fingered the uneven texture of the natural fibers and admired the simplicity of the designs before an array of save-the-date postcards caught my eye. What a great idea! Of course, Sean and I hadn't actually set the date yet, but hopefully . . . Anyway, I'd have to show this to Makayla later.

A whoosh of cold air brought me back to the moment. Turning back to the main doors, I saw Zach arriving with the first group of authors. Franklin and Flora joined me in greeting them and then offered to show the authors to their booths. I agreed to remain on standby waiting for the next group and any early-arriving vendors. Fine by me, I thought, heading back to the invitations. More time to check out the displays. I'd just picked up a beautifully printed invitation— cornflower blue with copper accents engraved on paper made out of bamboo, of all things!—when Jude Hudson sidled next to me.

"Hello, Lila." His eyes roamed over the table and then back to me with interest. "Invitations, huh? Does that mean you and lover boy have actually set the date?"

"You mean Sean?" I tried to play it cool and not let irritation show in my voice. "We're still trying to work out the date. It's difficult with our busy schedules," I explained. "If you're looking for something to do, Franklin could probably use some help getting authors situated."

He, of course, ignored my subtle suggestion to take a hike. Jude and I had a strange history. The first month I worked at the agency, his charm and his oh-so-sparkly brown eyes lured me into a foolish and regrettable kiss. I'd long ago come to my senses, realizing that Jude was a ladies' man and I . . . Well, I was a one-man type of lady, and that man was Sean. Nonetheless, there were times when a little leftover spark from that bygone kiss threatened to derail my best judgment. Like now. When he playfully snatched up my hand and pointed at my naked finger while making a *tsk-tsk* sound.

"No ring, Lila?" he said. "What *is* that man thinking? If you were my fiancée, I'd make sure the deal was sealed."

I slid my hand out of his, irritated that his touch made my heart beat faster. "He's still looking for the perfect ring. He wants to make sure I'm happy."

Jude shot me a wink, his full lips turning up at the corners. "If you say so, darlin'."

I sighed. Jude had been playing this little game with me ever since things turned serious between Sean and me. And much to my annoyance, he always knew just the right nerve to hit. Truth was, I'd dropped hint after hint of the type of ring I wanted. Something vintage, reflective of my personal style. But still, no ring. And the wedding date? Well, Sean and I couldn't agree on that, either. I was vying for next spring, while he wanted to push things off until Christmas of next year when he could get a little more time off work.

Suddenly, Jude's gaze hit on something behind me that caused his playful expression to turn serious. I wheeled around to see what had caught his attention. It was Bentley. She was thundering down the hallway, her arms swinging with determination. "We've got a problem," she said to Jude, her voice low and tight. "There's something wrong with the refrigeration system in the kitchen area. The walk-in cooler isn't working. There's a half-dozen buttercream cakes back there, ready for tomorrow afternoon's cake display and tasting. If the refrigeration goes out, the cakes will be ruined."

Jude turned his palms upward and shrugged. "What do you want me to do? I don't know anything about refrigerators."

"Doesn't this place have some sort of maintenance service?" Bentley wanted to know.

I immediately thought of the handyman at the Magnolia Bed and Breakfast. I remembered him saying he'd just taken a maintenance contract with the Arts Center. I told the others what I knew. "He's just down the road. I'm sure he could get here quickly."

"Guess he'll have to do," Bentley agreed reluctantly. She glanced at her watch and then turned back to Jude. "Call over to the Magnolia and see if that guy's still there. If so, tell him that I'm offering a generous tip if he can get over here fast."

Jude took out his cell and shuffled down the hall to make the call. In the meantime, Bentley and I turned our attention back to the front doors to wait for the next group of authors. Here and there, a vendor would stray outside and return with a box of extra supplies. They'd spent the last two days setting up their booths, and an almost palpable feeling of excitement hung in the air as they bustled about, putting the final touches on displays.

A few minutes later, Jude came back with some news. "Chuck, the handyman, said he could be here in about twenty minutes."

Bentley nodded. "Good. Let's hope it's something simple that he can fix quickly. Chef Belmonte has a demonstration later this afternoon."

"Belmonte?" I didn't recognize the name.

"He's the executive chef at Machiavelli's," Jude supplied. "The place opened last summer. It's good, too. All handmade pasta. I'm surprised you haven't been there. I just saw your mother there a couple of days ago."

"Mama?" *Huh. Strange she didn't mention it to me.* Then again, we didn't keep track of each other's every move.

"Speaking of the devil," Jude said, nodding toward the walk outside, where Mama was bent forward, struggling to carry a sign against the snowy wind. I ran out to give her a hand.

"Here, Mama. Let me help you."

She handed over the sign and adjusted her parka hood lower on her face. "Lawd, child. You're goin' to catch your death of cold out here." I agreed and quickly ushered her down the walk to where Jude was holding the door for us. Inside, I stomped the snow off my shoes and held out Mama's sign for inspection. It was painted deep purple and embellished with gold stars and half-moons. Whimsical script spelled out the words *The Amazing Althea, Babylonian Fortune-Teller.*

"The sign is perfect! Lila, your mother is going to be the hit of the expo," Bentley enthused, snatching the sign out of my hands and looping her other arm into Mama's. "Come on, Althea, I'll show you where to set up."

"Your mother sure is something," Jude muttered as we watched Bentley lead Mama toward the main room. I squinted his way, wondering if he was speaking flippantly about my mama, but the sincere expression on his face told me otherwise. Jude, like many of the town's folk, seemed charmed by my mama's eccentricities. I sighed. When was I ever going to learn to simply accept Mama for who she was and not worry about how others perceived her? After all, I *knew* she was amazing.

"Oh, there's Dr. Meyers," Jude said, pointing to a woman standing inside the doorway. I watched as she stomped the slush from her calf-hugging boots—which perfectly complemented her all-leather shoulder bag, I noticed—and brushed snowflakes from her cashmere blend coat. Dr. Sloan Meyers had a successful psychology practice in nearby Dunston. Later today, she was scheduled to read from her popular book *Strong Women, Strong Marriages.*

As I greeted Dr. Meyers, I told her how excited I was for her upcoming reading and discussion. She was planning to talk on how to transition into married life while maintaining your confidence and strength as a woman. Advice I certainly could use! While I couldn't wait to spend the rest of my life with Sean, I had a few niggling reservations. After all, I'd finally reached a time in my life when I was completely independent: Trey off to college, Mama in good health, a great job, good friends . . . Sometimes I worried about the transitions around the corner.

Just as Franklin appeared to show Dr. Meyers around, the door opened again and in strolled Chuck, the handyman. He was pulling a large tool bag behind him, the wheels leaving two wet lines on the carpet. I eyed the bag, hoping one of the tools inside would do the magic trick. Our chef demonstrations were a huge attraction; I would hate for them to be canceled.

As Jude rushed Chuck back to the service kitchen, Zach arrived with the other authors. I watched as they clamored out of the SUV, the bulk of their winter coats making them appear like puffy penguins waddling off the shore. Once inside, Lynn immediately came to my side, removing her stocking hat and running a hand through her layers of brown hair. She leaned in and whispered, "I saw Chuck's truck outside. What's he doing here?"

I noted the stress in her voice and explained about the kitchen's walk-in cooler, but the more I talked, the more agitated she seemed to become. "What is it, Lynn? How do you know him?"

"He's my ex-husband. And the reason I left the area and moved to Baytown. I thought he'd left the area, too."

I wanted to ask more, but Bentley poked her head into the hall and called for the authors and vendors to report to their booths. "Fifteen minutes until doors open, people. Let's all get into place."

There was a sudden bustle of activity as everyone

scrambled to their designated areas. Since I was on door duty for the first two hours, I decided to stay put and watch for early arrivals. I didn't have to wait for long. The entire female population of North Carolina seemed to arrive at once, ushered in on a cloud of excitement and sharp giggles, shaking snow from their coats and boots and dispersing into adrenalized groups of frenzied treasure hunters. For the next couple of hours, I kept busy taking tickets, pointing out the coat check, handing out the event schedule, and answering a bazillion questions, most of which had to do with the location of the restrooms. Ingeniously, Bentley had set up the book table just outside the coat check area. So when I told visitors where to check their coats, all I needed to say was, "Just down the hall next to the book table. Check out all the great selections while you're there. All the authors are on hand to answer questions and sign your books." So far, Bentley's little scheme was working well. Books were selling like hotcakes, with Pam's Reluctant Brides of Babylon series leading the pack. Speaking of which, I wondered how things were going for Amazing Althea the Babylonian Fortune-Teller. I really did need to check on Mama and Lynn, too.

I glanced around and checked my watch. My two hours were almost up and Jude was supposed to relieve me of door duty, but he was nowhere in sight. He might be checking on the refrigerator repair. Maybe I could just get one of the other agents to spell me for a . . . "Franklin!"

Franklin hurried to my side. "Is everything okay, dear?" Franklin was such a gentleman.

I nodded. "I just need to check on a couple of things. Jude was supposed to be here, but he must be tied up. Could you spell me for a few minutes?"

"Certainly." He looked around and lifted the sleeve of his herringbone jacket to peek at his watch. "I was just looking for Dr. Meyers, but I can catch up with her later. I'd be glad to help you out."

I thanked him and headed down the hall, working my way toward the center's main room and resisting the urge to veer off toward the textile rooms, where I knew a dress supplier from Raleigh had a vintage gown display. I was just dying to see it, but Makayla made me promise to wait until she could get here. She usually didn't finish at the coffee shop until four o'clock or after.

The Arts Center's main auditorium was designed for community plays and other performances and had a stage at one end and plenty of floor space to accommodate portable seating. Today, the spectator seating was stored away, and instead the floor was arranged with vendor booths, everything from photography to floral arrangements, party favors, and even spa packages. On the stage, a local string quartet was performing a classical piece by Bach while brides bustled about, notepads and pens in hand, their questions blending softly with the elegant music. I smiled to myself. Everything was going exactly as planned.

Except when I reached Lynn's booth, she was nowhere to be found. I looked around, finally interrupting the man in the adjacent booth. A popular local photographer, he had several women looking through his sample wedding albums. "No, miss. I haven't seen her for a while," he told me.

Thinking she was probably taking a well-deserved break, I decided to check back later. In the meantime, I headed for a quick check on the Babylonian Fortune-Teller. Only I hadn't gone far when Flora caught up to me. She seemed flustered. "Have you seen Jodi? She doesn't seem to be anywhere and she has readers waiting at her table."

I shook my head. "No, and I can't find Lynn, either. Maybe they went somewhere together. Let's go check the break rooms."

We'd just reached the hallway when Bentley flagged us down. She was carrying a large stack of hardcover books. "Good news, girls! The acquisitions librarian from the Dunston Public Library just purchased two copies of each of our nonfiction titles."

Flora's hands flew to her cheeks. "How wonderful! I do so love librarians."

"Me, too," agreed Bentley. "Be a dear, Flora, and help me out. She wants all these signed by the authors. Take the top four?"

Flora shot me a worried glance. "Go ahead," I told her. "I'll find Jodi and Lynn. I'm sure they're around here somewhere."

"And check in on the handyman while you're at it," Bentley added. "Chef Belmonte is due to present soon."

I nodded and took off toward the culinary area of the Arts Center, my heels echoing as I passed by the various rooms, which were all empty for now, but I was sure they would be teeming with brides later. We didn't plan to open this wing until later each day, after the keynote speaker was done presenting. Then brides could meet their favorite chefs, sample a few of their creations, and decide on foods and wines for their reception menus.

I reached the entrance to the service kitchen and pushed through the swinging door. "Chuck?" I called out. "Mr. Belmonte?"

No answer. Huh? Belmonte should have arrived by now to start setting up.

"Chuck?" I called again, making my way to the back of the kitchen and the large walk-in cooler.

Still no answer. What was it about today? No one was where they were supposed to be. First Lynn and Jodi disappeared and now Belmonte and the handyman were MIA.

"Chuck!" I called again, my toe hitting against something

on the ground. There was a scraping sound, followed by a loud hollow pinging noise as a wrench I'd inadvertently kicked slid across the floor and banked off the bottom of a set of steel cabinets. "Ouch!" I cried, cringing from stubbing my toe.

As I rounded the cabinet I noticed a lot of tools strewn across the floor: more wrenches, pliers, a drill, even one of those cordless, automatic nail gun things roofers always use. *How careless*, I thought. Someone could get easily get hurt. I bent over and picked a screwdriver off the floor as I headed toward the large steel door that accessed the walk-in fridge. Maybe Chuck was still working on the unit and couldn't hear me through the insulated door.

"Hey," I said, opening the door and holding up the screwdriver, the cold air making me shiver. At least it seemed he'd been able to fix things. "Looks like you dropped your tools out . . ." And that was when I saw him. I gasped, one hand flying to my mouth.

Chuck, the handyman, lay on the floor in a splattered mess of cake, blood, and buttercream frosting, a nail driven straight through his temple.

Chapter 5

I DROPPED THE SCREWDRIVER AND STARTED BACKING up. This couldn't be happening. It just couldn't. Memories flooded my brain of deadly garden spades and lethal explosions and . . . I started to shiver all over. I'd seen too many dead bodies under various circumstances and now this? No wonder half the town's people had dubbed me the local murder magnet.

I continued to inch backward until a scolding voice in my head snapped my mind away from past events. *Do something, Lila!* the voice screamed. Yet I couldn't move. What was wrong with me? Here an innocent, hardworking man was lying dead, obviously murdered, in a blob of frosting and all I could think about was my own reputation. I needed to do something . . . call someone . . .

My back hit something soft and squishy. I jumped just as a pair of strong hands clamped onto my shoulders. "What are you doing in here?" a husky male voice demanded.

"Hey! What did you do to that guy?" The hands gripped tighter, holding me in place.

Freaked-out, I lifted my foot and slammed my heel down as hard as I could on the shoe behind me. The hands instantly let go as an agonizing scream pierced the air, but I didn't bother to stick around to see what damage I'd caused. As soon as he released me, I made a break for it, running as fast as I could through the kitchen and back down the hallway, bumping into Zach and Jude as I rounded the corner to the main corridor.

"Lila!" Jude exclaimed. "What's wrong? We heard a scream."

I pointed behind me, sucking in a deep breath. My heart was slamming against my chest. "Murder," I managed to say.

Jude grabbed me and shook. "What do you mean, murder? Speak to me, Lila."

I pointed down the hall again. "The handyman . . . he's dead. In the fridge."

Zach's eyes popped. "What? You can't be serious." He threw his hands in the air and tipped his head back. "Whoa! I can't believe this. The Murder Magnet has struck again!"

Jude shot him a withering look before turning back to me. "How do you know he was murdered? Maybe he just had a heart attack."

"No, murdered. He's dead as . . ." *Dead as a doornail. Dead as a . . .* I stopped myself from actually saying the horrible phrase that suddenly popped to mind. Shaking my head, I tried to vanquish the gruesome image of the nail in Chuck's temple. *Dead as a doornail. Dead as . . .* The sound of heavy footsteps interrupted the automatic replay in my mind. We all looked up as the large man from the kitchen came flying around the corner, cell phone in his hand. I flinched and grasped Jude's arm.

"Don't let her get away," he cried, pointing at me. "She murdered a man! I've already called the cops."

"*Me?* It was *him*. And he tried to kill me, too," I blurted.

"Chef Belmonte tried to kill you?" Jude asked, pushing me behind him as he took a couple of aggressive steps toward the chef.

The chef's jaw went slack. "What? I didn't try to kill nobody. I just came into the kitchen and found this woman with a weapon in her hand, standing over a dead man."

My muscles tensed. "A weapon? What are you talking about?"

"Stop. Both of you." Jude cut us short. "No one say anything else until the police get here."

Within moments the sound of wailing sirens could be heard in the distance, muffled at first, then growing louder as they arrived outside. Zach started pacing, raking his hands through his tight black curls, causing them to shoot out in every direction. "Man, Bentley's going to be ticked when she finds out you discovered another dead body, Lila. And at our event, even! It's bad enough everyone in town thinks of you as a murder magnet. Now your reputation is rubbing off on *us*. No one's going to want to have anything to do with us, once this gets out. We'll be ruined!"

Belmonte furrowed his bushy brows at Zach. "Is he always so dramatic?" he asked Jude.

"He represents screenplays," Jude said by way of an explanation. Then, turning to Zach, he said, "You'd better go meet the cops and show them back here. See if you can do it quietly, without drawing too much attention." He pulled out his cell. "I'll call Bentley and let her know what's going on."

While Zach rushed down the hall to fetch the police, I took a moment to take a closer look at Belmonte. Strangely enough, the guy wasn't much taller than me, but something about the way he carried himself made him seem much taller, gigantic even. I let my eyes roam from the bald stripe down the center of his head to his fat hands. I could just imagine those short stubby fingers of his wrapped around a nail gun, finger pressed against the trigger . . . He caught me looking, wagged his fingers, and raised a brow, a strange little smile quirking the corners of his mouth. Oh for crying out loud! He thought I was checking him out for another reason. I scowled and looked away. Ego, that's what it was. Obviously, the man was full of himself.

I tuned into Jude's phone conversation. Poor guy was working hard to placate Bentley, whose irate voice was coming loud and clear over the line. I imagined at this very moment she was storming down the hallway, pushing her way through the crowds with her phone in hand, on her way to resolve this most recent crisis. "Yes," Jude was saying. "Lila discovered the body . . . Yup, afraid so . . . The police are here," he finally said in way of an excuse before quickly disconnecting.

Two uniformed officers had entered the hall and were quickly making their way toward us. "Where's the victim?" the first officer asked.

I pointed toward the service kitchen. "Back there. In the walk-in cooler. I found him there; he's got a . . ." I let my words trail off, shifting my focus to Belmonte. "This man was back there. He grabbed me."

Next to me, I could feel Jude grow tense.

"Grabbed you?" the man protested. "You backed into me." Okay. Maybe that was true. Still . . .

He turned to the officer. "She was standing over the dead guy with a screwdriver," he added.

One of the officers had taken out a notepad and was jotting down information. "Your names?"

"Oscar Belmonte. I own Machiavelli's."

Oh brother, I thought, noticing the way his chin lifted and his chest puffed out. "Lila Wilkins," I told the officer. "I'm an agent with Novel Idea Literary Agency."

"Wilkins?" one of the officers said, exchanging a look with his partner. The partner simply nodded in one of those all-knowing ways.

"Wilkins?" Belmonte echoed. "Do you know Althea Wilkins?"

I narrowed my eyes. "She's my mother. Why?"

He averted his gaze as his face flushed deep red. "She's a friend of mine."

IT DIDN'T TAKE long before the place was crawling with all sorts of officials: officers, crime scene techs, the coroner's team, and my fiancé, Detective Sean Griffiths. "Did you know the guy?" he was asking me. Belmonte and I had been sequestered to two of the small classrooms in this wing. Another officer was interviewing Belmonte, while Sean questioned me.

"Not really. I mean, I knew who he was. Actually, I suggested him for the job."

Sean waited for me to expand on my explanation. I'd come to learn that Sean's biggest asset as an interrogator was his patience. He knew how to wait it out, let the person being interrogated sweat a little. Make them nervous enough to start babbling. And it always seemed to work with me.

"I met him briefly yesterday at the Magnolia Bed and Breakfast. He's putting up some shelving in Cora's pantry. It irritated Bentley because he was so noisy." He raised a brow but didn't comment. "Not *that* much," I assured him. "Anyway, a few of our authors are staying at the inn: Pam, she writes erotic romance; Jodi, romantic suspense; and my client, Lynn. She doesn't actually have a book published, but she's a great—"

"So you met this Chuck once, but you recommended him for this job?"

"Well, not really. I remembered hearing that he worked maintenance for the Arts Center and it was sort of an emergency. The refrigerator died and we had the chef coming and the cakes . . ." I stopped, visions of buttercream frosting stained with blood swimming before my mind and mingling with echoes of yesterday . . .

Sean leaned forward. "What is it?"

"The cakes," I repeated. *Found facedown in a wedding cake.* Bentley's words from yesterday's meeting came rushing back to me. Of course! The way I found Chuck, facedown in a wedding cake, covered in frosting and blood . . . My own client had written that very same thing in her book, *Wed 'til Dead.* But certainly Lynn wasn't capable of such a thing. Suddenly I felt torn between my loyalty to Lynn and my obligation to tell Sean what I knew. In my heart I knew Lynn couldn't have done such an awful thing; there was just no way she could hold a nail gun to someone's head and . . . I cringed.

"Lila?"

I met Sean's eyes, deciding I needed to tell him about Lynn. He'd eventually find out they had been married anyway. "There's something I need to tell you. It's about one of my authors, Lynn Werner." I told him what I knew. That Lynn and Chuck were once married. The strange way Lynn acted when she discovered Chuck was working at the inn. The argument I witnessed between the two of them on the street yesterday. The murder scene in her book. But I did sort of leave out the fact that she was missing from her booth earlier. Surely she was taking a break to get some water or use the restroom. Wasn't she? I pushed away the strange thought creeping into my mind. There was just no way Lynn—shy, timid Lynn—was capable of something so violent. "I know it all sounds suspicious," I continued, "but she just doesn't seem like the type. She's so quiet and nice."

"Nice people do bad things, Lila."

He didn't have to tell me. Over the past two years, I'd encountered enough violence to last me a lifetime. "I just can't believe it. There's got to be another explanation."

He stood and reached out his hand. I took it, allowing him to pull me to my feet. "There might be," he said, pulling me close, his eyes staring intensely into mine. "But you're not going to look for one. I came too close to losing you last time, remember?"

I nodded, pressing a little closer and enjoying the warmth of his arms around me, even as my mind raced with doubt. Maybe I shouldn't have told him about Lynn. As her agent, didn't I owe her more? Maybe I should have warned her first. Given her a chance to get an attorney. I leaned in closer, my cheek sinking into the soft cotton blend of his dress shirt, inhaling his familiar soap scent, wishing more than anything that we could leave and go somewhere alone. I needed him to hold me, help me shake the horrible image of discovering the body.

"Ahem . . . excuse me."

We quickly pushed apart at the sound of Jude clearing his throat. He was standing in the doorway, looking directly at Sean. "Bentley sent me to ask you how long it was going to take your people to get the body out of the kitchen. We've got an event scheduled."

Sean cursed under his breath. "Tell Bentley—"

"It's okay, Sean." I squeezed his arm. "I'll talk to her, okay? Are you done questioning me?"

He nodded. "For now."

"Good." I took a deep breath, willing myself back to business mode. "Since the murder occurred in the kitchen at the end of the hallway, would you mind having your guys use the emergency exit back there? That way, we could partition off the front part of this wing for our events. It won't take us long to relocate a few things. And no one would get in the way of your investigation. Promise."

His lips pressed into a thin line as he contemplated my request.

Jude was still hovering in the doorway. I waved him on. "I'll be right out."

"Fine. But you'd better hurry. We're in the Potter's Room. Bentley's stressed out. She's called a DAC meeting and wants all the agents there, pronto." DAC was Bentley's abbreviation for Damage Assessment and Control. She must have felt desperate if she had already resorted to such measures.

"Tell her I'll be right there." Then, turning back to Sean, I leaned in close again and gave him a pleading look. "Please, Sean. If we lose the use of this wing this week, we'll have to cancel several events. This is a huge deal for our agency." I wrapped my arms around his midsection and gazed up into his eyes.

Finally his expression softened. He let out a long sigh and agreed, with a lot of provisions, of course. "Where is Lynn now?" he asked.

My heart dropped. How was Lynn going to take the news that her ex-husband was dead? And to be questioned as a suspect in his death? What had I done to poor Lynn? Suddenly overwhelmed with regret, I asked, "Can I be with you when you break the news to her? It was her ex-husband, after all. And I'm the only friend she really has here this week."

Another sigh. This one ringing with impatience. "All right. Tell me where to find her. I'll bring her back here and wait until you return before I break the news to her. In the meantime, go to your D . . . whatever meeting. And tell that boss of yours that she's not to get in the way of my investigation."

I described Lynn to him and explained where her booth was. Hopefully she'd be there now. An unwanted thought occurred to me: If Lynn was the killer—but I really didn't think she was—we might never find her again.

"THE MURDER MAGNET'S here," Zach said as soon as I entered the Potter's Room.

"Enough of that!" Bentley demanded, slapping her palm against the table. "Lila, take a seat over there." She pointed toward the chair between Flora and Franklin. Franklin stood and held it out for me as I approached, shooting me a pitiful look. And the second I sat down, Flora reached over and patted my back.

"You poor thing," she said, her expression mirroring Franklin's. "I can't imagine what you've been through, with finding the body and all."

"You didn't say how he was murdered," Zach said, tapping his pencil excitedly against the tabletop. "Stabbed with a butcher knife? Strangled with apron strings? Oh, I know . . ." His voice was growing more excited with each revelation. "Poisoned! Someone poisoned him. He *was* in the kitchen, right? Of course, the last time a murder happened in a kitchen around here"—he raised his hands and mimicked an explosion—*"Kaboom!"*

"Would you be quiet," Jude said. "Can't you see how upsetting this is to Lila?"

"I don't know why. It's not like this is the first dead person she's found. Let's see, first it was the homeless man in our office, then one of the editors from—"

"We get the picture," Bentley sneered. "The important thing is how are we going to keep this latest . . . uh . . . misfortune from affecting this week's expo. I don't have to remind you people of how much money the agency has invested in this event. It's paramount that it be successful." She turned to me. "Best scenario would be if the police could wrap this up quickly. Do they have any suspects in mind?"

I broke into an instant sweat, guilt welling inside me. *Suspect? Why, yes, Lynn is their primary suspect. Mostly because I pointed the finger of accusation at her. Never mind that she's one of our clients. That being accused of murder may ruin her career before it even gets started.* Oh my, what did I do? Only, I didn't verbalize any of that. First, Sean would kill me if he knew I leaked details of the case. Second, Bentley would kill me if she knew I'd handed over one of our clients to the cops. Either way, I'd end up dead. Dead as a doornail. I clasped my hand over my mouth.

"Lila, honey." It was Flora. She leaned forward, looking at me with a worried expression. "You look ill." Suddenly her chair slid back, and she stood and took me by the arm. "Excuse us, everyone. Lila and I are going to go powder our noses."

She ushered me down the hall and straight into the ladies' room. Ripping paper towels from the dispenser, she held them under cool water and then pressed them to the back of my neck. I could feel my resolve crumble. "Oh, Flora," I started. "I've got a mess going on."

"Tell me. Perhaps I can help."

The words started pouring out. "The guy that was murdered. Lynn, my client . . . you know, the new author? *Wed 'til Dead*?" She nodded and I continued, "She knew him. It was her ex-husband. I saw them arguing earlier today. And I told Sean. He's going to question her and it's all my fault that he suspects her. It's just that she wasn't at her booth . . . and that guy, the handyman, he was killed the very same way as the victim in her book."

"The same way? How do you mean?"

"I found him lying over the top of a wedding cake. The same as in her book. Only in her book the victim was stabbed with a cake knife. This poor guy had a nail driven through his head."

Flora gasped and faltered a bit.

I reached out to steady her. "I'm sorry. I shouldn't have given you the details. It's so horrible, I know."

She pressed the paper towel against her own forehead. "No, it's not that. I mean, yes, it is horrible, but . . ."

I realized she'd turned white as a ghost. "Flora? Are you okay?"

She nodded, leaning back against the washbasin. "It's what you just said, about the nail in the head." She shuddered.

"Yes?"

"It's exactly how my client Jodi Lee killed off the victim in her book *The Billionaire's Bride*."

Chapter 6

I WAS SHOCKED, TO SAY THE LEAST. I LIKED TO BELIEVE it was just a coincidence that Jodi's victim was killed the same way as the handyman, but there was no way. Besides, it was such an unusual method of murder. But honestly, I had a difficult time believing Jodi could shoot a nail through someone's skull. Of course, I'd only met her briefly, but she was just so nice. In my mind, I heard Sean's words again. *Nice people do bad things.* Still . . .

"Lila! There you are." Makayla caught up to me in the hallway just outside the ladies' room. After our discussion, Flora and I had decided the best bet was to come clean with the facts. She was going directly to the DAC meeting to break the bad news about both authors to Bentley.

"Oh, hi, Makayla. Is it after four already?"

"Four thirty. You said to meet you here, right? We were going to look at the booths together . . ." Her voice trailed off, her emerald green eyes clouding with concern. "Is something wrong? You don't look so good."

"I found another dead body. There's been another murder."

"What!" She clasped my hands, her silver hoop earrings glimmering as she shook her head. "Oh no! Not someone we know."

"His name was Chuck Richards," I told her, but she didn't recognize the name. "I probably shouldn't say much more. And I'm afraid I can't walk around with you like we'd planned. I'm sorry."

She pulled me in close for a quick hug. I inhaled, taking comfort in the familiar smell of coffee and cinnamon that seemed to follow her everywhere, even when she wasn't at her shop. "No need to apologize," she said. "I just hope you're okay. We can do this anytime this week—I bought a pass for the whole week anyway. Just take care of what you have to now, and we'll both enjoy the show together another day, okay? Call me later. Promise?"

I promised, and after one more hug we parted with plans to try again tomorrow. Next, I rushed to the break room, where I found a female police officer sitting by the door. As soon as I arrived, the officer made a call. Presumably to Sean to let him know I was back. I peeked inside and saw Lynn sitting alone.

"Lila! I'm so glad to see you," Lynn said as soon as I entered the room. "A police officer came to my booth and told me to come here and that he'd be back to question me."

My heart went out to her. She blinked a few times as if trying to wake herself from a bad dream. "That was probably my fiancé, Sean Griffiths. He's a detective."

"A detective?" Her fingers flew to her hair, where they

worried at the mousy brown strands that curled around her face. "Did I do something wrong?"

I took the chair next to her. Sean had asked me not to say anything to her about the murder until he was present, so I chose my words carefully. "Lynn, where were you earlier? I was looking for you, but you weren't at your booth."

She raised her brows and tapped her fingers on the book on the table next to her. "I'm sorry. I just took a little break to get a book. There wasn't much going on at my table, so I thought I'd do a little reading."

I glanced down at the title. It was Dr. Meyers's book, *Strong Women, Strong Marriages*. "Did you get it signed?"

She shook her head. "No. I mean, I didn't get a chance to go by her booth. I thought perhaps she'd sign it later for me."

"Lila?" Sean approached with a stern look.

I sat back and swallowed hard before attempting an explanation. "Lynn and I were just discussing a book. That's all."

He took the chair across from us, loosening his tie and running a finger between his neck and collar before addressing Lynn. "I'm sure Lila has told you that she's my fiancée," he started.

Lynn nodded. "And that you're a detective. Have I done something wrong?"

Sean glanced my way briefly. I scooted in a little closer to Lynn and placed my hand on her arm. "Do you know Chuck Richards?" Sean asked.

Her chin dipped slightly. "Yes. He's my ex-husband. Why? Has he . . . ?" Her eyes darted between Sean and me. "What's going on?"

"Has he what, Ms. Werner?" Sean wanted to know.

She shrugged, pulling her arms in close and wiping her

palms on her sweater. "I don't know. Is he in some sort of trouble?"

"Has he been in trouble before?" Sean pressed.

Another shrug. "No. Not really."

"Can you give me an idea of your schedule since arriving at the Arts Center this afternoon?"

"My schedule?" She looked at me for clarification, but I didn't dare speak out. Instead, I smiled encouragingly. Then another thought occurred to me. This was my client. Maybe what I should be doing instead of smiling encouragingly was advising her to get an attorney. What if she said something that could be misconstrued or held against her at a later time? And here Sean was asking all these questions without even telling her that her ex-husband had been murdered. What was he doing? I had thought he was going to tell her. That was why I wanted to be here, in case she needed comfort. Not as some sort of accomplice in the old good cop/bad cop routine. My eyes slid toward Sean, who steadily held my gaze. Either he just now sensed my conflict or he had anticipated it all along. Were those intense blue eyes of his daring me to step in and stand up for my client? Was this some sort of test of loyalty to him?

I took a deep breath and reached across the table toward Lynn. "Lynn, I think you—"

"Don't say a word, Lynn!" Bentley's voice interrupted. She blew right past the female officer sitting at the door and crossed the room with a perturbed look. I shrank back into my chair.

Across the table, I heard Sean curse under his breath. "This is official business, Ms. Duke, and you're interfering—"

"Has Detective Griffiths told you what these questions are about?" She ignored Sean and spoke directly to Lynn.

"No. I don't understand what's going on," Lynn said, looking to me again for some sort of answer.

"Ms. Duke!" Sean was on his feet now, motioning toward the female officer for assistance.

Bentley held up her hand. "I'm advising my client to remain silent."

"Remain silent? Client?" Sean chuckled. "You're a literary agent, not an attorney. And this is official police business."

The female officer had moved into position behind Bentley, apparently waiting for Sean's directive. Bentley shifted her stance, throwing her weight onto one hip and leveling her gaze on Sean. "An attorney is an excellent idea, Detective Griffiths. Thank you for the suggestion." Then, turning toward Lynn, she said, "Lynn, I'm sorry to tell you this, but your ex-husband has been murdered. And you're a suspect."

Lynn gasped, both her hands flying to her face. I immediately stood and moved next to her, leaning down and wrapping my arms around her shoulders. "I'm so sorry," I whispered.

Under my arms, I could feel her shoulders expand as she took a deep breath. "I'm not sorry," she said as she exhaled with a long sigh. I let go and stood back, surprised by her statement. Even more surprised by the fact that she didn't look upset at all. Instead, she looked . . . what? Relieved? Happy?

"Not another word," Bentley warned.

But Lynn shook her head, seemingly bent on saying more. "Chuck was a mean, horrible person. And I'm glad he's dead."

SOON AFTER THAT statement, Sean asked Lynn to come with him to the police station to answer a few more questions. Lynn readily agreed, insisting that she had nothing to hide and that she had no need for an attorney.

"Poor Lynn," I said, as soon as they left.

"No thanks to you," Bentley replied. "What were you

thinking, Lila? I can only assume the trauma of discovering the body addled your brain. Certainly you know better than to implicate a client in murder."

"What? You expect me to just keep information like that to myself? The fact that Chuck's murder and the murder in Lynn's book were so similar seemed important to the case. Not to mention he was her ex-husband."

"Important to your *fiancé's* case, you mean."

"That has nothing to do with it. And what about Jodi's book? Flora said—"

"Let me handle it. Okay?"

"But I feel obligated to say something to Sean. I mean, the guy was killed with one of those automatic nail guns. Flora said it was the same way Jodi killed off the victim in her book. We need to tell the police."

"And we will. Just as soon as I have time to prepare Jodi. Hopefully, she'll be smart about it and hire an attorney." She looked me up and down, possibly trying to decide if I was going to heed her advice or not. "Look, Lila. Just give me thirty minutes or so. It'll take Detective Griffiths that long to get back to the police department anyway. That'll give me enough time to talk to Jodi and place a phone call to a local attorney. It's the least I can do for one of our clients. Then I'll call the police and tell them what I know."

"But shouldn't you tell them right away?" In my mind, I was thinking that if Jodi was guilty, giving her the extra time might hinder the investigation.

Bentley shrugged. "The details of the murder haven't been released yet. For all intents and purposes, I don't even know the murder method in her book."

"Yeah, but Flora told you. And me."

"Have you read *The Billionaire's Bride*?"

I shook my head. I'd been wanting to read it but hadn't had the chance.

Bentley continued, "Then you don't really *know* anything. Like they say in court, it's just hearsay."

"I don't know. This doesn't seem right," I hedged.

"Look, Lila. If this were your mother, or your son, wouldn't you want someone to advise them during such a time?"

"Yes, of course."

"Well, when I sign an author into my agency, they become a part of the Novel Idea family. Do you understand what I'm saying?"

I nodded.

Her face softened a little. "I understand the conflict you're feeling. You're going to be married to that detective, after all. But I'm going to protect my family at all cost. Just the same as you would do for your family. Get it?"

I did. And I admired Bentley's loyalty to her family of authors, but . . .

"Good." Her brows furrowed as she glanced at her diamond-studded watch. "In the meantime, please go help the rest of the agents relocate the displays in the culinary wing. There's no reason these unfortunate circumstances need to disrupt our schedule any further." I could tell by the dismissive tone of her voice that Bentley felt a little angry with me. Not that I blamed her. Bentley's whole life revolved around the agency. In fact, I'd never heard her speak of any other family. As far as I knew, we were it. Maybe all this time I'd misjudged my hard-driven, tenacious boss. I'd always thought she was motivated by success, the lure of fame, and the final payout. Of course, I was still pretty sure those things did motivate her to some extent, but it was kind of nice to think that perhaps there were some kindred emotions motivating her, too. I liked the idea of everyone at Novel Idea, agents and authors, being one big family. Although judging by the way Bentley was eyeing me, it looked like I might have just become that family's very own black sheep.

I OVERSLEPT TUESDAY morning, the blast from Mama's horn jolting me—and my poor neighbors—as I ran through the house, shrugging into my coat and gathering last-minute items needed for the day. The air outside felt like a cold slap in the face, which I welcomed in a way. It was better than the warm grogginess that kept me in bed for too long. At least now I felt awake enough to take on another day. I shuffle-stepped down the walk, careful not to slip. Everywhere I looked, the world looked pristine and fresh, making me think that snow must be Mother Nature's favorite way to clean house.

"Tired, sugar?" Mama asked, as soon as I clambered into her truck.

I threw my satchel between us on the bench seat and adjusted the vent so that the heat was blasting my way. "A little. It was a long day yesterday." The other agents and I had succeeded in rearranging the displays in the culinary wing, putting a folding screen toward the end to mask off the glaring yellow crime scene tape. Thankfully, the rest of the day's events went off without a hitch, most of the attendees delightfully oblivious to the fact that a murder had even occurred. Or at least they would be until they read about it in the *Dunston Herald* today. I thought back to when I'd worked at the *Herald*, writing about church bazaars and Girl Scout cookie sales for the Features section of the paper. The news of a local murder would have certainly sent our staff into a frenzied race to scoop the story and put out a blazing headline.

"I still can't stop thinkin' of that poor man," Mama continued. "And killed in such a nasty way. Sorry you had to see it, hon. It worries me that you keep comin' so close to death. But I trust Sean's going to work to get this cleared up and bring the murderer to justice. So you won't be gettin' involved, right?"

I glanced across the seat, noticing that the lines around her eyes seemed deeper than usual. She'd been worrying again. I hated it that I caused her so much stress. But maybe stress was just an inevitable part of motherhood. Heaven knows, Trey had caused me enough stress to last a lifetime. Enough joy, too, I thought with a bittersweet twinge. I'd tried to call his dorm room last night, but he never answered. Probably off doing whatever it was college kids did late at night. I really didn't want to know. "Two of our authors are suspects," I finally replied, skirting her question. I knew I couldn't promise her that I wouldn't get involved. I'd just stayed up half the night trying to put together pieces of the puzzle, hoping that the image they formed had nothing to do with Lynn or Jodi. Actually, the picture that kept popping to mind was that of Oscar Belmonte. Now, there was a man that couldn't be trusted.

"Not Pam," she said, gripping the steering wheel a little tighter. I assumed that sitting next to Pam at her author's booth yesterday had made Mama fond of the woman.

"No, not Pam," I assured her. "My client, Lynn, and another author named Jodi." I went on to explain everything I knew about the case.

"Do you think one of them did it?"

"No," I answered right away. I'd asked myself the same question all night and finally decided that it couldn't have been either author. And not just because I thought they were too nice, or because they were part of the Novel Idea family, as Bentley put it, but because the method of murder was just too coincidental. "If one of them was the killer, I don't think they would have used the same method as in their book," I explained. "It had to be someone else. Someone who had access to the kitchen area." *Someone like Oscar Belmonte*, I thought.

I suddenly had a great idea for lunch. "What's on your agenda for today, Mama? Besides being the Amazing Althea, Babylonian Fortune-Teller?"

She chuckled. "Thought maybe a little later we could grab a bite at that new place, Machiavelli's."

I did a double take. "Did you just read my mind?"

"Huh?"

"I was just going to ask if you'd go with me to lunch there." I shook my head. "Amazing."

Mama smiled.

We'd just tuned into the lot behind Novel Idea. She pulled up close to the stairs leading to the back door. "Lila, I've been wanting to talk to you about a few things."

"Sure," I said, one hand on the door handle, the other reaching for my satchel. "We'll talk at lunch, okay? I've got to run. Love you, Mama."

"Love you, too, sugar."

I hopped out and headed straight for Espresso Yourself. I still needed to fill in Makayla on everything that had happened at the expo the day before.

WALKING INTO ESPRESSO Yourself felt like being engulfed in a warm blanket. A blanket that smelled deliciously of coffee, cinnamon, and chocolate. Smiling, I made my way to the counter, where my friend was busy whipping up one of her marvelous creations, her melodic voice carrying over the piped-in acoustic guitar music as she visited with the young woman at the counter.

While waiting, I looked over the artwork displayed on the walls. Makayla was a huge supporter of the local art scene. Every month she'd change the display to showcase a different group of artists. This month, in support of Booked for a Wedding, she'd featured area wedding photographers and their best work. My eye scanned the gorgeous prints, stopping on a black-and-white close-up of a couple's intertwined hands. The engagement ring on the bride-to-be's hand dazzled, almost jumping out of the photo. I ran my own bare-fingered hand along the edge of the frame, dreaming a bit about the ring I'd be wearing soon. That was, if Sean ever got around to giving me one.

"Latte?" I turned to see Makayla leaning over the counter, a to-go cup in hand. "Your usual."

"Oh heavens, yes!" I grasped the warm cup and inhaled the slightly burnt coffee smell laced with rich caramel sweetness before taking my first gratifying sip.

"How ya doing, sweetie?" she asked, her emerald eyes shining with concern. "I didn't hear from you last night and was going to call, but I thought you might have been tied up with the murder and everything." She reached under the counter and brought up a handful of coffee stirrers, restocking a basket on the counter.

"I'm sorry. I should have called. By the time I got home I was exhausted."

"I'm sure. Were you able to sleep at all?"

I shrugged and took another sip of my latte, taking comfort in its warm sweetness.

"Did you know the man?" she asked, moving on to restocking napkins.

"No, not really. But he used to be married to one of my authors. Lynn Werner."

She gasped. "The poor thing!"

"She's not all that upset about it. It wasn't an amicable divorce," I said, thinking back to the way Lynn reacted when she found out the news. Surprised, yes. But not sad. More like relieved. Thrilled, if I had to be honest. "She's a suspect. And so is one of our other authors."

"Really? Why?"

"Because of the way he was murdered. They'd both sort of written about it in their books."

She shook her head. "I don't understand. What do you mean, they'd already written about it?"

I went on to explain how Chuck's murder mimicked the scenes in Lynn's and Jodi's books. When I told her the exact way he was killed, she gasped and raised her hand to her chest. "That's horrible!"

I shook my head slowly, letting silence settle between us as I raised my cup to my lips and squeezed my eyes shut against the horrible image that kept resurfacing in my mind. When I reopened them again, I found Makayla working over an invisible spot on the counter with a rag and cleaner. "So much wickedness in the world," she said.

"There's a lot of goodness, too," I maintained, feeling sorry that I'd burdened my friend at a time when there should be nothing but wedding plans and happiness in her life. "So, are we still on for this afternoon?" I asked.

She stopped scrubbing and her shoulders seemed to relax. "That would be great." She indicated toward the photo I'd admired earlier. "The photographer who took that shot has a booth. Thought I'd stop by to see if I could schedule an appointment for Jay and me. Maybe get some prewedding shots." She looked at her ring and then back to the wall, her eyes taking on a slight dreamy look. "You know, when Jay and I hold hands, they fit perfectly together. Like puzzle pieces.

I'd like for the photographer to capture that feeling. Maybe in a picture like that one."

My gaze drifted to her hand, coveting how the elegantly set diamonds seemed to sparkle against her dark skin. Then I checked my emotions, trying to conjure the happiness I should be feeling for my best friend. "*So we stood hand in hand like two children, and there was peace in our hearts for all the dark things that surrounded us,*" I quoted.

Her emerald eyes lit up. "That's perfect! And so beautiful."

"Arthur Conan Doyle, Sherlock Holmes," I told her with a smile.

"Sherlock. Really?" she said, a grin spreading across her face. "Guess there was something more than reasoning and logical deduction going on under that deerstalker cap of his. But that quote sums up just how I feel when I'm with Jay. Like we can take on the world as long as we're together."

I nodded in reply, happy that I'd vanquished the thought of the murder scene with something that made her happy.

"And what about you and Sean?" she continued. "Been shopping for rings yet?"

I shrugged, trying to keep my voice light. "He says he wants it to be a surprise."

She raised a brow. "That's . . . romantic."

I laughed. "Scary, you mean. Don't worry, I've given him plenty of hints about the type of ring I'd like." *Lots and lots of hints.* "So, what time do you want to meet this afternoon?"

Another customer came in, so we quickly finalized our plans and said good-bye. Outside, I was surprised to run into Sean on the steps leading up to Novel Idea. He'd worn a heavy overcoat over his suit and a brimmed hat, bringing to mind a pleasant image of the blond, well-built, and ever-so-broody

Sam Spade, Dashiell Hammett's famous detective character in the book *The Maltese Falcon*.

I leaned in for a quick kiss but hit nothing but air. I stepped back and steeled myself. He must have found out about Jodi and was ticked at me for not saying something before she lawyered up.

"Got a call yesterday from an attorney representing another one of your agency's authors. Jodi Lee?" His features remained neutral, but I could tell he was angry. Over the last couple of years, I'd picked up on his tells, the little physical things that betrayed his emotions. Like the twitch in his jaw, or the way his neck muscles tensed when he was angry. Both those things were happening now.

For a second, I contemplated lying to him. After all, he didn't need to know that I even knew about Jodi's book. She was Flora's client. I could just feign ignorance. But I knew that lies had a way of driving wedges between people. I didn't want that for Sean and me. "She's Flora's client," I said. "I'd never read her book, but Flora told me about it yesterday. I was going to tell you, but Bentley asked me to wait until she could make sure Jodi had an attorney."

I waited, but all he did was nod.

"Are you angry with me?" I finally asked.

He sighed, his muscles noticeably relaxing. "Actually, no. I probably would have done the same thing in your position. Can't really blame Bentley, either. Getting Jodi a lawyer was smart."

I lowered my gaze. Maybe I should have been smarter when it came to Lynn. "So, you must be here about the case," I said, coming back to my original question.

"I am."

A feeling of dread settled over me. "Were any prints found on the nail gun?"

"No. It appears to have been wiped clean. Or the perp was wearing gloves."

Which currently described everyone in town, I thought, staring down at Sean's own hands. I'd given him a nice pair of leather gloves for Christmas after he complained that his police-issued pair had worn thin. "That means there's no real evidence against Jodi or Lynn."

"Not yet." A resolved look settled over his face as he turned to make his way up the steps. I followed, my eyes riveted to the backs of his boots as they clunked against the metal edging on the staircase steps. His walk was determined, meaning he had something serious on his mind, reminding me again of the pertinacious Sam Spade. Come to think of it, Sean was a lot like Hammett's main character, not just in physical appearance but also in demeanor. Especially his single-minded determination and notable detachment from everything and everyone when he was working on a case. I sighed. I might as well forget about coming up with a wedding date or a ring anytime in the near future. Sean's mind would be on nothing but this case until it was solved.

"Detective Griffiths," Vicky said, immediately standing and coming out from behind her desk, picking a few stray orange hairs from her skirt. Eliot remained curled up on his usual chair in our waiting area, acknowledging our sudden presence with a little flick of his tail. "Can I offer you some coffee?" Vicky was saying.

"No thank you," he said, pausing to take note of her sweater. "That color becomes you, Ms. Crump."

Oh brother. He must need something important from her.

Vicky's hand flew to her chest, her gaze moving downward over her teal green sweater with white angora trim along the mock turtleneck and sleeve edges. It certainly did set off her silky white hair and was a bit brighter than the usual conservative apparel of our office manager, but I could see through his ploy. Another of Sean's tells. Vicky's cheeks flushed with pleasure. "That's so kind of you to say, Detective."

Sean dipped his chin. "Is Ms. Duke in?"

"No, I'm expecting her at any moment. She called earlier to say that she was going to call a DA . . . an emergency meeting," she corrected. "Would you like to wait?" She motioned to the chair adjacent to Eliot's perch.

"No, I'm sure you can help me. I need a copy of Ms. Werner's book."

Vicky faltered, her eyes darting my way. "Oh, I'm not sure if that's possible."

"Sure it is," Sean cajoled. "One of you must have access to it." He looked my way. "Lila?"

My mind reeled. Bentley would kill me if I handed over Lynn's as-yet-unpublished manuscript. Not to mention how damning it would be to Lynn's case. I was just about to ask if he had a warrant, a question sure to slide our relationship even further away from setting any wedding date, when the door opened and Bentley came in, Olive in tow.

Eliot immediately arched his back and started hissing. Bentley nodded down the hall and shot Vicky a look, prompting her to sequester the cat to the break room. Then she turned and leveled her gaze on Sean. "Why are you here, Detective?"

I noticed Sean's shoulders tightening. Vicky had returned to her desk, wringing her hands nervously on her lap. "I'm here to pick up a copy of Lynn Werner's manuscript."

"Why don't you get a copy from her?"

"It's on her computer at home. She has no way to access it here. So, I'll need to get a copy from your office."

Bentley squared her shoulders. "Do you have a warrant?"

Sean's shifted his feet. "No."

Bentley threw up a gloved hand. "Well then, we have nothing else to discuss. Good day, Detective." She started down the hall, Olive prancing proudly at her side. "Come with me, Lila," she called over her shoulder.

After casting an apologetic look Sean's way, I shuffled down the hall after her. Instead of her office, she went directly to the conference room.

"Shut the door, please," she told me, shrugging off her coat, which I quickly took and hung on the coatrack, along with my own. In the meantime, she laid her briefcase on the table and was pulling out a list of papers. Next, she extracted her reading glasses. After slipping the attached bejeweled chain around her neck, she adjusted the frames on the end of her nose and started flipping through a notepad. I settled at my usual spot on the other end of the table. Olive took a spot on the floor next to Bentley's feet. "There's something I want to discuss with you before the other agents arrive."

I gripped the side of the table. "Okay."

"Things look bad for our clients. Well, not so bad for Jodi. She doesn't have any clear motive for murder. But Lynn sure does. And she refuses to get an attorney, told the cops all sorts of ugly things about Chuck, her ex, and seems oblivious to how all this could affect her career."

"I think maybe she's relieved that he's dead." I told Bentley about the argument I'd witnessed between the two of them, calling to mind the way I saw her cower during the exchange. "She almost seemed afraid of him. But I don't think she killed him. I can't see her murdering someone that way. It doesn't seem in character. At least not in real life."

"Of course it isn't. They're both innocent. I'm sure of it."

"But, like you said, the evidence is stacked against them. Especially Lynn."

"Yes, it is," Bentley agreed. "And as long as they stand

accused, it's going to look bad for our agency. I can't let that happen. Nor can I stand by and let one of the Novel Idea family members be prosecuted for something they didn't do."

I was listening, wondering what exactly it was she planned to do about all this. But I didn't have to wonder long, because she lifted her chin, her eyes taking on a determined look as she declared, "That's why we're going to help the police solve this case."

Chapter 7

MY MOUTH FELL OPEN. *DID SHE JUST SAY THAT WE'RE going to solve the case? As in the whole agency?* Before I could ask, the door opened and the rest of the crew filed into the room. Flora sat next to me, giving me a reassuring pat on the arm as she settled into her chair.

After a couple of seconds of small talk and paper shuffling, Bentley cleared her throat and started in on the meeting's agenda. "As you all know, with the unfortunate murder of Chuck Richards at our book event, our agency has incurred another blow to our reputation."

"Thanks to Ms. Murder Magnet," Zach threw out.

"You can't put the blame on Lila," Flora defended me. "None of this is her fault."

"That's right," chimed in Franklin. "It's not her fault she keeps finding murder victims. She just seems to . . ." He stopped himself from saying the obvious. But I could fill in the blank. I just seemed to attract dead bodies. Like a magnet. A murder magnet. I sank lower in my chair. Across from me Zach wore a smug look. He was right, after all. I'd definitely earned my reputation.

"Not only has our reputation suffered," Bentley continued, "but two of our authors have become suspects in the crime. Just think how detrimental this could become to their careers. Not to mention the shadow it casts over our agency." She moved to the whiteboard, removed the cap from a dry-erase marker, and drew a long arrow. On one end she wrote the word *Monday*. Then she started marking off increments, labeling each with thirty-minute intervals.

"A timeline?" Vicky asked. Her head was bobbing up and down as she glanced from her own notepad to the whiteboard. Vicky was a dutiful note taker.

"Exactly," Bentley confirmed. "What time did you discover the body, Lila?"

"Just a little before four o'clock, I think."

"Do you remember what time Chuck arrived at the Arts Center?" she asked Jude.

He tapped his pencil a few times before replying, "I'd say right around one thirty. It was just a little after the authors started arriving."

Bentley nodded and marked the timeline intervals between one thirty and four o'clock. "So we know the murder occurred within this time frame."

"What are we doing?" Jude asked. "This feels like a scene out of one of those television detective shows."

"Yeah," Zach piped up, the tone of his voice exciting Olive. She let out an excited *woo-woo* sound, her tail thumping against the floor. "I'm reading a screenplay now for a police drama. The cops are always in the case room, laying out the crime facts on a big whiteboard, just like this."

Vicky's normally serious expression turned to delight.

"We're going to participate in solving the case," she deduced. "A brilliant idea, Ms. Duke. And the sooner we crack the case, the sooner our clients will be exonerated."

Bentley nodded her approval. "My thoughts exactly, Vicky."

A couple of chairs down, Franklin cleared his throat. "This seems a little unconventional, doesn't it?"

"I'd say!" Flora glanced nervously around the table. "And it sounds dangerous. I don't like this idea one bit."

Jude held up his hands. "Hold on, everyone. Let's give Bentley an opportunity to explain." He looked to where she was standing, marker still in hand. "Because certainly you're not asking us to interfere with police business."

"Or do something that would put us in harm's way," Flora added.

"Not at all," Bentley assured us. "All I'm asking is that we pool our brain power. Keep our eyes and ears open. Besides, it's obvious that this killer is a reader, and who knows readers better than us?"

The room fell silent. I wondered if everyone else was as perplexed by that statement as I was.

"I'm not following you," Jude finally said.

She briefly explained the circumstances surrounding the discovery of the body, concluding with, "So, whoever did this used pieces of both Jodi and Lynn's plots in order to frame them for the crime. That means they read the books. They're readers."

My heart started thumping. "But Lynn's book hasn't been published. There's only a handful of people who could have read it." *And except for the editor and a few select people at the publishing house, they are all in this room.* Once again, the room fell silent as nervous eyes darted around the table. Was it my imagination, or was everyone looking at me? Then

I remembered Bentley's little joke the other day at the James Joyce Pub. "The murder victim in her mystery was found facedown in a wedding cake," she'd said about Lynn's book. That was how the killer knew. He or she was at that meeting. That had to be it! I explained my revelation to the group.

"Good!" Bentley exclaimed as soon as I finished. "That's what I'm talking about, people. Brain power." She turned back to the board and made a few notations.

"But there were at least a dozen authors there," Flora said.

Zach nodded. "And all of us."

"And don't forget the waitstaff and restaurant workers," Franklin said, reluctantly getting into the spirit of things. "Any one of them could have overheard that tidbit of information."

"Including Ms. Lambert," Bentley interjected. We all knew there was no love lost between Trudy Lambert, the liaison from Southern Belles Bridal, and Bentley. They'd been butting heads all week. I was sure Bentley would just love to see Ms. Lambert go to jail, and the sooner, the better.

"It sounds like we have more suspects now than when we started," Vicky observed. "And how do we know for sure that Jodi or Lynn *didn't* have something to do with the murder?"

"Certainly not Jodi! I've known her for years. It's just not possible." Flora's tone rose sharply, eliciting a series of high-pitched yaps from Olive.

"Shh, shh," Bentley cooed, bending down to calm the dog with a few strokes on the back.

I shifted in my chair and chewed my lip. No one had mentioned anything about Oscar Belmonte. Although maybe I shouldn't mention anything, either, not until I had something solid—or at least something more than just a feeling. Besides, he hadn't been around to overhear that detail of Lynn's murder plot. Hopefully I'd learn something more over lunch at Machiavelli's. Maybe Bentley's idea was a good one after all. If we all just kept our eyes and ears open, certainly we'd find out something beneficial to the case.

For the next twenty minutes, I listened as the conversation continued back and forth until everyone had voiced their opinions. As expected, Vicky and Franklin were eager to help in any way possible. Zach seemed ambivalent while Jude professed his reluctance to get involved in police business. And Flora, while usually the first to lend a helping hand, was dead set against any sort of involvement. Too dangerous, she maintained. Not that I could disagree with her—I'd found out the hard way in times past that stepping into police business could be deadly. In the end, however, we all agreed to do what Bentley asked—keep our eyes and ears open and report back with any new findings. After all, it couldn't hurt to stay alert for the possibilities.

The rest of the meeting was spent finalizing details for the afternoon's Booked for a Wedding events. Today's scheduled highlight was a cake display and tasting. Apparently Ms. Lambert and the Southern Belles Bridal people were able to secure over twenty local and statewide bakers to participate in today's showing. Of course, one of the bakers who had hoped his cake would make an impression on soon-to-be-brides instead had an impression of a dead man's face smushed into his buttercream creation. I couldn't help but wonder how *that* bit of news had been broken to, and taken by, the shopkeeper.

"Cakes have such a terrible habit of turning out bad just when you especially want them to be good."

"What?" Franklin asked as several heads turned to me.

"Oh, sorry. I was just recalling a verse—"

"From one of Lucy Montgomery's Anne books, isn't it?" Flora interrupted, her eyes alight at the familiarity of the quote from the famous children's book author.

"Yes, actually." I nodded. *"Anne of Green Gables."*

Bentley stared at me over the top of her glasses. "Well, thank you for that tidbit of literary history, Lila; now let's get back to the present, shall we?"

I nodded and quickly informed them that everything was set for Lynn's reading from her debut, *Wed 'til Dead*, later today. Bentley gave a curt nod and proceeded to her final orders for our troupe. I sat back with a sigh; well, at least I hoped, with everything going on, Lynn would still be up to the task. I made a note to meet with her for a practice run prior to her big event. One destroyed cake could be replaced, but the confidence of a new author could be tough enough to shore up, even without all the additional trauma surrounding this event.

After the meeting, I spent the next couple of hours at my desk, reading the proposals that had piled up in my inbox. With the added events of the week and only working half days in the office, I knew I'd fall behind on this task, but I hated to make expectant authors wait. I could just imagine them checking their inboxes, hoping to hear back from me. I let out a long sigh and nestled in for some solid reading.

A LITTLE BEFORE eleven thirty, I made my way out to the back lot, where Mama picked me up for our lunch at Machiavelli's. She was unusually quiet on the way to the restaurant. Probably all the activity and her new responsibility as the Babylonian Fortune-Teller wearing her down. I certainly hoped this wasn't going to be too much for her.

"Looks like we've beat the lunch crowd," I commented as we scooted into the corner booth at Machiavelli's. I rubbed my hand across the red and white checkered tablecloth and then fingered the layers of colored wax dripping down the side of an old Italian wine bottle being used as a candle holder. I looked over at my mother. "Are you okay, Mama?"

"Why wouldn't I be okay?"

I eyed her from across the table and shrugged. "You seem quiet. You needed to discuss something with me?"

"I did?"

This was turning out to be a strange conversation. "That's what you said this morning when you dropped me off at work. That there was something you wanted to tell me at lunch."

"Yes, I did say that, didn't I?" She glanced around, nervously it seemed, before leaning across the table. Just as she began, the waitress arrived with the menus and a pitcher of ice water. "Hi, Althea. How are you today?" she asked, filling our glasses.

"Uh . . . fine, Anna. This is my daughter, Lila. Lila, Anna Maria."

Anna's eyes lit up. "Your daughter! Then you must be Trey's mother." She placed the pitcher on the table and swiped her hand across her apron before holding it out to me. "It's so nice to finally meet you! I'm Anna Maria Belmonte."

I took her hand, immediately recognizing her last name and finding it hard to believe that such a cute, young girl could be related in any way to the big buffoon I'd met the day before. "So you must know Trey from school?" I asked, wondering if Trey and this girl had been classmates.

"From school?" She cast a strange look Mama's way. "Why, no, Ms. Wilkins. Trey and I met here. At the restaurant. My grandfather owns this place."

"I think I'll have the spaghetti and meatball special and a Coke," Mama said.

Caught off guard, I reached for the menu, but with Anna

waiting with notepad and pen in hand, I felt rushed. I ordered the first item my eyes landed on, manicotti with a tomato basil sauce.

"I would have liked more time to look over the menu," I said as soon as Anna retreated to the kitchen with our orders.

"Don't worry. Everything here is delicious. They only hire the best cooks."

I raised a brow, first wondering how she knew this, then remembering Belmonte's comment yesterday about knowing Mama. "I must be the last person to try this place. You've obviously been here a few times." Trey, too, guessing from the waitress's comment. I felt a pang of jealousy. Mama and Trey must have come here together before he left to go back to school. Wonder why they didn't ask me to go with them? "Speaking of Trey. Have you talked to him lately? I've called his dorm several times but haven't been able to reach him."

Mama nodded and took a quick gulp of water, some splashing over the edge as she placed the glass back on the table. She quickly unrolled her silverware and used the red cloth napkin to dab up the spill. "No need to worry. He's doin' just fine."

Aw, so she'd been able to reach him. Figured. Mama and Trey were like two peas in a pod. Truthfully, their tight relationship cut a little close to my heart sometimes. As a single mom, I'd been busy being trying to fulfill both parental roles all these years, which meant while I was busy making sure homework was done, enforcing curfews, and doling out consequences, Mama had stepped in to become the "fun parent." Not that I begrudged her the role, and heaven knows I could never have raised Trey without her, but still there were times I envied the easy way she had with Trey. "Did you ask him how his classes were going? He was worried about his math class this semester. Calculus, I think. I'll probably call and tell him to get a tutor. I'd hate to see his grade point average suffer." As I spoke, I kept a lookout for Oscar. I was hoping to get a better sense of what type of person he really was. Ultimately, I needed to figure out if there was a connection between him and Chuck Richards.

"You miss him, don't ya, sugar?"

Mama's question brought my focus back to the table. "Of course I do. We had such a nice Christmas, don't you think?" My mind floated back to Christmas Day. It was the first time Sean had spent an entire holiday with us and it was wonderful, almost magical actually. I remember feeling blessed that he and Trey got along so well. Sean was going to be an excellent stepdad. "It was sure hard seeing him go back to school, though. Hasn't he grown up this past year? Do you remember some of those stunts he pulled in high school?" I placed my hand on my cheek and shook my head. "I'll never forget the time he and those other boys got busted for tearing up the football field with the car. Then there was that time he—"

"Honey, I gotta tell ya something. It's important."

I reached for my glass of water. "Sure. What is it, Mama?"

She drew in her breath. "It's about Trey. He wasn't happy at school."

"Not happy at school? He's doing so well." What was she saying? And why did she say it in the past tense?

The kitchen door swung open and Anna emerged carrying a tray with our drinks and what I hoped was a bread basket. I was starved. But suddenly her foot caught on something and she pitched forward, the tray flying from her hands.

"Lawdy!" Mama cried as we both sprang from the booth and scurried to help her.

"Anna! Are you okay?" I sidestepped shards of broken glass and squatted next to her on the floor. "Are you cut?"

Behind me, the kitchen door swung open. Then, to my utter astonishment, I heard a familiar voice. Trey's voice. "Anna!"

He joined me in helping her to her feet, his hands resting on her arms as he checked her over. "Are you hurt?" he asked, turning her hands over and looking for glass cuts.

She shook her head. "No. I'm fine. Really. I'll go get a broom and get this cleaned up before the lunch crowd starts arriving."

"Trey?" My voice came out as barely a whisper.

Slowly he turned to face me, his dark brown eyes anxious. "Hi, Mom."

"'Hi, Mom'? Is that all you have to say for yourself? 'Hi, Mom'?" I looked over the stained apron he was wearing. "You're working here? Why aren't you at school?" My voice turned shrill. Over Trey's shoulder, I could see Anna hovering about, broom in hand, afraid to approach us.

"Take it easy, Mom." He glanced around the room and sent a pleading look toward my mother.

I lowered my voice. "Just exactly when did you get back?" I hissed. "And when were you planning on letting me know?" Then something occurred to me. I whipped around and faced my mother. "And you *knew* about this?"

She shooed Trey back toward the kitchen, but he didn't go. Instead he walked over to Anna and took the broom from her hands. "Go get them some more bread and drinks. I'll clean this up."

"I don't want more drinks or bread. I want answers. Now." That stopped everyone cold as my blood ran hot from being so flagrantly lied to. Arms crossed, I stepped toward this now pale-faced boy of mine, when my toe started to catch the edge of something. I looked down, afraid of stepping on glass, and noticed several protruding floor tiles. That must have been what Anna tripped over, I thought.

"Careful." Anna held out a hand to me. She looked up at Trey, back at the floor, and then at Trey again. "You're not going to tell Grandpapa, are you, Trey? He's stressed about this already. You saw how he was the other day."

Trey shook his head. "Did I ever! I thought he was going to kill that guy."

Then, looking around some more, I noticed the whole floor was uneven, some of the tiles cracked and coming loose. Suddenly a light went off in my mind, temporarily eclipsing my anger. "What do you mean, Trey? What guy?"

"Some handyman he hired to do a bunch of stuff around here. I can't remember his name."

Anna spoke up, "I think it was Chuck something."

"Chuck Richards?" I asked.

Her eyes registered recognition. "Yeah! That's it. Don't ever have him do any work for you. He's a terrible contractor."

"Don't worry," I told her. "There's absolutely no chance that anyone will be hiring Chuck for any more jobs."

Chapter 8

"YOO-HOO, MS. WILKINS!"

I stopped short, squeezing my eyes shut for a second before turning around to face Trudy Lambert. "Yes, Ms. Lambert. Is there something I can do for you?" She was the last person I needed to see, especially after everything that had happened today.

"Perhaps you can be of some assistance, especially since Ms. Duke seems preoccupied with other things. We have a slight problem."

It took all of my self-control to keep from rolling my eyes. She didn't have to tell me about problems—I was up to my eyebrows in problems: my client accused of murder, my son leaving school and not even telling me . . . I shook it off and put on my professional face. "I'd be glad to help, if I can."

"It's about your author, Pam Fox."

"Pam? Yes, what is it?"

She lowered her chin and tucked a strand of platinum

blond hair behind her ear. "It seems Pam has some sort of fortune-teller at her booth."

"Oh? Is that a problem?"

"Not necessarily. It's just that the line for fortunes is blocking the other booths. I've received several complaints from the vendors in that area."

I took a deep breath and exhaled slowly. "Okay. I'll see what I can do."

She sent me a sappy smile to match her sugary tone. "Soon, I hope."

I had been on my way to find Lynn in order to do a couple of practice runs on her presentation, but I guessed I could take a few minutes to stop by Pam's booth. "Sure," I sighed. "I'll head over there now."

"I knew I could count on you, Lila." She stepped to the side, opening up the path toward Pam's booth. "I wouldn't think of keeping you another second."

As soon as I was out of earshot, I mumbled a few choice words under my breath. It was easy to see why Bentley butted heads with this woman. Ms. Lambert and my boss were complete antitheses. While both were equally demanding, Bentley dished out directives and orders like a drill sergeant, while Ms. Lambert coated them in sugar and handed them over on a doily-covered platter. I preferred the drill sergeant tactic.

Then again, as I neared the area of Pam's booth, I realized the line, more of a clump actually, really was blocking several other booths. The good news was that Pam was busy on her end of the table, signing books like crazy. Flora's idea of using the Babylonian Fortune-Teller was paying off big-time, but I couldn't even catch a glimpse of Mama behind the starry-eyed and giggling ladies vying to be next. One woman, heading the opposite direction, clogged traffic all the more as she excitedly whispered to others waiting, showing her palm to them, as if it held some secret treasure. I sighed; no doubt this one had just left the Amazing Althea with "good signs," as Mama would say.

"Excuse me," a man's voice called out. "Would y'all mind moving over, please?" I glanced over the heads in the crowd to see a hand waving through the air. "Excuse me, ladies," the deep voice continued, a little more agitated this time. "You're blocking my booth."

Oh, boy. This is a recipe for disaster. I quickly pulled out my phone and called Zach, asking if he wouldn't mind bringing some stanchions to the area. I'd seen some earlier in a storage closet off the main hall.

As I spoke, the voice continued growing more irritated. Pushing through the crowd, I made my way toward the waving hand, finding it attached to a now angry-looking young man. His skin was flushed the same color red as his hair. "Hi," I greeted, with my cheeriest voice, hoping to defuse his anger before he exploded.

His expression softened as he regarded me as a possible customer. "Are you looking for information about my photography services?" The banner on his booth said *Rufus Manning Photography*. A little more excitement crept into his voice as he continued, "I can provide you with a total package from engagement photos all the way through the reception. Perhaps you'd like to look at my portfolio."

"Are you Rufus?" He nodded. I shook his hand and introduced myself. "I just wanted to let you know that I'm going to get this problem taken care of quickly." I explained about bringing in stanchions to cordon off a waiting line for the Babylonian Fortune-Teller.

"Thank you," he replied. "I haven't had a single visitor so far. I don't think anyone can even see my booth." I felt the crowd pressing against my backside as a group of ladies pushed forward to catch a glimpse of Mama in action. I swear, she'd turned into a fortune-telling rock star overnight.

"Well, I'm glad *I* made it through," I commented, admiring a collection of his work displayed behind the booth on a large black partition. There was something about his photographs, something that couldn't quite be put into words. It was as if he'd captured all the unseen moments that happen at a wedding: the prick of a tear in a father's eye, the devilish look on a flower girl's face, the bride's veil dancing in the wind as she embraced her groom under the widespread branches of a live oak. He'd not only captured beautiful images of his subjects, but also absorbed their emotions, archived them for all time. "Your work. It's exquisite."

His eyes followed mine as I studied his work. "Funny you should say that. I'm never quite satisfied with my work. There's always the shot I missed. The one that got away, so to say."

A burst of giggles drew my attention back to the ladies in front of Mama's table. She was looking up at a young blonde and saying, "This card here tells me you're in for smooth sailin' ahead. Maybe you just fixed some problem, or got rid of somethin' agitatin' you."

The blonde tipped her head back and laughed. "I just told my mother-in-law to go jump in a lake. Does that count?"

Another round of laughter ensued as the crowd continued pressing in tighter. I shuffled sideways, trying to open up a little breathing space between me and the edge of Rufus's booth. *Where is Zach with those stanchions?*

Rufus shoved a large album my way. "Here, take a look and tell me what you think of these."

I flipped through the pages, each photo more stunning than the last, until my eye stopped on a photo that looked like the same close-up I'd seen earlier in Makayla's shop. My finger traced the outer edge of the couple's entwined hands, pausing on the engagement ring. It *was* the same. There was no mistaking the unique setting . . .

The sound of rusty tires rolled closer and screeched to a halt somewhere on the other side of the spectators. Then Zach astonished the crowd into silence as he cried out, "Zach to the rescue!"

I gave Rufus an apologetic look and excused myself. Then I weaved back through the bystanders to help Zach unload the full cart of stanchions. It took a while, but we were able to erect a dozen posts and organize the line in front of Pam's table. When we finished, we'd opened up access to all the adjacent booths.

"Much better," I said to Zach, thanking him for his assistance.

"No problem." Then, leaning in closer, he asked with a mischievous glint, "Found the murderer yet?"

I hesitated, wondering if he was serious.

"No, huh? Well, no worries." He hitched both his thumbs to his chest. "Zach's on the case. And I guarantee I can crack it before you." He held out his hand. "Wanna bet on it?"

"No!" I said, letting his hand hang. "I don't think that's what Bentley meant this morning. She just wants us to keep a lookout for the obvious, not actively pursue leads. That could be dangerous, Zach."

He rotated his palms up in a mocking gesture. "Whoa. I never pegged you as someone afraid of a little competition. Scared you'll lose?"

"Lose?" I shook my head. "I'm not even playing the game."

He narrowed his eyes. "Oh, I see. Forfeiting, huh?"

I squeezed my eyes shut and rubbed my temples. "We'll

talk about this later, okay?" Zach was a good guy, just a little overenthusiastic at times, an admirable trait when it came to signing screen and sport contracts, but not so much the rest of the time. Right now, I needed to find Lynn. I glanced at my watch. She was on in fifteen minutes. So I left Zach standing there with an empty roller cart and a smug look on his face as I searched out my author.

I FINALLY FOUND her in the hall outside the textile room, where she was deep in conversation with Dr. Meyers. Hesitant to disrupt them, I hovered down the hall a ways, amusing myself by checking over a display of spa items. However, a sideways glance told me Lynn and the doctor were discussing more than just books. I could tell by the way Lynn swiped at a tear and Dr. Meyers leaned in closer to place a comforting hand on her shoulder. Was I witnessing a bit of the doctor's bedside manner? Was Lynn upset about something—perhaps delayed grief over her ex-husband's death—or was she unburdening details of a crime that would later be classified as privileged information shared between a doctor and client? I quickly dismissed that last thought. Call it gut instinct, or whatever, but I still believed Lynn was innocent.

I waited until the doctor walked away before approaching Lynn. "Hey, everything okay?"

She nodded, her still-moist eyes darting about nervously. "I'm fine," she said, but to me, it looked like she was about to have a breakdown, and she was due to present in just a few minutes. I took her arm and guided her toward the Potter's Room, where I hoped we could find a quiet spot.

"Do you want to go over your reading? We probably have time to run through it before your event starts," I said as we settled at a quiet table in the corner of the room.

She shook her head. "No, I practiced out loud in front of Jodi and Pam last night. They've been so helpful. And Dr. Meyers, too. She's been helping me come to grips with some feelings I have."

"I saw you two talking just a few minutes ago. I'm sure this has been difficult for you."

She lifted her chin and looked me straight in the eye. "The hard part is the guilt I feel."

My heart dropped. "Guilt?"

"Yes, guilt over the relief I feel. I can finally rest easy now. Move on with my life." Her eyes grew wide at my shocked expression. "Not that I killed him," she quickly added, then narrowed her eyes. "You don't think I killed him, do you?"

"No, of course not."

She exhaled. "You see, when Chuck and I first got married, things were wonderful." She fiddled with the table covering as she spoke. "Then slowly, everything began to change. Small things at first. A cross word here and there. Then he started constantly picking me apart. Do you know what I mean?"

I nodded.

"Things kept going downhill from there, until one day, he lost his temper and hit me."

"Oh, Lynn! I'm so sorry."

"It's okay. I got out of the relationship in time. So many women don't, you know. I was lucky. Did you know Dr. Meyers runs a home for abused women over in Dunston? I wished it'd been there when Chuck . . . Well, that's all over now. Really over. And like Dr. Meyers was telling me, I don't need to feel guilty because I'm happy about Chuck's death. She said there's no wrong or right feelings, just feelings. And it's natural for me to feel relieved after everything I went through."

I found myself blinking back tears as she spoke. What an incredible story of strength and courage. "I'm so glad Dr. Meyers was here for you, Lynn. And you're right. You are very fortunate to have escaped that type of relationship. I'm so proud of you. You've overcome the odds and accomplished so much for yourself. I mean, here you are, embarking on a new and fabulous career as an author."

The corners of her lips tipped upward. A tiny smile, but the first one I'd seen for a while. "And if I want to keep my career, I'd better get down the hall and do my presentation."

I gave her hand a little squeeze before we stood. "That's right. Your future readers are waiting."

THE SUNDANCE ROOM, located down the hall from the main auditorium, was a smallish theater, able to seat only a hundred or so, and used mainly for debuting local independent films. Currently, only the first few rows were filled, but it was enough to make Lynn noticeably nervous. I held my breath, my eyes riveted on the stage where she was beginning her reading. After a couple of wobbly starts, she surprised me by finding her groove. After a few more lines, she started to become more confident, showing everyone a little animation and an ability to captivate a crowd. Up to now, I thought she was a very shy, timid person. But over the course of the week, despite Chuck's death and everything going on, she seemed to have blossomed. Now, in front of this crowd, she appeared almost vibrant. And by the end of the first page, she had the audience sitting on the edges of their seats, including someone I didn't expect to see—Sean.

I'd caught sight of him in the second row from the back, notepad in hand as he hung on Lynn's every word. He jotted down several notes as she read up to the point of a page-turning cliff-hanger—the discovery of the murder victim. His scribbling picked up to a feverish pace during that part and I was pretty sure it wasn't because he was a fan.

As Lynn wrapped up her reading, she received a nice round of applause. I started toward the stage to offer my congratulations, but before I could reach her, she was surrounded by a small group of future readers. I turned away and set my sights on Sean instead. "Did you get everything you needed?" I asked, my tone more than slightly sarcastic.

He patted the suit pocket where he kept his notepad. "Believe so. She did a good job, by the way. I liked the sound of the book. Any chance I could get a sneak preview?"

I shook my head.

He shrugged. "Doesn't really matter. I should have the warrant in my hands anytime now."

"Lynn's not your killer," I told him again. "I'm sure of it, Sean. Sure, she seems relieved that he's dead, but that's only because . . ." I stopped short, realizing I was about to relay more information that might be damaging to Lynn's case.

"Because Chuck was abusive," he finished for me. "She already told me about it."

"Oh. Well, then you can kind of understand why she might feel a little relief upon his death. It must have been horrible to endure that type of relationship."

"I'm sure. She must have lived in constant fear. Seeing him again might have caused all those old emotions to resurface. Maybe she just cracked."

I sighed, deciding to change the subject. "Guess who I saw today? Trey."

"Trey? Is everything okay?"

"No, it isn't. He decided to quit school and try making his way as a chef. He's been staying over at Mama's for a while. Can you believe she didn't even tell me?"

"Maybe she was afraid you'd be upset."

"Well, of course I'm upset! He's giving up his education, for crying out loud. He's wasting his chance to go to college. Not to mention the money I shelled out for this semester's tuition." I rolled my neck, trying to relieve some of the tension building there.

"Look, I see your point. Being a chef wouldn't be an easy job. Long hours, crappy starting pay, and it can't be easy work."

This from a guy who practically burned down my kitchen last year. He was speaking from experience.

"But he's going to be twenty years old in just a couple of months," he added. "He's certainly old enough to decide what he wants to do with his life. If it's cooking, then good for him. Look on the bright side—if he gets his own restaurant one day, he'll probably let us eat there for free."

He chuckled. I didn't. Obviously Sean just didn't get it. He'd probably be singing a different tune if it were his kid, and his wasted money. I could feel myself quickly slipping into a dark place, so I decided to refocus the conversation. "Anyway, he's working at Machiavelli's. I ran into him today. I also learned something that might be of interest to your case."

Sean leaned in, all ears.

I continued, "Trey mentioned that Belmonte was really upset over work Chuck had done at the restaurant. Actually, I'd be upset, too. I saw some of his handiwork up close and it wasn't safe, let alone pretty. Anyway, guess they had a huge argument over it the day before Chuck ended up dead. Pretty suspicious, huh? And remember Belmonte was here at the time of the murder; he had the means to kill him as well as a motive."

"That is interesting," Sean said. "Belmonte didn't say anything about Chuck doing work for him."

"Really? Then obviously he's trying to hide something."

Sean's lips pressed into a thin line. "Maybe. I'll see what I can find out. I appreciate you telling me about this, but I absolutely don't want you out looking for information. I've got a whole team of professionals working on this. And last time . . ." He came a little closer and placed his hand discreetly on my hip. "I just couldn't stand it if anything ever happened to you, Lila," he whispered in my ear. With the heat of his breath sending prickles down my neck and my insides going all mushy, I decided it probably wasn't the best time to mention that Bentley had put her own team of professionals on the job.

I FOUND MAKAYLA working her way around the Dragonfly Room with a plate in hand. I'd had enough of Sean and Trey and murder and work for the moment. The expo crowd seemed content to drool over the bridal treats, with not even a whisper about the article on the murder in yesterday's paper penetrating their happy spirits. I wished to join them. All I wanted to do was take my dinner break, enjoy a few sweet confections, and dream of my own wedding. "Thank goodness you're here," Makayla said. "I've already tested three cakes. They're all so good; I can't decide. Jay's favorite is chocolate, but this champagne cake is so moist." She rolled her eyes. "And the frosting has just a touch of orange Cointreau liqueur. Here, try it." She handed me her plate.

I took a bite. The cake, which was both fluffy and moist at the same time, was indescribably good, with a sweet creamy custard between the layers and topped with a rich buttercream frosting containing just the right hint of orange liqueur. "Oh my goodness," I said, stealing another bite. "This is melt-in-your-mouth good!"

She nodded. "Isn't it? Come on." She tugged excitedly on my sleeve. "Let's try some more."

For the next hour or so, we circumvented the room, admiring each stunning display. Cakes of every shape, size, and theme were exhibited. Some showcased intricate detailing and artistic piped designs, while others were textured and decorated with fresh flowers. Makayla loved the more traditional designs, while I was drawn to the whimsical ones like a two-layer square 1920s-themed cake with metallic gold and black art deco designs. It was cleverly accented with a waggish peacock feather.

"Do you like that cake?" Makayla asked, joining me in front of the display. "You've been gawking at it for a few minutes."

"Oh, sorry," I said. "Guess my mind wandered for a second. It reminds me of a query I just received for a mystery set in a 1920s speakeasy." I hadn't heard back yet from the author who'd sent me the query for *Death of a Dame*, the Roaring Twenties mystery. I was anxious to read the rest of the manuscript. That was how it was with good queries— they always stayed on my mind.

"Sounds wonderful."

I shrugged. "I haven't seen the full manuscript yet, but I'm intrigued. Which reminds me, your cover art should be in any day now."

A beaming smile broke out on her face. "I'm so excited about my book. And I have you to thank. You're very good at your job, my friend. Any author who has you for an agent is very lucky indeed." She looped her arm in mine. "But let's not get too distracted. We're here to find our dream wedding cakes, remember?"

Never before had I thought there was such a thing as eating too much cake, but by the time we'd finally finished checking out all twenty-some displays and sampling almost as much cake, I was feeling the beginnings of a sugar coma. "I could use something solid to counteract all this sugar," I told Makayla.

"Oh, really? I was going to suggest we head over to the wine sampling room." I grasped my midsection as my stomach gurgled in protest. Makayla laughed and threw me a mischievous wink. "Just kidding. Actually, I should be going. Promised Jay I'd meet him for dinner later this evening."

"You wouldn't be heading to Machiavelli's, by chance?"

She shook her head. "No, just over to the pub for a quick bite. Jay has some work to do tonight. Why?"

I explained to her about running into Trey and how he'd been hiding out at my mother's and working at Machiavelli's. "He thinks he wants to become a chef. Can you believe it?"

"Yeah, I can. When he worked for me last summer, he always wanted to try out new recipes on the customers." A smirk played on her lips as she thought back to the time. "I have to admit, I tried to get Althea's banana bread recipe from him, but he wouldn't give it up."

"You what?"

She laughed. "Seriously, Lila. He was good in the kitchen. I think he has a knack for cooking. Probably gets it from your mother."

"Probably. I just . . . I mean, giving up an opportunity to go to college to work in a restaurant . . ."

"It's okay," she said. "You've gone through this with him before, remember?"

She was referring to his stint a year or so ago with a commune on Red Fox Mountain. "I remember. And that didn't turn out so well."

"Relax." She reached over and touched my wrist. "I've met

Machiavelli's owner, Oscar, and he's an okay guy. And I've heard he's a gifted chef. Trained at some famous culinary school in New York."

"New York?" Oh, heavens. That'd be the next thing. Trey would want to go off and study in New York.

"Don't worry, Lila. Trey's going to be fine. He's a hard worker and he'll make his own way."

"You sound like my mother."

"She's a smart woman." She gave a little grin. "Different, but smart." Which brought a smile to me as well. She gave me a quick hug and turned to leave just as Cora Scott walked up. "Oh hey, Cora. Good to see you," Makayla said. "Sorry I can't stay and visit, but I've gotta run." She looked at me and added, "We'll talk more later, okay?"

"I've been looking all over for Ms. Duke. Have you seen her?" Cora said as soon as Makayla left. "There's something I feel I should discuss with her. A serious matter."

"No, I haven't seen her lately. Is this about Chuck? The news of his death must have been a shock to you."

Her head bobbed up and down. "Yes, yes, it was quite a shock. Not that I knew him well. It's just, to know he was murdered . . . well, it's all so horrible. And now I feel caught in the middle of things."

"Caught in the middle? How so?"

"Well . . ." She hesitated, wringing her hands and glancing about.

I placed my hand on her shoulder. "Does this have something to do with one of our authors?"

She pressed her lips tight, then opened them again and let out a long sigh. "Yes, yes, it does. You see, your Detective Griffiths stopped by a little while ago and was asking all sorts of questions about the two authors staying at my inn."

"Lynn and Jodi?"

"Uh-huh. And I'm afraid I had to be truthful about something I observed happening, even though it probably caused trouble for Jodi."

Uh-oh. "Of course you had to be truthful," I said, trying to ease the discomfort she was obviously feeling. "Can you tell me what it was?"

"Perhaps I shouldn't, but I feel you should know so you can be prepared. I think the police officer might arrest her. And all because of what I told them."

"Arrest her?" I said, louder than I intended. A woman passing by turned her head and regarded us suspiciously. "Would you mind stepping over here?" I asked, pointing to a quiet spot in the corner of the room. "What is it you saw, Cora?" I asked as soon as we were out of the flow of traffic. I had a feeling this was going to be a doozy.

She brought her hands in front of her hips and began wringing them together. "I think Jodi and Chuck had a tryst."

"Jodi and Chuck? Why do you say that?"

"Because I saw him coming out of her room the morning he was murdered. And when Jodi came down for breakfast that day, she seemed preoccupied with something."

"What did Sean—I mean Detective Griffiths—say when you told him what you saw?"

"He thanked me. Said it was just the connection he was looking for. Then he made a phone call. I heard him requesting a search warrant. He left, but there's still a police officer parked outside the inn."

Sean had gone to pick up a warrant. I was sure of it. He was probably going to search Jodi's room, maybe Lynn's, too. "Thank you for telling me, Cora." I reached out and touched her shoulder. "Can you excuse me, though? I'll go see if I can find Bentley and let her know about this." I started to leave, then turned back and gave her arm a quick squeeze. "You did the right thing letting us know, Cora. I know Ms. Duke will appreciate it."

I stepped away and took out my cell to call Bentley right away. There was no answer. *Shoot!* I moved out to the main hallway and looked about, spying Jude not too far away. "Have you seen Bentley?" I asked.

"She went back to the office to get the dog. Said she'd be right back. Why?"

I wasn't sure I'd heard him correctly about the dog, but it didn't really matter. Bentley must not have answered her phone because she was en route. "How about Flora?" I asked.

"The last I saw her, she was at Jodi's—"

Before he could even finish, I turned on my heel and made a beeline for Jodi's booth, but she was surrounded by fans waiting for her autograph and Flora was nowhere in sight. Hovering nearby, I watched for Jodi's line to dwindle down, but more people just kept coming. Finally, I decided to interrupt. "Do you have a couple of minutes, Jodi? It's important." But as I spoke, I noticed the female officer I'd met yesterday making her way down the aisle toward us. She was accompanied by another officer whom I didn't recognize. They both looked like they meant business.

"Ms. Jodi Lee," the lady cop said as they reached the booth. "You need to come with us. You're wanted on suspicion of murder in connection to Chuck Richards's death."

Chapter 9

THE MOOD IN THE CONFERENCE ROOM WAS BLEAK
Wednesday morning as we rehashed the events leading up
to Jodi's arrest. After being taken in yesterday, Jodi was
officially charged with murder. Apparently, the police had
searched her room and found a strip of pneumatic nails, the
same type that were used to kill Chuck.

"Jodi's waiting for her arraignment," Bentley was telling
us. "Hopefully the attorney can get her out on bond. But I'm
afraid the news of her arrest will do irreversible damage to
her career."

Flora, who was devastated by the arrest of her longtime
client, had called in ill this morning, saying she'd try to catch
up with us later at the expo. As for the rest of us, we were
all shocked by the latest turn in the case, each of us reacting
in our own unique way: Franklin stared off with a pensive
expression, Jude absently doodled on his legal pad, Zach
bounced his knees and tapped his pen annoyingly, and

Vicky . . . well, Vicky kicked her sleuthing mind into high gear.

"This doesn't make one iota of sense," she declared, pushing back her chair and standing to straighten her skirt. She stepped around Olive and made her way to the whiteboard. "Let's reexamine the facts," she said, uncapping a dry-erase marker. "Starting with any new information pertinent to the case."

Zach stopped tapping and sat a little straighter. "You don't think Jodi did it? I mean, they found the same type of nail in her room. And that lady who runs the inn, what's her name?"

"Cora Scott," I supplied.

"Yeah, Cora. She said she saw Chuck leaving Jodi's room early that morning." Zach's gaze danced around the table. "Y'all know what that means, right?"

Franklin cleared his throat and straightened his bow tie. "Actually, Zach, it could mean any number of things, not just what you're insinuating."

"Exactly," Bentley agreed. "We haven't even heard Jodi's side of the story yet. Let's hold off on making any presumptions."

Vicky tapped the dry-erase marker against the board. "Any new information, people? We were supposed to be keeping our eyes and ears open." She gave us "the look" that told us we'd better have something for that board. I wasn't sure at the moment who was the most formidable to answer to: Bentley or our all-too-able Vicky.

I spoke up, telling the crew everything I'd learned yesterday at Machiavelli's. Well, not everything. I left out the part about discovering that my own son had left school, hid out at my mother's for over a week, and started a new job, all without consulting or even saying a word to his own mother. But I did tell them about the second-rate job Chuck did when he renovated Belmonte's restaurant. "The grand-daughter said he was really angry about it."

"That's a great point, and Oscar Belmonte had been present immediately after the murder as well," Jude concurred. "But it brings up another factor: There could be others out there like Belmonte, too. People who are out big money because of Chuck's shoddy work."

Vicky wrote Belmonte's name under our list of suspects and then added yet another name.

"Matt Reynolds?" I gasped. "The pet store owner?"

Vicky nodded smugly. "Yes, I've been spending a lot of time at the pet store lately, picking up things for Ms. Duke's new friend." She cast a dubious look Olive's way. "Yesterday, I overheard Mr. Reynolds talking on the phone with an insurance agent about a recent loss he incurred."

"What type of loss?" Jude asked.

I already knew the answer to that question. It was the large saltwater aquarium that had fallen and crashed to the floor. Matt had blamed Olive for causing the accident. And was he ever angry about it.

"A large aquarium," Vicky answered, confirming my thoughts. "He was telling the person on the phone that he'd discovered that the cause of the accident was an inadequate support structure. Meaning the aquarium stand wasn't built correctly," she clarified, looking to us with a hint of triumph in her tone.

I was starting to put the pieces together in my mind. "Did Chuck build it?"

"I can't say for sure," she answered, removing a tissue from her sweater pocket and dabbing an ink smudge on her hand. "I couldn't think of a prudent way to ask such a question, so instead, before I left the shop, I casually asked Mr. Reynolds

if there were any contractors in town he could recommend.
I told him I needed some work done in my home."

"Very clever, Ms. Crump," Franklin said. "You're turning out to be a regular Miss Marple." Vicky looked down,
her cheeks blushing from the compliment.

Bentley cleared her throat. "What was Mr. Reynolds's
response?" she asked, trying to keep the conversation on
track. Sometime during our discussion, Olive had found her
way to Bentley's lap, where she was snuggled in close. Surprisingly, with everything going on this week, my normally
high-strung boss had remained relatively calm. Maybe what
Franklin said was true. Dogs do have a calming effect on
people. In fact, I'd never seen Bentley so calm. I wondered if
she'd make Olive a permanent addition in her life.

Vicky's voice brought me back to focus. "He didn't actually give me a name, but he did say that thankfully the worst
contractor in town was no longer in business." She shuddered.
"And he said it with such a menacing smile. So out of character for such a nice man."

I heard Sean's words echo in my mind: *Nice people do
bad things.* He was right, of course. It was hard telling what
might push someone over the edge. Cause them to do the
unthinkable. Had Matt been pushed too far? Was the financial stress of the ruined aquarium enough to make Matt resort
to murder? When he'd thought the cause was Olive, pet lover
that he is, he was willing let the poor thing freeze to death
out in the cold streets, at least in the heat of the moment. But,
eventually, he'd realized it was an accident. How would he
feel when he discovered a person he'd paid had been the
cause of the loss? And that it was no accident at all, just plain
negligence? I didn't want to, but I had to admit, his name did
belong on our list of suspects, which seemed to be growing
longer by the day.

"Yoo-hoo!" A voice came from outside the conference room. It was followed with a sharp knock on the conference room door. "Are y'all in here?"

Olive let go with a series of high-pitched yelps, jumped to the floor, and ran to the door. Unfortunately, I recognized that *yoo-hoo*. It belonged to Ms. Lambert.

Bentley threw open the conference room door and smiled through gritted teeth. "Yes, Ms. Lambert. Is there something I can do for you?"

The woman pushed past Bentley and came right on into the room, passing around her sugary smile like she was sharing a box of chocolates with old friends. "Hi, y'all. I just stopped by to talk a little about what happened yesterday. The author being arrested in front of attendees, well, it was so distasteful. When Southern Belles Bridal signed on with you people, we didn't know y'all had a reputation for this sort of thing. Now I'm hearing around town that this type of stuff happens at most of your events. Something that you should have disclosed before we entered into an agreement, Ms. Duke."

"Disclosed what? That we anticipated a murder at the expo?" Bentley asked with an incredulous expression.

From the floor, Olive started growling. Obviously she didn't think much of Ms. Lambert's attitude, either. Ms. Lambert looked down her nose at the pup and curled her lip with disdain. "What a feisty little dog you are."

Bentley signaled Vicky. "Ms. Crump, would you mind taking Olive for a walk? I think she needs a little exercise."

Vicky let out her own little growl as she stood and scooped up the dog. The rest of us remained silent, waiting for the inevitable row that was about to occur. Ms. Lambert had a lot of nerve waltzing into Bentley's domain and addressing her in such a way. Then insulting Olive? Oh boy. She was about to get blasted.

As soon as the door shut behind Vicky and Olive, Bentley turned back to the insufferable woman and scowled. To my surprise, though, and probably the surprise of everyone in the room, Bentley remained controlled. She even managed to match the woman's saccharine smile with one of her own. "Ms. Lambert. I can assure you that our reputation is impeccable. That's why authors from around the world seek our representation. The fact that the crime rate has risen in this area has nothing to do with us. And the idea that you would buy into the canards of scandalmongers and muckrakers is an insult to your obvious intelligence."

Somewhere buried in there was a compliment, and Mrs. Lambert was, if anything, easily flattered. Two bright circles of pink appeared on her cheeks as she started backtracking her statements. "Yes, of course, Ms. Duke. I do apologize. I'm sure that's all it was: silly gossip. I should have realized that when someone made mention of a murder magnet." She chuckled. "I mean, really, isn't that the silliest thing y'all have ever heard?"

THERE IT WAS again. That phrase, *murder magnet*. I carried the title the rest of the day as if it'd been emblazed in scarlet on my forehead. Cloaked in paranoia, I imagined the glare of accusing eyes and the sting of bated whispers behind me. It made for a long day.

Finally, around eight o'clock that evening, after the day's expo events wrapped up, I gladly made my way across the parking lot toward Mama's truck. Tight little snowflakes danced under the light illuminating from the parking lot poles and pelted my face as I stepped carefully over the snow-packed areas of the pavement. I could see exhaust from the truck's tailpipe and uttered a word or two of gratitude that she already had the heater going.

Despite everything hanging over our heads, we'd managed to pull off a successful day. The authors and vendors had been busy enough that they didn't have time to gossip over the yellow tape that many of them had spied yesterday. Plus, of course, they had a vested interest in not letting anything taint the attitudes of their potential clients. So the crowds remained mostly oblivious to everything but vintage lace veils and Hawaiian honeymoon packages. As expected, the wine tasting event was completely sold out. And with all the refreshments as a primer, the crowd was ready to buy, buy, buy when it came time for Franklin's author to read from his hit book, *Wines for All Occasions.*

Before leaving the Arts Center, I'd stopped by Lynn's booth and we talked about Jodi's arrest. She'd been shocked by the news because she didn't think Jodi and Chuck even knew each other. When I'd asked her about Chuck's work record, she'd told me he had never held a job for more than a few months at a time and his current occupation as a handyman surprised her, because, as she'd put it, "He was about as useful as a chocolate teapot." Apparently, he'd never done as much as change a lightbulb when they were married.

I tried to push all that out of my mind, though, as I climbed into the passenger seat and greeted Mama. "How was your day?" I asked. Things had been so busy, I'd really only had a chance to check on her a few times throughout the afternoon. Each time she'd been so involved in giving tittering groups of ladies glimpses into their futures that she'd barely had time to say hello to me.

"Exhaustin'! I don't think I've told this many fortunes my whole life. I've 'bout worn out my gift. And am I ever bone tired." She stretched a few kinks out before looking over her shoulder and putting the truck in gear.

I eyed her closely. Mama was so vibrant and youthful-looking, it was easy to forget she was in her seventies. "Really? You shouldn't be overdoing it, Mama. Maybe you should take some time off tomorrow. I'm sure Pam could spare you for a few hours."

"*Pssh!* Don't you be worryin' none 'bout me. I can take it. Besides, it isn't nothin' a sit-down with my best man can't cure."

I smiled. Mama and her best man, Mr. Jim Beam, had been consorting for many years now. In fact, I was just sure her veins probably flowed with the stuff by now.

She continued, "Well, that and a little pasta."

I let out a little groan. "No, I'm not up for that tonight, Mama. Sorry. Anyway, aren't they going to close up soon? It's getting close to nine o'clock."

"Good point." She kept her focus on the road, and I was relieved we were headed home and not to a confrontation with my son. "How was your day, sugar? Any more news on the killin' of that handyman?"

"Not really. Jodi's arraignment should be tomorrow, but I haven't heard for sure." I'd already told Mama all about Jodi's arrest earlier that morning.

"Now, I can't keep all these authors straight. She's the gal that writes those romantic suspense novels, like Pam's, right?"

"Well, no . . ." I hedged. I couldn't believe she hadn't read Pam's books yet. Was she ever going to be surprised! "Pam's books aren't quite like Jodi's. They're a little heavier on romance and definitely lighter on suspense."

She shrugged. "Been meanin' to read them, just haven't found the time yet. Anyway, sugar. Tell me who the suspects are. Maybe somethin' will come to me."

I drew in a deep breath, knowing darn well she wasn't going to like what she was about to hear. "Well, there's Lynn and Jodi, of course." She waved those two names off. "And we added someone new today. Matt Reynolds. He owns the pet store in town." I told her about how Chuck had done a poor job constructing the aquarium stand. "I was in the store after it collapsed. It was a huge mess and Matt lost so many fish. He was very angry about it."

"Angry enough to kill?"

I shrugged. "I don't want to think so."

"Well, I'm not gettin' a feeling from any one of them folks. Is that all you have?"

"No. There's one more. Oscar Belmonte."

"Oscar?" She slapped the steering wheel and let out a robust belly laugh. "Why, he's nothing but a big ol' teddy bear. He couldn't hurt a fly. Did y'all know he's raisin' that granddaughter of his all by himself? Poor dear. Lost her parents a few years back in a terrible accident. He moved here from New Jersey just to make a better life for her." She shook her head again. "No, Oscar's not your man. Listen to your mama on this one, hon, and don't be wastin' time barkin' up the wrong tree."

I sighed. "If you say so." But I couldn't help but wonder if her instincts weren't being derailed by her personal feelings. Obviously she felt some sort of friendship with this man. I was about to ask her about it when I noticed we were pulling onto Walden Woods Circle. "I'll make you some of that pasta you were talking about, if you like, Mama."

"No need. I ordered takeout." A sly smile played on her lips.

As we rounded the corner, my heart gave a little leap. Trey's blue Honda was parked outside my cottage! Then it fell flat when the angry thoughts came flooding back. "What's going on? Why is Trey here? Has he moved back home?" A little part of me hoped that was the case. That he'd come by asking for my forgiveness, admitting that he'd made a horrible mistake and begging to come home for a little while until he could get reenrolled in classes. I exited the truck and stomped through the snow to the front door. *He better not want me to pay for this crazy little excursion from reality.* One thing on tonight's plate was going to be a heart-to-heart about how he planned to make up for the tuition I'd already paid out for this semester.

Inside, I zipped out of my boots and tossed my coat over the back of the recliner in the front room. The wonderful smell drifting from the kitchen momentarily quelled my anger as I realized I hadn't really eaten anything more than a few pretzels at the wine tasting.

"Trey?" I called into the kitchen, ready to get to the bottom of things.

He turned from the counter and stood facing me, a smudge of red sauce under his dark eyes and his hair all whooshed to one side. I had a sudden flashback to the little boy who used to swipe Mama's baking tins and wooden spoons, disappearing in the backyard to make mud pies. I remembered clumsy little hands mixing and stirring, patting and pouring and painstakingly decorating with bits and pieces of nature. How delighted he'd be when I'd make gobble noises and eat it all up!

Next to me, Mama whispered in my ear, "He's his own man, Lila. Let him prove himself."

I looked from Trey down to the stove, where he was tending to a large pan filled with bubbling red sauce, chunks of juicy-looking meat, and plump garlic cloves. The kitchen smelled wonderfully of tangy tomatoes, spicy pork, and starchy pasta. It was enough to make anyone else want to yell out *Buon appetito!* and make a pig of themselves, but it only made my own heart ache all the more to think this would be the extent of my son's life—a cook, with his only security held by his next restaurant owner's whim. I swallowed back my reaction, cautiously weighing my next move. But when I spoke—"Why do you want to be a chef, Trey?"—I heard my voice crack with a mix of desperation, anger, and confusion.

He looked down, gathering his thoughts as I waited patiently for his reply. "It's like art to me, Mom. Putting together ingredients to make something beautiful for people to enjoy. And every time I'm in the kitchen there's something new and challenging. How can I make this better, spicier, or more delicious? And then there's the joy of watching people eat my food." He shrugged. "I don't know, Mom. Guess it probably seems weird to you."

There it was. A simple but heartfelt reason why my son had left school, even though he knew I'd be upset. He'd found his calling. Not one I'd have chosen for him. Not one that was safe or secure or prestigious. But it was his choice, what he loved. I'd often regretted that it took me until I was forty-five to stumble into my dream job, and here he was, so fortunate to have found his at a young age. And here I was, trying to keep him from pursuing this dream of his. *What was wrong with me?* I crossed the room and engulfed him in a giant hug. "It doesn't seem weird to me, Trey. It just sounds like you've found your passion." Then I pulled away, holding him at arm's length, smiling through tears of happiness. "I'm glad you're home, son."

"So am I, Mom. So am I."

"But I'm angry that you didn't tell me yourself, Trey. You lied to me! I thought you were still at school all this time. And what about your tuition? Can we get it back?"

Mama came over to us and put her hands on our shoulders. "All good questions, sugar. Why don't we tackle 'em over dinner? I've really worked up an appetite today. I'm feelin' 'bout half starved." She gave me a little push toward the chair. "Go on, now. Sit down."

I did as she said, sinking into the chair as if it were a hammock. I remembered what Mama had said earlier: *bone tired*. That was exactly how I felt. I'd been trying to push this stuff with Trey to the back of my mind, but it seemed to have caught up with me all at once. I looked over and saw Mama pouring herself a glass of whiskey. "Would you mind pouring me one of those, Mama?"

"You must be thinkin' the same thing I am, hon?"

"What's that?"

She passed a glass of amber liquid my way. "That Mr. Beam would be a welcome dinner guest tonight."

Chapter 10

LATER THAT NIGHT, I LAY IN BED CURSING MYSELF FOR eating pasta so late in the evening. Not to mention that the warm glow of Mr. Beam's libation was likely part of the roiling effects I was now suffering. A bit of delicate chardonnay with dinner or a sip of a sweet after-dinner cognac was more my style, but oh, no, I'd joined in with Mama's dear friend tonight. Now my stomach lurched like a ship caught on stormy ocean waves as my brain tried—and failed—to keep an even keel. Of course, no meal could possibly pair well with the discussion at our table tonight. After a lot of back-and-forth, Trey and I had finally come to an agreement. If cooking was really what he thought he wanted to do, then so be it. I supported his decision and would help him in any way I could. But he was going to give me a portion of his paycheck until he'd fully paid for the tuition I'd lost. I could tell he wasn't thrilled with that, but, really, how could he expect otherwise? That was only reasonable, after all.

Sighing, I rolled over, slapped my pillow a few times, and plopped my head back down. Not only was my stomach rolling, but my thoughts were reeling. Or maybe it wasn't the pasta and dinner conversation upsetting my stomach, but the awful thought that'd been niggling at my mind all day: Lynn might really be guilty.

After all, someone had to have planted those nails in Jodi's room. Because what motive did Jodi possibly have for wanting Chuck dead? As far as I or anyone knew, she and Chuck had never met before this weekend. Even if what Cora thought was true, that Jodi and Chuck had a fling, so what? Although I didn't quite take Jodi for the "fling" type. But even if she had, why kill him? And those nails so conveniently found in her room? It just seemed too easy. Too coincidental, especially when combined with the very same murder method she'd used in her own book. Of course, maybe Chuck was in her room for some reason related to the remodel and simply dropped the nails. But wouldn't he have noticed? Heard them drop to the floor? No, more than likely the real murderer planted the nails in Jodi's room to cinch the deal. Knowing that if they were discovered, Jodi would be arrested and all the focus would be put on her. The question was, who had that type of access to her room? The rooms had locks, so surely Jodi would have locked her room when she left the house. But while she was there? She might have left it unlocked, so anyone also in the house at that time could get in. There were only three people that I knew of: Lynn, Pam, and Cora. And here's the part that really bugged me: Out of those three, Lynn was the only one who had any sort of reason to want Chuck dead.

Letting out another sigh, I squinted at my nightstand clock. After midnight. Giving up on sleep, I turned on my lamp and slipped out of the covers. Then I quickly traversed the cold pine-planked floor to retrieve some papers from my purse before diving back under covers. Earlier that day, I'd snatched a pile of queries from my desk, hoping I'd find some free time to read over a few. Now seemed as good a time as any. Maybe they'd take my mind off the case and my queasy stomach.

Surprisingly enough, the first one I read appealed to me. Even from just a one-page query, I could tell the author had a remarkable knack for character development. Her protagonist's personality shone through from the first line and carried through the entire query. Best of all, the author had taken a risk when developing her main character. She'd painted a picture of an older female protagonist, rough around the edges, street-wise and prone to bad habits like heavy drinking and swearing. *Interesting.* I marked it and set it aside. I'd be asking to see more of the author's work.

I kept working my way through the pile but didn't really find anything else of interest. Eventually, I must have drifted off because sometime in the early morning I was jostled from sleep by the ringing of my cell phone.

Had I overslept? Was something wrong? Trey? Then I remembered he was here, sleeping in his room just down the hall. *Mama? Was something wrong with . . . ?* "Hello," I said, trying to shake my brain fog.

"Lila. It's me, Makayla. I'm sorry to wake you."

"Makayla?" Her voice sounded strange. I sat up straight, on full alert now. "No, it's okay. What's wrong? Are you okay?"

"Yeah. I'm fine. It's just that . . . Can you come over to the café? Someone's broken in and they've torn up the place. Jay's here, but we need help."

"You were robbed? Have you called the police?" I was already heading for the bathroom, phone in hand.

"Yes, they've been here and gone. They asked some questions and made out a report. That's about it. I can't tell for sure, but I don't think anything was stolen."

I used my free hand to load my toothbrush with toothpaste as I spoke. "Okay. I'm on my way. I'll bring Trey with me." Hanging up, I did a quick brush and turned the shower on full force. As the water heated, I headed down the hall to rouse Trey. I stopped just inside his door. It did my heart good to see him back in his own bed. His breathing was deep and punctuated with little snores. "Trey," I said, rubbing the tuft of brown hair peeking out from the covers. He was wrapped up in his blankets like a mummy. He always was a hard sleeper. "Trey?"

For a brief second, his eyelids parted, but then his eyes rolled back and closed again. I shook him and patted his face. "Trey! Get up. Makayla needs our help."

I HAD NO idea just how much she needed our help until about a half hour later, when Trey and I walked through the bashed-in back door of Espresso Yourself. Tables were overturned, chairs broken, artwork torn off the walls. But behind the counter was the real mess. Containers of coffee and loose tea overturned and spilled on the floor and counter, packages of napkins ripped open and coffee mugs broken. Next to me, Trey shook his head and asked, "Who would do this?"

Good question. The whole thing seemed so senseless. And undoubtedly costly. Sure, insurance would most likely cover the cost of missing or destroyed items, but there was no accounting for the time and emotional costs of such a malicious act.

I heard some noise coming from the kitchen and hurried back to find Makayla and Jay sweeping up shards of glass and piles of dumped flour and spices. I crossed the room and pulled Makayla into an embrace. "I'm so sorry. Any idea who would have done something like this?"

"No idea," she responded, fiddling nervously with her apron strings. "I'd just got here and noticed the back door was ajar. I could tell it'd been forced open, so I called the police."

"Then she called me," Jay added. He must have come over as soon as Makayla called. He wore a hooded sweatshirt over plaid pajama bottoms and loafer-style slippers.

"What time was that?" I asked.

"Must have been a little before five," Makayla answered. "I usually come in around then to start my baking."

"Nothing's missing?"

She shook her head. "Not that I can tell. Thankfully, there wasn't much money here. I took in a deposit after closing yesterday. All I had on hand was enough change to open up this morning."

Jay tenderly placed his arm around her shoulders. "I'm just glad you didn't run into these lunatics. I couldn't bear it if anything ever happened to you." He swallowed hard, obviously shook up. "I'm getting a security system installed today."

"I can't let you do that," Makayla protested. "It's too expensive. And I can't afford one right now." She looked around, her features falling as she seemed to shrink into herself. "Especially after all this," she whispered.

Trey took a deep breath and stepped up. "How about Mom and I start out front? I remember how everything goes from when I used to work here. We'll get it whipped back into shape, I promise."

Makayla started nodding, pressing her trembling lips tightly together. After taking a quick swipe at her cheek, she looked up with bright eyes. "Just don't know what I'd do without y'all." We hugged again, and this time when we pulled apart, she took a ragged breath and straightened her shoulders. "But first things first. I'm going to put some coffee on, 'cuz if y'all are going to help me tackle this mess, you'll need to fuel up."

The air instantly seemed lighter. Jay smiled and clapped his hands together. "Now, that's a good idea."

We all kicked it into gear: Makayla brewing up some motivation, Jay going back to sweeping up flour, and Trey and I sweeping clean enough floor space out front to start flipping tables and chairs back into position. In short order we all had steaming mugs of bold breakfast-brew coffee close at hand while we dug into the mess. Soon, the aftereffects of last night's whiskey and words were dissipated with the generous jolts of caffeine and my desire to help my dearest friend.

"Do you think we can save some of the photographs?" Trey asked a little while later. We were still working in the front of the café, sweeping up the final pile of mangled frames and broken glass. We'd already removed the prints from their broken frames and laid them out on the tables. Most were so crumpled and torn that they were unsalvageable.

"At least they're only photographs," I commented, and then shook my head. "I didn't mean that the way it sounded. It's just that the only things really lost are the mats and frames. The photos can be reprinted." I shuddered to think if this had been an exhibition of original watercolors or sketches—the artist's vision and talent lost forever.

I stacked the prints and stashed them under the counter so Makayla could contact the artists later, then joined Trey in cleaning up the piles of overturned coffee beans. Before long, we had everything nearly back in order. We were sweeping away the last bit of coffee grounds when a knock on the front door interrupted us.

"Customers are already here," Trey said, a note of panic in his tone. I ducked into the kitchen to let Makayla know.

She came right out and opened the door, with her usual cheerful smile. "Good morning. Sorry about that. Come on in. I'm just a little slow opening up this morning."

Another customer, then another, shuffled in, leaving little puddles of melted snow on a path to the counter. Soon the whole place was crawling with people ordering their morning caffeine fix. A few people commented about the missing artwork, but other than that, nobody seemed to notice anything out of the ordinary in the shop.

Trey stayed behind the counter, and he and Makayla worked in tandem to take care of customers. Since they had lost so many supplies, they had to make a few order adjustments here and there, but overall things were going smoothly. So, after double-checking to make sure Jay had things under control in the kitchen, I put on my coat and left quietly to head up to work.

But once outside, I hesitated. It was only a little after eight o'clock. I usually didn't show up at the office until nine, so there was a little over forty-five minutes to spare. Just enough time to head over to the pet shop and pay Matt Reynolds a visit.

MATT LOOKED UP from stocking his lower shelves with bulk-sized bags of various shapes of kibble. "Good morning, Lila. You're here early." As soon as I told him about Makayla's shop being vandalized, he stopped working and stood up, peering toward the window. "That's terrible. Who would do something like that?"

"The cops seemed to think it was kids. Guess there's

been quite a few incidents like this in Dunston lately. They think it's moving to our area."

Matt scratched his early-morning stubble of a beard. "That's all we need. We moved to this area because we thought it was a quiet community. Seems there's been a lot of crime lately."

"You mean Chuck Richards's murder?"

He shook his head and squatted down to finish unpacking the box. "Yeah, I read about that in the paper. Can't say I'm surprised." I must have had a shocked look on my face, because he immediately started backtracking. "Oh, heck. I didn't mean that to come out the way it sounded. No one deserves something like that. Forget I said anything, okay? It's just that I've been under a lot of stress lately."

"You mean with losing the aquarium and everything?"

"Yeah, that was a huge hit. The tank and the equipment were covered on my insurance plan, but not the fish. Or the damage caused by the water." He sighed and shook his head. "Running a small business is difficult these days. There's not a lot of margin for error. And that Richards guy?"

"Yeah?"

"Well, I hired him to do a few things around here. He came cheap. Now I know why."

"What do you mean?"

"Follow me." We were working our way through the aisle toward the back of the store when he said, "By the way, how's Olive doing? Giving Bentley fits?"

I chuckled. "Well, you were right. She's a handful. Seems to have a calming effect on Bentley, though. You know how high-strung she can be."

"Dogs do that for people, you know? That's why they're used so much in hospital therapy."

"I believe it. I've never seen my boss this content before."
Of course, I couldn't say the same for Vicky and Eliot.

We'd reached the puppy area, where a couple of yellow
Lab pups were frolicking in the pen, rolling around together
in a cartwheel of paws and ears. Unable to resist, I paused
to watch their play.

"Aren't they cute?" Matt asked. He reached in and picked
one up. "This little girl is Ethel. The other's Lucille. They're
sisters."

"Lucy and Ethel? I love their names." I bent down and
ran my fingers along a tuft of downy-soft fur under Ethel's
ears. "They're so sweet."

"Aren't they? Seeing them now, it's hard to believe all
they've been through."

"Been through? What do you mean?"

"They're rescue pups. Just came in yesterday. A couple
of months ago, they were removed from a breeder who'd
been neglecting them. Poor things were starving to death."
Ethel started squirming in his arms, bending her nose
toward the floor. He gently put her back to play with her
sister. "Ethel was really underweight and had infected sores
on two of her paws."

"That's horrible. Who would do such a thing?"

Matt shoved his hands into his pockets and took a deep
breath. "There's a lot of bad people out there, Lila. That's
just a fact."

There were. I also knew there were a lot of people working
every day to right the wrongs in the world. Matt was one of
those people, caring for these animals the way he did. It was
hard to believe that anyone so nice could be a murderer. Again,
Sean's words came back to mind: *Nice people do bad things*.

"Anyway," Matt was saying. "I hope things work out

between Bentley and Olive. It hasn't been easy finding a good match for that dog." He turned to head for the back room, so I gave Lucy and Ethel each a parting belly rub and followed. "Watch your step," he called back to me. "Things are kinda messy back here."

He wasn't kidding. The whole room was torn apart, including the floor and even part of the drywall. "I had no idea you'd had this type of damage," I said, stepping over a long roll of carpet.

"Yeah, well, a couple hundred gallons of salt water can do that." His eyes flashed with anger. "Richards assured me the stand was going to be strong enough to support that type of weight, but . . ." Matt shook his head and muttered something unrepeatable under his breath. "Then, after I took up the carpet, I found that parts of the subflooring hadn't been nailed to the floor joists. What a mess." He pointed down at the plywood covering the floor. I could see a few nail heads here and there, most of them driven into the wood at a crooked angle. Some even bent and sticking out of the wood. Whoever did the floor wasn't too handy with a hammer.

"Let me guess. Chuck did your floor, too." I was reminded of Belmonte's tile job. Matt nodded. Chuck had definitely left a trail of destruction behind. "So how long will this take you to repair?"

He glanced around the room, hands on his hips. "Well, the carpet's in bad shape. The salt water from the tank caused a lot of damage. I'll have to have someone come in and install another rug. But the subfloors are no problem. I can nail that back down myself." He pointed to the corner of the room where he'd already started working. My eyes were instantly drawn to one of the tools—a nail gun. I searched my brain trying to remember if the article in the paper had mentioned the way Chuck was killed, but I couldn't recall. Seeing one now, though, made my blood run cold. I'd have to add nail guns to my running list of tools I could no longer tolerate, like garden spades.

"You okay, Lila? You look like you've seen a ghost."

I blinked a few times and swallowed hard. "Is that a nail gun?"

He walked over and picked it up. "This thing? Yeah, I rented it for the day. It sure makes the job easier."

I couldn't help but notice how well it fit his giant hands. I nodded. "Those things can be dangerous, can't they?"

"Heck yeah. Gotta be careful with these things. You could really hurt someone with one of these." As if to demonstrate, he bent down, pressed the tip against the floor, and pulled the trigger: *click-thunk!*

Or kill someone, I thought.

Chapter 11

THE NOISE FROM THE NAIL GUN STILL HAUNTED ME AS I stomped my feet on the mat just inside the office door. Olive greeted me with a little bark and scurried over for a quick sniff of my boots. "Hello there," I said, scratching between her ears. "And good morning to you, Vicky." I did my best to put on a cheerful tone, despite the fact that my stomach was in knots from everything that had happened this morning. I quickly told Vicky about the break-in at Espresso Yourself.

"That's simply dreadful. Who would do such a thing? Did they apprehend the perpetrators?"

"No. The police think it's related to some vandalism incidents in Dunston. Kids, they think. We were able to get most of it cleaned up in time for her to open this morning."

"That poor girl. I'll go down on my break and see if there's anything else she needs."

"I also paid a visit to Matt over at All Creatures, Feathered and Furry. You were right. The accident was caused by a faulty stand. And he told me that Chuck built it."

Vicky nodded triumphantly. "Just as I presumed."

"The worst part is, when the aquarium broke, it flooded the whole back room. The carpet, even part of the drywall, was destroyed. And insurance won't cover all the costs."

"The repairs sound expensive."

I nodded. "And there's more." I almost hated to mention the rest, because it painted an ugly picture of Matt. And the truth was, he was a good guy. I really liked him. Still, the destruction caused by Chuck's subpar work could easily have been motive for murder. "Apparently, Chuck did some work on the shop before it opened last summer. When Matt tore out the carpet, he found that Chuck hadn't properly nailed down the subflooring. So he was taking care of it himself. With a cordless pneumatic nail gun."

"That's what—"

"Yeah. That's what the killer used on Chuck. Gave me the creeps to see Matt holding one. And the sound . . ." I shuddered.

"Yes, but it does establish the fact that Matt knew how to use one. I was thinking that I'd have no idea how to operate one of those things. I bet a lot of people wouldn't."

She was right. The killer would have to have some knowledge of how to handle a nail gun. Of course, if they'd planned the murder to set up Jodi, or Lynn, they would have had plenty of time to learn how to use one. But . . . "I just thought of something. I keep assuming we had to consider Jodi or maybe Lynn, too, on our suspect list. But now, with the nails found in Jodi's room, it's looking like someone really intended to frame Jodi all along. I mean, it makes sense, right? Why would she use the same method that was used in her book and then be careless enough to just leave a strip of pneumatic nails in her room?"

Vicky nodded. "I agree. It would seem that she's being framed." Suddenly she darted from her chair. "Stop that! Bad dog!" She ran over to where Olive was chewing on the leg of one of the waiting room chairs. She pulled her away and placed her on her doggie mat in the corner of the room before returning to her desk with a disgruntled sigh. "Sorry. Please go on."

"I'm just wondering, if Jodi was framed, how did the killer know Chuck was going to be in the kitchen at that very moment with a nail gun in his tool bag? And why'd Chuck bring in a nail gun in the first place? It wouldn't seem a likely tool for fixing a refrigerator."

"Perhaps he always carried one in his bag," Vicky supplied.

"Maybe." Although it was kind of a big thing to carry around all the time. "Still. The timing was incredible. And getting back to Matt. We don't know if he was anywhere near the Arts Center that afternoon."

"You're right. We'll need to find out if he had an alibi." A whining noise drew our attention to the door, where Olive was pawing to go out. "Oh for Pete's sake!" Vicky grumbled, reaching under the desk, where she kept a small tote bag with her winter boots. She started slipping off her sensible pumps and sliding on her boots. "You'll have to excuse you, Lila. *Olive* needs to be walked." Her tone on the dog's name left no doubt as to her feelings about this task.

I glanced down the hall toward Bentley's office door. "Where's Bentley? Shouldn't she be taking care of Olive?"

Vicky pressed her lips tightly together and let out an exaggerated harrumph. "Jodi's arraignment was scheduled first thing this morning. Both she and Flora went to the court-house. I'm supposed to remind everyone to keep their ears and eyes open for anything that will exonerate Jodi." She lifted her heavy wool coat from the coat stand and wrapped a hand-knitted muffler around her neck. Next to her, Olive yapped and jumped with excitement. Vicky turned to me before opening the door. "I would do a little checking around on my own, but I've been busy dog sitting. Of course, it seems dog sitting is all I've been doing lately. By the way, would you mind checking in on Eliot? He's in the break room. He might need some extra water." Her voice was almost sorrow-ful as she asked. I was starting to wonder just how wise it was for Bentley to take on Olive's care, even if it was just tempo-rary. Sure, Olive needed a home and she did seem to have a soothing effect on our high-strung boss. But was Bentley's on-the-go lifestyle really suitable for caring for the lovable but highly demanding Olive? Sloughing off that responsibil-ity to Vicky might seem a simple fix to her, but the repercus-sions could be disastrous. Vicky was a considerable asset to our agency; her thorough and no-nonsense personality had created a smoothly functioning office, something that was hard enough to find in any office staff, especially one with such high energy and eclectic personalities as our agency. Bentley really couldn't afford to jeopardize that. I shook my head. I had a feeling that what started out as a good intention was going to end up as a bad dilemma.

ON THE WAY to my office, I stepped into the break room, picked up Eliot, and took him with me. After throwing my shoulder bag in the bottom desk drawer and flipping on my computer, I set him on the floor. Then I went back to the break room and retrieved his water and food bowls. "You can just hang out with me for a while, buddy," I said, placing them on the floor by my desk. In response, he rubbed against my legs and let out a purr that sounded like a motorboat starting up. I think he liked the idea of hanging with me.

Just as I settled behind my desk, my phone rang. It was Sean.

"Hey, there," he said. "Glad I caught you in your office."

"Yeah. Good timing. I was about to give you a call. There's something I need to talk to you about."

"Bet there is. Just got in. Saw that someone broke into Makayla's shop this morning. There wasn't anything in the report about injuries or anything. Is Makayla doing okay?"

"She's fine. Shook up a little, but you know Makayla . . . She's already back up and running. Didn't really miss a beat."

"The report said nothing was stolen."

"She hasn't noticed anything missing yet. They might have been after cash, but she'd taken in a deposit the night before, so there wasn't much there. Just enough to open with this morning." Eliot jumped up on my desk and started rubbing his cheeks against my computer screen.

"And it wasn't touched?" he asked.

"No, guess not." *That was strange.* Someone breaking in for money would have stolen whatever cash was at hand. In fact, I'd think they would have taken it even if they'd broken in just to cause havoc. "I had something else I wanted to tell you about, though. It has to do with the case."

"I'm listening." His voice suddenly seemed tight, but he listened patiently while I relayed what I'd learned at the pet shop. "Seeing Matt with the nail gun made me think of something important, Sean. I know you don't believe me, but what if I'm right and someone is really framing Jodi. I mean, at first I thought Lynn was the one being framed, but after the nails being discovered in Jodi's room, I'm thinking the killer set out to frame her all along."

"Or she's guilty. Not all killers are smart about it. It could be she just thought she could get by with it, that no one would suspect her enough to search her room."

"But there's no real connection between her and Chuck. Is there?" I ran my fingertips along Eliot's ginger-colored fur, tracing the line of his spine until his tail rose and bushed out like a feather duster. Glancing at my frost-covered window, I couldn't help but think there was something comforting about a warm cat on a cold day. Even when discussing something as gruesome as murder.

After a few beats, Sean still hadn't replied, so I jumped back in with, "It's just that the method of murder was so unique. Either someone read about it in Jodi's book and copied it, or they purposefully set out to frame her. No matter what you think, I know Jodi's too smart to kill someone the same way she killed off one of her characters. And the nails cinched it for me. It just seems too convenient that they were found in her room. And were her fingerprints on the nails?"

"No. No prints at all."

More proof that they were probably planted, I thought.

Sean continued, "And I've considered the same things you're telling me, Lila. And I agree. But there's also a lot of evidence stacked against Jodi. At this point, it's up to the court to sort it all out."

He was right, but I still persisted. "True. But if you're considering the possibility of a frame job, then you'd have to ask yourself how the killer knew Chuck would be alone in the kitchen, with a nail gun, at just the right moment."

He paused a few beats before replying. "That just proves my point. It wasn't a frame job."

Boy, he sure was stuck on that point. "It's the nail gun that's bothering me, Sean. The day I met Chuck, he was doing some work over at the Magnolia Bed and Breakfast. Putting

up shelves, I think. Anyway, he was using a hammer and
nails. I remember because the hammering was driving everyone crazy. Then at the pet shop this morning, Matt showed
me some work Chuck had done on the subfloor. He'd missed
nailing down a bunch of boards, but the ones he did nail down
looked like they were done with a hammer. I could tell
because there were little dig marks in the wood where he'd
missed the nail head in spots. Anyway, the point is, if he had
a nail gun, why wasn't he using it for those jobs? Or, what I
find even weirder, why did he take one into the Arts Center
when he was going to be working on a refrigerator? Does that
seem likely to you?"

"No, it sure doesn't. You've made some really good
points. Really good points," he reiterated.

My heart did a little flip. I didn't ever remember Sean
praising my detecting efforts before. It felt good. Really
good. I smiled into the phone. "Thank you, Detective. I'm
glad you approve of my sleuthing capabilities."

"Who said I approved?" And just like that, I stopped smiling. "Look," he continued. "Don't get the wrong idea. A little
armchair detecting is fine. And you're good at it. Just please
don't go and do something that might be dangerous. Like last
time."

I pressed my lips together and rolled my eyes at the phone.
Like I'd purposefully set out looking for danger last summer
when I found myself at the mercy of a crazed killer. Or those
other times, for that matter. No, I didn't look for trouble; it
simply found me. Or if what everyone said was true, I
attracted trouble like a magnet. Still, it wasn't something I
could control. I sighed heavily and sank deeper into my desk
chair as Sean continued with his lecture. The sudden movement of the phone cord being pulled tautly prompted a tail
twitch from Eliot.

"So, I have your word that you'll let my team handle things?" Sean was saying.

I was about to answer just as Eliot rose on his haunches and started batting at the phone cord with his paw. "No!" I scolded, causing him to stop mid-action and plop back down on the desk. Only when he landed, he landed on my phone receiver. I heard a click.

"Hello, Sean? Sean?" *Uh-oh.* I lifted Eliot off my phone and quickly punched in Sean's number. It went straight to his voicemail, so I left a message.

"That wasn't very nice of you," I told Eliot as I hung up the phone. He responded with a twitch of his whiskers and a soft purr before circling his favorite spot next to my keyboard and plopping down for a nap.

I decided to push my conversation with Sean to the back of my mind and focus on some work. I certainly had a long enough to-do list. In addition to the orange bundle of fur next to my keyboard, my desktop was cluttered with queries, flyers, and event schedules for the expo, and about a thousand little yellow sticky notes with *ASAP* written across the top. My email was overflowing with proposals that I'd requested as well as correspondence from clients.

I tackled the emails first, happy to find one from Makayla's editor. Last year Makayla had approached me with a book she'd written, *The Barista Diaries.* Of course, I was delighted to read something written by my dear friend, but after only a few pages I found I was completely sold on the premise of the book. She'd penned a charming collection of six interwoven short stories, all narrated from the point of view of the barista and set entirely in a coffee shop. But what really struck me was the sincerity of Makayla's writing voice. Her talent definitely resided in the simple, heartfelt way she put together words. I could hardly wait to get her work out there in front of readers. And it looked like we were right on track for a spring release. The editor had copied me on the first round of edits sent to Makayla and let me know that the cover art would be finished soon. This was one of the things I loved most about my job. The process of discovering an author, helping them refine their talent and then walking with them, step by step, as their dream became reality. With *The Barista Diaries*, it was all the sweeter, because this time the dream was coming true for my best friend.

BY THE TIME I wrapped up my work for the morning, I was half starved. I stood for a couple of stretches before I went for my coat. Outside my window, the entire town seemed to be coming alive. After several days of freezing temperatures and snow, the sun was shining bright and the snow had begun to melt. People were out and about, scuttling between shops catching up on errands they'd put off during the inclement weather.

I was glad to see the thaw. Mostly because I'd been missing my daily commute on my Vespa. I'd purchased the banana yellow beauty from my friend Addison Eckhart at the Secret Garden nursery a couple of years back and had been in love ever since. There was just nothing that could equal the happy feeling I got from zipping around town on my Vespa. Although bumming rides from my mother this past week was also nice—and warmer by far. Plus it'd given us more time together.

Speaking of Mama, as I looked out the window I saw her turquoise pickup pulling into a parking spot across the street. *What in the world?* I leaned forward, fogging up the window with my breath. I stepped back. *It couldn't be!* Pulling my sweater over my hand, I rubbed away the fog and looked again. *It was!* Oscar Belmonte was driving my mother's pickup truck. It was hard to miss. He looked like a clown crammed into one of those tiny circus cars, the way he was all scrunched up behind the wheel. As I looked on, he swung open the truck's door, unfolded his bulk onto the curb, and scurried around to open the passenger door. I blinked a couple of extra times. *What was she doing letting that man drive her truck?* My heart kicked up a notch as I saw Mama take his outstretched hand and step out of the passenger side, as if she were the queen being assisted from her carriage by a footman. Then she did something I never thought I'd see my mama do: She leaned forward, stretched up on her tiptoes, and planted a kiss on his cheek!

Chapter 12

I GASPED AND STEPPED BACK FROM THE WINDOW, SHAK-
ing my head to clear away the image. Then, curious, I stepped
forward again, rubbed another clear spot in the pane, and
craned my neck to see them walking arm in arm down the
sidewalk. They were laughing like schoolkids as they entered
the Catcher in the Rye sandwich shop.

*Mama was going out to lunch with Oscar Belmonte? Was
it a date? It looked like a date.* The blushing tingle on my
cheeks certainly made it feel like I was watching my mother
on a date. I crossed the room to my desk, retrieved my purse,
and shut down my computer. "Keep an eye on things, okay,
buddy?" I told Eliot, leaving him curled up in his favorite spot
as I put on my coat and wrapped my cashmere scarf—a
Christmas gift from Sean—around my neck.

"I'm heading out for lunch," I told Vicky on my way out.
Bentley must have still been at the courthouse because Olive
was still in the reception area, eyeing another chair leg, tail

switching, ready to wreak havoc on the wood furniture again.

"Very well," Vicky replied. Her voice held a hint of melancholy or irritation; I wasn't sure which. But there wasn't time to stop and find out. I was on a mission.

A FEW MINUTES later, I entered Catcher in the Rye and was immediately greeted by the cheerful owner, Big Ed. "Hello, sunshine." Big Ed never actually called anyone by their real name, preferring instead to assign clever monikers to his waiting customers in lieu of numbers. Sunshine was a good start, but I couldn't wait to see the name he'd assign after I placed my order.

"What can I get for you today?" he asked.

I didn't even have to think about it. I simply ordered one of my favorites: the Homer—chicken souvlaki covered with shredded lettuce, diced onions, fresh tomatoes, and Big Ed's homemade yogurt sauce, all served on toasted pita bread.

"One Homer," he called over his shoulder. "May be a few minutes. They're training a new guy in the back." Ed sucked in his stomach and ran a finger along his apron strings before letting out a long sigh. I noticed that the string ends on the knot of his apron had become noticeably shorter since he and Nell from the Sixpence Bakery had tied the proverbial knot. Nell was a true baking genius. Just walking by her bakery added inches to my own hips. I couldn't imagine being tempted by her treats on a daily basis.

"What a coincidence that you're here," Big Ed was saying as he scribbled out my card. "Your beautiful mother showed up just a few minutes ago."

I eyed him suspiciously. Was I detecting a hint of goading in his voice? "Oh, she's here?" I feigned innocence as I glanced over the crowd. It seemed like the whole town was crammed into his shop. "Sure is crowded in here today."

"The Dirty Dozen is having their monthly meeting here. They take up a lot of space." The Dirty Dozen was the governing body of our village's garden club, a very active group of ladies who took their responsibility of beautifying Inspiration Valley seriously. Every year they planted over sixteen barrels in the town's center as well as the gardens surrounding the Nine Muses fountain. I'd come to learn a lot about the club and its service to our community through Vicky, who due to unforeseen circumstances several months ago had become the club's new president. Which explained her melancholy mood. Undoubtedly she'd planned to attend the club meeting over her lunch hour but had been waylaid by her dog-sitting duties.

"If you're looking for your mother and her friend," Big Ed said as he handed me my card, "they're at the corner table."

I rose on my tiptoes and raised my chin in an attempt to see around the flouncy hats of a couple of the garden club ladies. All I could see from my vantage point was the top of Mama's head. I did notice, though, that Mama had finally worn the jeweled barrette I'd given her for Christmas. I'd been a bit chagrined before that she hadn't worn it yet; now it irritated me that she'd chosen to wear it for the first time on her date with Oscar.

A young man brought a bag out and set it on the counter. Ed gave it a quick once-over and yelled out, "Tom Sawyer!" A man wearing stained painter's pants under his winter parka stepped up and grabbed his order. I smiled. Clever. Tom Sawyer and the whitewashed fence.

I glanced down at my own card and raised a brow. "Cordelia Gray?" P. D. James's famous lady detective.

"You are on the case, aren't you?" Ed winked. "I heard

one of your authors has been arrested for Chuck Richards's murder."

I sighed. At least he hadn't written *Murder Magnet* on my card. "Yes," I said. "But I don't believe she did it. Did you know Chuck?"

"Not personally. I knew *of* him, though. He didn't have the best reputation in town." He thumbed toward the seating area. "So, your mother and Oscar Belmonte, huh?"

"What do you mean? They're just having lunch together."

He chuckled. "If you say so, Cordelia. She could do worse. He's an okay guy and a hell of a cook. Course, so is your son."

I blinked back my surprise.

Big Ed was going on. "Belmonte's lucky to have him on his team. Did Trey tell ya what I did?"

Suddenly I felt like I was on the outside of my world looking in, watching as my life unfolded. How much had I missed lately? Guilt washed over me as I realized I'd been so wrapped up in my job, consumed with dreams of my wedding . . . that I'd neglected my family. Hadn't Mama told me more than once that she wanted to talk with me? And each time, I'd put it off until "later." Then, when I'd heard about Trey's situation, I'd been angry that Mama hadn't kept me in the loop . . . but she'd tried. I was the one too busy, too self-absorbed to listen. And what type of daughter was I that I hadn't noticed there was someone special in my mother's life? And now it seemed that even Big Ed knew more about my own son than me. I stammered for a response, finally just shaking my head and shrugging.

Big Ed continued, "Tried to lure him away. Offered him more than Belmonte's paying him, too. Know what he said?"

Again, I shook my head.

"That he appreciated my offer, but that he intended to open

his own restaurant one day and needed to learn the complex-
ities of cooking a full menu. That fine dining was where he'd
find his niche. His words, not mine. But his enthusiasm was
evident. That, combined with his obvious work ethic . . . Well,
that kid of yours is going places. You must be so proud." The
guy from the back appeared again. This time carrying a tray
with a wrapped sandwich and a soft drink. Ed took the tray
and passed it my way. "Here you go, Cordelia. Enjoy."

"Thanks," I replied, still a little dazed by what he'd told
me about Trey. Yes, I should be proud, and, yes, I should have
recognized his fire for cooking. But I hadn't seen it, or at least
I hadn't recognized the depth of it anyway, and what else had
I missed? My thoughts quickly turned back to my current
dilemma—Mama and Oscar Belmonte. A man who had spirited my son from college to his workforce. More importantly,
a man I'd run up against immediately as I'd backed up from
a nail-gunned dead body. A man who then accused *me* of
murder! In reality, how honest and safe was this man? How
safe was Mama in the hands of this new "special friend" of
hers? I turned to scout a place to sit. Someplace out of the
way, but where I could keep an eye on the lovebirds. Suddenly, I noticed Lynn waving to me from a table not too far
away. Pam and Dr. Meyers were seated with her.

Pam reached over and pulled out a chair as I approached.
"Come sit with us," she said. "Or were you planning on eating lunch with your mother and her friend?"

I glanced over, wondering if Mama had even noticed I was
in the café. She hadn't. She was too wrapped up in her dining
partner, her eyes glued on the man whose face glowed as he
spoke with a hand-waving flourish about something or other.
I sighed. "I'd love to join you ladies," I said, settling in and
unwrapping my sandwich.

"This is going to be my go-to place for lunch whenever I'm in the area," Dr. Meyers said. "The sandwiches are unbelievable. I'm having something called the Hamlet."

"*Mmm* . . . Black Forest ham on rye with Dijon. One of my favorites," I told her. We slipped into a long discussion about food before the subject turned to the expo. Two of Franklin's authors were due to speak that afternoon: the authors of *Tie the Knot on a Shoestring Budget* and *A Handmade Wedding*. Afterward, Ms. Lambert had arranged for several local craftspeople to hold a crafting seminar, focusing on hand-crafted centerpieces and homemade wedding favors. I'd hoped to get some ideas for my own ceremony, maybe special placeholders for the reception tables or memorable party favors to say a special thank-you to our wedding guests.

"Oh, don't look now, but here comes your mother and her beau," Pam giggled. "They do make a cute couple." I looked up from my sandwich to see Mama coming our way. Oscar was on her heels, following like a puppy dog.

"Hi, hon. I didn't even notice y'all were here."

So much for my mother's psychic abilities! Apparently her crystal ball was clouded when the aura of romance filled the air around her. "Well, you were busy enjoying your lunch. With your friend," I added, nodding his way and not bothering to try to sound pleasant. "How are you today, Mr. Belmonte?"

"Oscar, please." He extended his hand, which I shook quickly, without making eye contact. He shuffled his feet and made another attempt at conversation. "Guess we didn't get off to such a great start the other day."

I shrugged, still not looking his way. "Guess not." *Sort of difficult with a dead body in the room.* An awkwardness fell over the group. I picked up my sandwich for another bite.

Mama spoke up. "Well, guess we'd best be goin'. Oscar

needs to get back to the restaurant. Trey's been holdin' down the fort for him while he's out."

Out of the corner of my eye, I could see Oscar shift his stance and lean forward. "That boy of yours has the makings of a fine chef, Ms. Wilkins."

I should have said, "Call me Lila, please." Or at least maybe a simple *thank you*. Or anything except nibbling on my sandwich without bothering to respond. It was rude and I knew it. I felt it in the crawling warmth up my neck, the cold stares of the others at the table. But I simply couldn't help myself.

Casting a sideways glance toward Mama, I could see telltale spots of red breaking across her cheeks. My behavior was embarrassing her. "Well, guess I'll be seeing y'all later this afternoon at the expo," she said. A round of good-byes ensued from the table, but I kept my focus on my food.

After they left, Dr. Meyers tentatively said, "Your mother's friend seemed nice. Don't you think?" She dipped her chin and tried to engage my eyes, using a tone of voice I imagined she used to coax secrets and innermost thoughts from her clients.

I shrugged and pretended to be enjoying my sandwich. But the truth was, the hurt look on Mama's face had ruined my appetite. I'd behaved horribly toward Oscar. Not without good reason, I reminded myself. Look at all the havoc the man had created in my life! First, he hired Trey away from a good college education; now he was . . . what? Trying to take Mama from me, too? And for all anyone knew he could be a crazed killer.

Pam thumped the table, bringing me out of my reverie. "Now I know where I've heard that man's voice before. At the Magnolia Bed and Breakfast."

"Oscar?" I asked. "When?"

Pam rolled her eyes to the ceiling. "It must have been the first day I arrived. Before you and Jodi got there," she said to Lynn.

"We came in Sunday morning," Lynn supplied.

"That's right. It was Saturday afternoon. I remember now because Flora picked me up at the airport that morning and dropped me at the inn. She was coming back to pick me up for an early dinner, so I was hanging around the front room waiting for her. I remember a huge argument breaking out in the kitchen between Chuck and someone else. Someone who sounded just like Oscar."

"Did you happen to hear what they were arguing about?"

"Oh sure. I couldn't help but hear. It was over some work Chuck had done. I didn't quite get the gist of what type of work, but Oscar was really mad. He said something like, "You'll regret this, Richards. When I'm done with you, you'll never work in this town again." She shrugged. "Well, I don't know if those were his exact words, but something like that."

"You're sure it was Oscar."

"Pretty sure. It was a raspy voice like his and with that slight Jersey accent."

"His voice *is* distinctive," Lynn commented. "Do you suppose he was angry enough to . . . ?" She rubbed the tops of her arms and shuddered.

"We shouldn't jump to conclusions," Dr. Meyers started. "People exchange angry words all the time. In fact, arguing is an acceptable form of direct communications. If done properly, it can provide a healthy emotional release and help pave the way for further discussion. That is, if both participants refrain from becoming contemptuous and express their differences in a respectful manner."

Pam was listening with raised brows. "If you say so, Doc. But I'm telling you girls, there wasn't anything courteous about this argument. And there sure as heck wasn't any mutual respect floating around. Leastways, all I heard was a whole lot of pissed off. And mostly on Oscar's part. I wouldn't have wanted to be Chuck Richards for anything."

"And it'd be much easier to believe that a guy like that killed Chuck than it is to believe Jodi did it," Lynn said. "Although that would mean your mother is dating a . . ." Lynn let the last word drop off, biting her lip.

Suddenly a sense of self-righteousness swept over me. *See?* I wanted to say. *I was right not to be nice to the guy.* But I didn't say anything, just held my head a little higher.

"Well, being angry doesn't make one a killer," Dr. Meyers said. "Thank goodness, or everyone who comes into my office would be wanted for murder." She ended with a raised eyebrow and half smile. She started wrapping up her leftover sandwich. "Speaking of which, I've got to head back to my office to see a client. Can I give either of you a lift back to the inn?"

"Me," said Pam. She took a final drag on the straw from her cherry Coke, grabbing the stem of the cherry and biting off the sweet morsel. Then she wadded up her sandwich wrapper. "Think I'll try to get some writing in before this afternoon's events get started." She looked toward Lynn and cracked a smile. "Unless you want to challenge me to another game of pool this afternoon?" Then, noticing my double take, she offered an explanation. "Cora's got a nifty game room up on the second floor of the inn. It's fun, but little did I know Lynn's a pool shark. She's about taken me for all of last quarter's royalties."

Lynn laughed. "Maybe later this evening, Pam. Right now I think I'll stay and finish my sandwich." Then she smiled up at Dr. Meyers. "And thanks for the offer of a ride, but I think I'll walk back. I may want to browse some of the shops anyway."

After they departed, Lynn grew quiet. "Are you doing okay?" I asked. "This has been quite the week, hasn't it?"

"Yes, it has. I need to ask you a favor." She fiddled nervously with her napkin as she spoke. "I want to go to Chuck's funeral."

I was surprised, not sure exactly what she wanted from me—encouragement or dissuasion. "Of course. I'll go with you, if you wish, but do you think it's a good idea to dredge up all those bad memories?"

She sighed. "I understand what you're saying, and believe me, I've gone back and forth myself. It's complicated. I'm not even sure I can explain."

"There's no need to explain."

"But I want to try," she insisted. She took a deep breath, her eyes not quite meeting mine as she started to explain. "Whenever Chuck lost his temper and . . . and hurt me, he'd say how bad he felt, how he couldn't help it. Then he'd apologize and say the sweetest things, promising me it'd never happen again." Her cheeks flushed as she nervously tore at the edges of her napkin. "I always believed him." She sighed. "Over and over, I made excuses for his behavior until one day he almost killed me."

I reached for her hand, sending little white flakes of paper napkin everywhere. "Oh, Lynn. I'm so sorry."

She pulled away and sat straighter in her chair. "It was so bad . . . I was in the hospital for two days. As soon as they released me, I left. Didn't even say good-bye. I couldn't. Didn't trust myself to go back to him. And ever since then, I've been trying to push it all behind me. Build my own life, become stronger so I never fall into anything like that again."

"And you have. Look at you, Lynn. You've written a book and it's going to be a huge success. I just know it."

She nodded, her stare fixated on the table. "Anyway, I think going to the funeral will help me close that part of my life. I just need to know it's really over. Can you understand that?"

I nodded. "I think I can. And I'd be happy to go with you."

"Dr. Meyers doesn't think I should go. She said the same thing you did. That it might bring back too many unhappy emotions."

I nodded. "Yes, but now that you've explained it to me, I understand your need to go. For a sense of closure. To put those emotions finally behind you."

"Thanks for understanding," she said. And for the first time in our conversation, she looked across the table and met my gaze. A little shiver ran down my spine, because what I saw in her eyes didn't bespeak a woman lacking confidence or struggling with inner strength. Instead, they were filled with cold determination. "Besides, I'm a different woman now," she professed. "And I'll never let another man hurt me again. Never."

LATER THAT AFTERNOON at the expo, I kept busy trying to avoid my mother. Or, perhaps, trying to avoid my own thoughts of her dating Oscar Belmonte. Of all the men to pick! Not only was his ego as large as his waistband, but if what Pam said was true, he had a supersized temper to match. Knowing about his argument with Chuck had definitely moved him up a notch on my suspect list. For all I knew, Mama *was* dating a cold-blooded murderer. And my son was working in his kitchen!

Despite my best efforts to keep busy, my mind still reeled with worry as I popped into the Dragonfly Room to check on the progress being made for this afternoon's crafting events. Inside, I found Ms. Lambert busy directing her minions through the rigors of setting up several crafting stations.

The idea behind tonight's events was to appeal to the more budget-minded gals who hoped to not only save some money but add a personalized touch to their big day.

As I walked between the craft stations, I found all manner of interesting—and sometimes intimidating—craft projects. I especially liked a giant faux floral arrangement I saw Ms. Lambert's people haul into the room, dipping the tops under the doorway. It sported what appeared to be giant alliums created with large foam balls covered in those oversized cotton swabs found in medical supply houses. Each swab had been cut in half and pierced into the balls, the resulting flower "head" sprayed in pale lavender paint. The flowers were then attached to flexible tubes wrapped in green floral tape, accompanied with green silk leaf spears and towering high over the heads of attendees. Stunning!

I continued to circumvent the room, trying to gain inspiration for my own wedding, admiring hand-stamped place-holders, dried flower arrangements, and easy-to-do party favors. I felt in awe of the vision these crafters had for taking simple things and making them into extraordinary pieces of art, but I found my enthusiasm waning as my mind kept becoming sidetracked by thoughts of the case.

I was so deep in thought that I didn't notice Flora until she tapped me on the shoulder. "Hey, Lila," she said. Her face was deeply flushed with tiny beads of perspiration forming above her upper lip.

"Flora. Are you okay?"

She shook her head. "I'm fine. But have you heard the news?"

"About?"

"Jodi. The judge denied bail. Said she was a flight risk because she didn't have any ties to the community."

"Oh no." My heart sank. "What does that mean, exactly?

Will she have to stay in jail until the trial? That could be a long time."

Flora shrugged and removed a tiny lace handkerchief from the pocket of her sweater. She began dabbing at her face. "I don't really know. The lawyers are working on it." She swallowed hard. "I just feel so awful for Jodi. And now these accusations from Cora about Chuck and Jodi having an affair. Jodi's torn up over it."

"What's Jodi have to say about Chuck being in her room?"

"She said he came by with one of her books saying that his friend was a huge fan and wanted to know if she'd sign it."

"The Billionaire's Bride?"

"Yes. A paperback copy. She said it was brand-new and still in a bag from the bookstore."

"Probably from the Constant Reader," I observed. "Did she remember who he wanted it inscribed to?"

Flora shook her head, refolded her handkerchief, and slid it back into her pocket.

I thought of another question. "Did she mention if he was wearing his tool belt when he came into her room? I was wondering how those nails could've got there." And hoping the explanation had nothing to do with Lynn.

"I don't know." She shrugged. "I didn't even think to ask, but Bentley will probably fill us in on the details later. I do know that because of those nails, a couple of the agents believe Jodi is guilty." Her eyes shot over to where Ms. Lambert was directing the efforts of a worker who sorted and arranged sprigs of dried flowers. "Ms. Lambert maintains that our author is bringing down her company's reputation and affecting the expo sales. But the real tragedy is the damage to Jodi's own reputation. She may not have much of a career to come back to after all this is over. Already her book sales have plummeted. Her editor called me yesterday. They're considering pulling the contract on the new book she has scheduled to release this spring."

"But you were able to talk them out of it, right?"

"Bentley did. She got right on the phone and straightened it out. For now, anyway. I hate to think what'll happen if the real killer isn't found." She let out a long sigh and touched my shoulder. "I do so appreciate your support through all this, Lila. It's good to know you're on our side."

Reaching over, I cupped her hand in my own and gave a little reassuring squeeze. "Hang in there, Flora. It'll all work out, I promise." Although my words sounded hollow, even to me. Things would work out, sure; one way or the other they always did. But there was no guarantee that things would work out for Jodi. Not unless the real killer was found.

Chapter 13

DESPITE MS. LAMBERT'S COMPLAINT THAT JODI'S INCAR-
ceration had generated negative publicity, attendance at the
expo this evening didn't seem to be affected. The Arts Center was yet again packed with happy brides-to-be browsing
booths with nothing more serious than murmurs of dress
fittings and reception venues punctuating their lighthearted
conversations. Soon I found myself immersed in their jovi-
ality, ruminations of suspects and clues quickly replaced by
daydreams of bouquets and receiving lines.

Tickets to hear Franklin's two authors and the subsequent
do-it-yourself seminar sold out in the first hour after the
doors opened. Fortunately, I was able to slip away from the
book sale table, where I was on duty with Jude and Zach,
long enough to catch the tail end of the talk given by the
author of *Tie the Knot on a Shoestring Budget*. I jotted down
a few helpful notes and planned to get a copy of her book
later for a closer look. Even though I dreamed of a simple,

elegant affair, it was shocking how quickly costs accumulated. And with Trey's education to consider—or maybe not—I didn't have a lot of wiggle room in my budget.

I returned to the book sale table to find Jude leaning back and relaxing with his feet propped on the table. With most of the clientele currently attending the author presentations and craft seminars, the hallway was empty. Jude told me that Zach had taken the opportunity to grab a quick bite to eat but would be back soon. As I settled into my own chair, Jude regarded me with a pensive expression. "Been getting some ideas for your own wedding?"

"A few." Wariness crept over me. Every time the conversation turned to my wedding, Jude became contentious. I quickly picked up a random book and feigned interest, hoping to avoid any more talk on the subject. A red-hot flush overcame me as my eyes skimmed the page and I realized I'd picked up one of Pam's racier novels.

"I'm happy for you, you know," Jude was saying.

I briefly glanced over the top of the book and nodded. "Thanks."

"I hope you're planning to invite me to the wedding."

I closed the book, setting it aside as casually as I could muster. I reached for *A Handmade Wedding* and shrugged. "Sure." I half expected him to follow up with a smart quip or something condescending toward Sean, but this time there was no razzing, no playful goading, no annoying comments. Instead he reached over and placed his hand on my arm, drawing my attention away from the book.

I looked up, caught off guard by the intensity in his brown eyes. "You're going to make a beautiful bride."

I froze. His sparkly eyes, the warmth of his hand on my arm . . . My whole world stopped. Then he slid his hand up to where my hair grazed my shoulder and playfully tugged

on a strand. Sparks shot through me; his full lips, oh so very
close to mine, turned up at the corners as if he knew some
sort of secret. His long lashes swept down to half cover those
warm chocolate brown eyes of his, tempting me to drink in
his soft gaze. We remained there, suspended in a moment
of lusty ambiguity while my insides screamed for me to pull
back, get away, and put a stop to this nonsense while another
teensy-tiny part of me remembered, with all the tingly thrill,
the time that we'd shared a kiss so long ago . . .

"Lila?"

I startled, a shaky hand flying to my ready lips, guilt
glaring in my mind's eye. I kept my hand there, holding back
the excuses that threatened to spill from my mouth as I
looked at Makayla, who was staring down at me with . . .
with what? An accusing look. That was what it was. Then
I looked back at Jude, who was sitting smugly, that mischievous glint dancing in his eyes as his lips now spread into a
knowing grin. He winked. My insides screamed: *I would
not have kissed him! I wouldn't have!*

Then Makayla cleared her throat and stepped forward,
choosing a book from the pile and thrusting a bill my way. "I
just came by to pick up this book." There was a hint of disap-
pointment in her voice. *Disappointed in me? She had it all
wrong. It looked bad, but I wasn't really going to kiss Jude.
Was I?* "And to see if you were getting ready for your dinner
break. I have a ticket to the do-it-yourself seminar."

"Sure." I fumbled to make her change, my hands shaking
with shame. Could I really say what would have happened
if she hadn't shown up? What was wrong with me? I loved
Sean. This thing with Jude . . . well, it was just plain stupid.
After handing Makayla her change, I turned back to Jude.
"I'm heading for my dinner break," I told him, joining
Makayla on the other side of the table. "If you need help, I

suggest you call Zach or one of the other agents. I won't be back here this evening."

"Sure, darlin'," he replied in his easy way. "I'll be seeing you tomorrow."

"That wasn't what it looked like," I said to Makayla as soon as we'd walked out of earshot.

She kept walking, pursing her lips and shooting me a sideways glance while she tucked the book she'd bought into her shoulder bag. "Then what was it? Because to me, it looked like y'all were heading into major lip-lock." Suddenly she stopped and turned to face me straight on. "What's this all about, Lila? Do you have a thing for Jude Hudson?"

I shook my head. "No, not at all. It's just . . ." I hesitated, not knowing how to articulate my feelings. *Why couldn't I shake the attraction I felt toward Jude?*

Her eyebrows shot skyward. "Just what?"

Shaking my head, all I could answer was, "I guess I don't know. I don't understand it myself." I told her all about Jude and me, the kiss we shared the first week we worked together, his continuous flirtations, my sometimes attraction to him. "What you just saw . . . I wasn't going to . . . I just . . . I just don't know." I brought both hands to my cheeks. "What *is* wrong with me?"

Makayla reached up, grabbed my hands, and held them in hers. "Look. I've known Jude since long before you moved to the Valley. He's used to getting what he wants with women. The fact that he can't have you must really bother him. That's all it is, Lila. A silly game to him. Do you really want to throw away everything you have with Sean on a guy like that?"

A silly game. I knew she was right, of course. It was all just a game to Jude. He agented thrillers and suspenseful adventures. And his love life offered the same genre of intrigue and conquests with an ultimate lone—and satisfied—hero striding off into the sunset, leaving a string of broken hearts behind him. Life imitating art; Jude imitating fiction. "No. Of course not."

"Then keep your distance from Jude. Okay?" She gave my hands a final squeeze before letting go. Sighing, she plastered on a smile and nodded in the direction of the Dragonfly Room. "Come on. Let's go check out those crafts. After what happened to my café this morning, I'm going to need every budget tip I can get." We started walking again.

"Have the police come up with anything yet?"

"Nope. I don't think they will, either. They didn't even bother dusting for prints. Said it would be fruitless in such a public place." She shrugged. "Guess it could have been worse. I've just lost a few supplies. Nothing major. I just can't figure out why someone would do something so malicious."

I shook my head. "It doesn't make sense, does it? Especially since nothing was taken. I mean, I could understand it if you had a bunch of cash on hand. But even what you had wasn't touched. Maybe the police are right. It was just a bunch of kids up to no good."

Once we reached the Dragonfly Room, we dropped the subject, choosing to focus instead on the spectacular displays and fun-filled craft seminars. However, my heart wasn't into tonight's special events. What I really wanted to do was sit down over a warm, soothing caramel latte and talk to Makayla about all the things weighing on my mind: Trey's newfound career as a chef, Mama's "special" friend, my niggling suspicions about Lynn, and now this "thing" with Jude. I knew Makayla would listen attentively and offer me some little tidbit of insight that would soothe my worries. Just as I would do the same for her. Because, even though she was only in her midtwenties, Makayla possessed the self-assurance and prudence of a much older woman and over the last couple of years, we'd grown to become each other's best confidante.

The last thing I wanted, however, was to drag her down with my problems. She had enough of her own problems with her business trashed just this morning. I'd been there for her physically to help clean it up, sure, but I needed to be there for her emotionally now as well. She deserved to enjoy this time focusing on the joy of preparing for her wedding. So for Makayla's sake, I worked extra hard to push aside all my worries. Instead, I put on my best happy face, mingled with other, more lighthearted brides-to-be, and did my best to pick up a few money-saving craft ideas that might come in handy when I started finalizing my own wedding plans.

BY THE TIME my dinner break was over, Makayla and I were both atwitter with ideas—and feeling like we were plenty capable of pulling off many of the grand ideas offered. As I said good-bye to Makayla, she gave me a warm hug and I knew we both felt better for this little time together.

Now it was time for me to make the rounds checking on our authors. I started with Lynn's booth. She wasn't there, but the vendor next to her informed me that she'd just left for a short dinner break. So, for twenty minutes or so, I kept busy, delivering snacks and bottled water, tissues, or anything else needed to keep our other authors comfortable while they worked. After everyone seemed settled, I picked up a steaming hot cup of coffee to take to Mama. A peace offering of sorts. I'd started to feel guilty about my bad behavior earlier that day. Maybe I didn't like Oscar Belmonte, and even if I had good reasons for it, Mama certainly hadn't deserved my rudeness.

Carefully worming my way through the crowds, I was just

about to Pam's booth when I heard Lynn call out my name. She was standing at Rufus Manning's photography booth, admiring his portfolio. A quick glance told me Mama was busy with a client anyway, so I held on to the coffee while I stepped aside to say hello to Lynn. "I'm just getting ready to head back to my own booth," she was saying. "I came over to say hi to Pam but got sidetracked by these beautiful photos." She flipped through a couple of pages while Rufus looked on with pride. "Aren't they lovely?"

"They sure are," I agreed. I was suddenly reminded of Rufus's photo of a bride and groom's hands clasped together. The one that had been destroyed at Makayla's shop. "Oh, Rufus. Did Makayla get hold of you today?"

"Makayla from Espresso Yourself?" He squinted with confusion. "No, I haven't talked to her today. Why?"

I explained about the break-in at her shop. "The vandals really made a mess of things. Including much of the artwork, I'm afraid."

"That's just awful," Rufus replied.

"Yes, it is," Lynn reiterated. "You didn't mention that at lunch today."

"I didn't?" *I guess I didn't. Probably because I was too distracted by other things.* My eyes slid over to where Mama was tracing the lines on a young lady's palm. The gal's friends were leaning forward, anxiously anticipating Mama's verdict. Whatever she said elicited a loud burst of laughter, followed by several more outstretched palms and urgent pleas for more readings. Mama could sure captivate a crowd, I thought. Then I shook my head and refocused on the conversation at hand. "Well, anyway. Makayla will probably be contacting you soon. She may need another copy for her display."

"That's no problem," Rufus said. "I'll print up another one first thing in the morning."

"Thanks." I raised the cup. "Well, I'd better get this over to the Amazing Althea, Babylonian Fortune-Teller, before it goes cold."

"Hold up a second," Lynn said, trotting after me. "Could you tell Zach that I won't be needing a ride back to the inn? Sloan and I are going to go out for a drink after we finish tonight." It took me a second to remember that Sloan was Dr. Meyers's first name. I was glad to see that she and Lynn were becoming friends. "But we're still on for tomorrow morning, right?" she asked. I nodded, and after we confirmed our plans to attend Chuck's funeral the next day, she threw a quick wave Pam's way and headed back to her own booth.

"Excuse me, ladies," I said, pushing my way through the crowd around Mama. "Hot coffee coming through."

Upon seeing me, Mama stood up and held out her hand like a traffic cop. "Give me just a moment, girls. I'll be right back." She came around the table and pulled me aside. "Thank ya, sugar. Coffee sounds good 'bout now." She took a sip and then leveled her gaze on me. "I've been hopin' you'd come by the booth. You still gonna need a ride home tonight?"

I forced myself not to overtly sigh as I realized the implication. "If you need to be somewhere else, I can find another way home. I mean, I understand if you have other plans," I said, figuring she was probably picking up Oscar for a nightcap. My heart fell as I realized I'd have to get used to sharing my mother with someone else.

"Other plans?" She squinted. "No, sugar. I don't have any plans, except to have a talk with you. If you're willin', that is. Seems seeing Oscar and me together has upset ya some."

Now I did sigh. "Just surprised, I guess." *And worried that you may be falling for a crazed killer.* "But I had no reason to act so rudely. I'm sorry, Mama."

She nodded, stealing a glance back at the throng of

women eagerly awaiting their readings. "We'll talk some more tonight, hon."

She settled back into her side of the table, while I popped in on Pam. "Do you need anything?" I asked.

"Nope. I'm doing just fine. Thanks to your mother, that is. I owe most of my sales this week to her energy and enthusiasm." She leaned in and whispered conspiratorially, "You know, I had her do a reading for me."

"You did?"

Pam nodded. "Yeah. It was so enlightening, too. Said she saw that I'd been struggling with a big decision lately."

"Was she right?"

Pam's head bobbed up and down enthusiastically. "What do you mean, was she right? Of course, she was! And you know what else she said?"

I shrugged.

"'Life,' she said, 'is too short to put off trying all the things we want to do.' She said you taught her that."

"Me?"

"Yes, Lila. You know, your mama's so proud of all you've done, admires how you bounced back from a failed marriage, raised your son. How when you lost your job, and that boy of yours was giving you fits, like most boys that age do, I suppose, how you were strong enough to follow your passion, and make a new, better life for the two of you. Said you're a wonderful mother."

"She did?"

Pam nodded.

I swallowed hard. Mama had told all that to Pam? Was that really how she felt? She thought I was a good mother. Strong?

Pam was still going on. "After I heard about your struggles and all you went through, making my decision was easy. Remember the other morning at the Magnolia when I told you and Ms. Duke that I love to read mysteries?"

I furrowed my brow and nodded, sort of remembering her saying something about mysteries.

She continued, "I'm going to stop writing romance for a while and try my hand at mysteries. It's always something I've wanted to try. It'll be like starting my career all over again, but I'm going to do it."

"You are?" I wondered what Flora might have to say about this. Pam was her top-selling author. She'd hit the *New York Times* bestseller list numerous times. And Bentley? Pam's bestselling romance series brought a lot of money into the agency.

Pam was gushing with excitement. "I haven't told any-body, but I've been working on a mystery for a while and I think it's good. It needs some polishing, but when it's done, would you take a look at it?"

"Absolutely. I'd be honored." And I meant it. Pam was an extraordinary writer; I had no doubt her mystery would be terrific. Although Flora and Bentley might not feel as enthu-siastic about this new endeavor of hers, I viewed it as a won-derful opportunity for new growth for Pam as a person and as a writer. With Pam's writing talents, and an already enthu-siastic and huge fan base, any editor would be happy to sign her. Of course, romance writing and mystery writing required different mind-sets and different literary skill sets. But if she was successful, she could very easily end up being a bestseller in both genres. On a selfish note, the thought of representing her was thrilling to me. While I had a few high-selling authors, I had yet to have a client's book grace the bestseller lists. "I'll look forward to reading your mystery, Pam."

Pam let out a little squeal. "Thank you, Lila." Then she turned and glanced at my mother, who was holding a tarot card in front of a captivated audience. "You know, I hope you're not upset that your mother told me all that personal stuff about you. I don't think she could help herself, she's just so proud. And sometimes I think we need to hear other people's stories in order to understand our own. Do you know what I mean?"

I nodded. Still, I'd never thought of my story as anything special. Certainly not anything to inspire others. The fact that Mama did truly touched me. It reminded me that we all have our own stories, even Mama. I thought about all the years she'd lived without Daddy—alone and devoted to Trey and me. Was Oscar just an indication that Mama was ready to turn the page on a new chapter in her life? One that included someone to grow old with? At the very least, she deserved that type of happiness. And she deserved to have her own daughter support her. Just like she'd supported me all these years. I still wasn't sure about Oscar, but I *was* sure that from now on, I'd be more sensitive to Mama's needs. After all, she was one truly amazing woman.

I turned back to Pam and, to her surprise, embraced her in a hug. Pulling back, I said, "You're right, Pam. Other people's stories can teach us a lot about ourselves. Thank you."

Chapter 14

THE WARMER WEATHER HAD BEGUN TO WEAR DOWN the snow, leaving only small patches of dirty slush here and there. The pavement on the parking lot was practically bare, giving me hope that I'd be back on my scooter by the weekend. Did I ever miss jaunting around town on my Vespa!

I'd told Mama I'd meet her as soon as the expo events wrapped up, but I'd been delayed helping reorganize the Dragonfly Room after a few gals tried to mix wine sampling with craft assembling. Not a good combination. Anyway, it was almost eight thirty by the time I finally made my way out to Mama's truck. I found her standing outside the passenger door, staring down at a flat tire and talking on her cell.

"What happened?"

She hung up and waved her hand through the air. "It's as flat as a pancake, that's what. Must've hit somethin' on my way into town this mornin'." She moved around to the back end of the truck and threw open the tailgate. "I've got a jack back here someplace. I usually keep a spare mounted under the chassis, but I used it last summer and didn't replace it. I called Oscar. He's got an extra that should fit my truck. Said he'd bring it right over."

"Isn't he busy at the restaurant?"

She shrugged. "Not too busy to give a friend a hand, I guess."

Her tone spoke volumes. She was still upset about my earlier behavior. I wrapped my coat tighter around my midsection and took a deep breath. "Look, Mama. I'm sorry about the way I acted toward Oscar today. I was rude and it was wrong of me."

Having retrieved a jack and wrench from the toolbox in the bed of her truck, she slid off the tailgate. "It's not me you need to apologize to, sugar."

My breath caught. *She wanted me to apologize to Oscar?* I sighed. She was probably right. I did owe him an apology. "Of course. And I'm sorry I embarrassed you in front of everyone."

She was squatting in front of the flat, sliding the jack under the truck's carriage. "Well, I probably should've told y'all about Oscar before ya saw us out like that. Must have been quite the shocker."

I nodded. "You could say that." I watched as she started pumping the jack. I stepped in and squatted next to her. "Let me do that, Mama."

Her strong arms kept working the jack. "I've got it." She paused and looked over at me, her eyes bright and clear blue. "I'm not as old as y'all might think. I'm still plenty capable of doin' lots of things."

"Sure you are. I know that, Mama!"

She kept pumping until the truck rose off the ground. Then she grabbed the wrench and started loosening the lug nuts. "Like to have this thing off here before Oscar shows up. Hate to keep him too long."

I stood by, helplessly watching. Wishing I could go back and undo my earlier behavior. I couldn't, so I did the next best thing. "If you like Oscar, then I'll try to like him, too." I didn't sound quite as sincere as I'd hoped to, but Mama stopped working and looked my way.

"I'm glad to hear you say that. I don't know where this is going with Oscar and me. I can tell ya he's a good guy. Treats me like a queen, he does. And cooks like it's nobody's business." Her face lit up a bit when she mentioned his cooking. "But the truth is it's been a long time since your daddy left this world. And I miss him every day, sug. Don't you go thinkin' that any man could ever take his place. But I'm lonely. You've got yourself a fiancé now. And Trey, well, he's making his own way." She shrugged. "I dunno. It's hard to figure. Doesn't make sense for an old woman like me to be thinkin' of such things . . ."

I put my hand on her shoulder. "No, Mama. It makes perfect sense. And, I'm trying to be happy for you. Really I am."

She nodded and smiled at me, relief evident in her eyes. Then she turned back to the task at hand, working the rusty lug nuts with all her might. "Well, shoot! These damn things are on here tighter than bark on a tree."

At that very moment, Oscar drove up in a powder blue Cadillac, circa 1970-something. He threw open the driver's door and heaved his girth out onto the pavement. He must have come right over from the restaurant because he was still wearing his customary ankle-length black apron over a white button-down shirt and black trousers. "Let me take care of that, Althea." He walked around the back of his Caddy, threw open the trunk, and hefted out a spare tire. "I'll get you fixed right up," he added, rolling the tire our way.

It was dark, with only the light from a nearby lamp pole to illuminate the scene, and still I could tell Mama was blushing with pleasure. "Well, thank ya, Oscar," she said, stepping aside to make room for him. "It's so good of you to drop what ya were doin' just to come help me."

I hung back to watch, a little surprised by Mama's helpless act. I had no doubt that given just a little more time, she would have weaseled out those lug nuts by herself. For years she'd taken care of tires and all sorts of other thing—much bigger things!—on her own. I cleared my throat. "Mr. Belmonte?"

He looked up my way and stood up. "Oscar. Call me Oscar, please."

I nodded and swallowed down the hitch in my throat. "Okay. Oscar. I just wanted to apologize for my rude behavior today at Catcher in the Rye." I held out my hand.

To my relief, he didn't hesitate to grasp it in his own, a broad smile on his face as he enthusiastically shook it. "Don't mention it again, Lila. I understand."

I smiled back. A bit of a weak smile, perhaps. Because I couldn't help but remember what Pam told me at lunch about overhearing Oscar and Chuck Richards arguing the day before Chuck was murdered. Then there was the fact that Oscar was at the murder scene and, well . . . disliking Oscar was just so easy for me. But for Mama's sake, I was going to try to stay open-minded.

Oscar was back to working the lug nuts, which didn't seem to be any easier for him than it was for Mama. After a few minutes of huffing, puffing, and a wee bit of swearing, he glanced over his shoulder. "Lila, would you pull my Caddy over and fix the headlights on me. I need some more light."

"Sure," I said, walking to the back of his car to shut the trunk before I moved it. Just before slamming it shut, I glanced inside. Obviously the back of his car doubled as a tool chest.

Every sort of tool imaginable was crammed in the tiny space. Including a nail gun. A cordless nail gun, just like the one I'd seen at the crime scene, lying not too far from Chuck's lifeless body. My eyes darted from the contents of the trunk to where Mama and Oscar were standing, looking down at the flat. Oscar leaned in and whispered something in her ear, causing Mama to let loose a raucous belly laugh. Then she playfully wrapped her arm around his midsection and rested her head against his shoulder. My heart stood still as I offered up a silent plea that my mother wasn't falling for a killer.

OSCAR FINALLY GOT the tire changed and Mama dropped me off at my cottage. I was surprised to find Sean's Ford Explorer parked on my curb.

I bid Mama a quick good-bye and hopped out of her truck to greet Sean. "This is a nice surprise," I said, as he stepped out of his car. "What brings you over?"

He reached back into his vehicle and pulled out a to-go bag from Machiavelli's. "Peace offering?"

"Peace offering. For what?" Guilt pricked at my conscience as I thought back to that reckless moment with Jude earlier. How could I have been so stupid? But Sean couldn't have known. Could he?

He shrugged. "Why don't you tell me?"

A flush warmed my face and, though shadowed in the dark, I felt sure Sean could spy this obvious declaration of guilt. Probably knew everything that happened—or actually didn't happen—at the author's table with Jude. After all, he was a detective. He knew how to figure things out, sweat out suspects, get confessions. But how . . .

He went on, "I figured I did something wrong. You hung up on me this morning."

Every fiber in me loosened as my mind swung around to this morning's call. I tipped my head back and laughed. With everything that'd happened, I'd forgotten about the mishap with Eliot. "Oh no, Sean! Didn't you get my voicemail? I tried calling you right back. It wasn't me that hung up on you. It was Eliot."

The lines around Sean's eyes crinkled. "Eliot?"

I quickly explained how the cat had inadvertently caused my shout and the resultant abrupt hang-up.

"Well, I'm going to have to have a talk with that cat." He laughed and nodded toward the cottage. "How about we head inside where it's warmer. There's a few other things I want to talk with you about, too."

A few minutes later, we were settled on the couch, two heaping plates of shrimp scampi with capellini pasta on the coffee table in front of us and a warm fire crackling in my fireplace. I'd found some red wine in the fridge and poured us a couple of glasses. I sighed with contentment and nestled in close to Sean.

"Wait until you try this," he said between forkfuls of pasta. "It's delicious."

I took my own bite, savoring the tender shrimp sautéed in a delicate white wine sauce with just the right amount of garlic and a fresh lemon taste. I rolled my eyes. "Really good," I mumbled, digging in for more.

"Trey was running the kitchen. I talked to him for just a second. He seemed to be doing well."

I nodded, still chewing.

Sean went on, "I don't think you need to worry so much about him, Lila. He's doing fine. Working hard."

I swallowed and reached for my wine. "I hope you're right. Actually, at the moment, I'm more worried about my mother." He kept eating as I told him all about seeing Mama with Oscar

Belmonte at Catcher in the Rye and how they'd been dating for a while, and what Pam had told me about overhearing the argument between Oscar and Chuck Richards before the murder. I finished by telling him that I saw a nail gun in Oscar's trunk. "I'm worried that Mama may be dating a killer. She seems to be absolutely smitten with the man."

Sean placed his empty plate back on the coffee table. "I'll follow up about that argument Pam overheard. There might be more to it."

"Good, because I simply don't trust the man."

"It could be that you're letting your personal emotions affect your judgment." He leaned forward and took my empty plate, returning it to the table, handing me my wineglass, and pulling me closer. "I know it's probably not easy to see your mother dating someone."

Was I letting my personal sentiments taint my judgment of Oscar? Perhaps. But the facts still stood: He was at the murder scene, he had motive, Pam witnessed him arguing with the murder victim, and he knew how to use a nail gun. That was a whole lot of evidence stacked against him, whether he was dating Mama or not.

Sean continued, "Anyway, I wanted to let you know that we're checking into the nail gun. I think what you said today was correct. It doesn't make sense that Chuck Richards would have a nail gun at the expo job. Especially since he didn't seem to use one on previous jobs. Either he recently purchased one or the killer brought it to the scene of the crime. I've got a couple of guys checking sales reports at local hardware stores."

I sat up and turned his way. "Really?" I tried to keep my voice calm, even though I was secretly thrilled I'd made a small contribution to his investigation. I wondered if after we were married, he might discuss his cases with me over dinner, asking my opinion on this and that. Sort of like Agatha Christie's Tommy and Tuppence, or maybe more like Annie Laurence and Max Darling from Carolyn Hart's Death on Demand series. I loved those books! "Have you found out anything yet?"

He shook his head. "Not yet. I'm also checking with some of Chuck's other clients to see if he used a gun on any previous jobs. I can't put a lot of time into it. As far as my sergeant's concerned, we've got our killer. And I've got a full caseload, so I'm not going to be allocating as much time to following up on loose ends."

"Loose ends? What other loose ends are there? Something other than the nail gun?"

He reached for his wine, taking a long sip and avoiding my question.

I pressed on, "If you're still checking into things, then you must not be completely convinced of Jodi's guilt."

He held up his hand. "Don't read too much into it, Lila. I just thought you brought up a valid point about the nail gun. I'm checking into it, that's all."

I sighed. It wouldn't do to press him any further. I recognized that tight-lipped expression of his. Getting any more information out of him would be impossible. So I finished up my wine and moved on to other topics. "Flora told me that Jodi was denied bail. What'll happen now?"

"She'll have to stay in jail until the trial."

"That's horrible."

Sean shrugged. "It's how the system works. At this point, it's up to her defense lawyer to prove her innocence. She's lucky. Bentley got her the best lawyer money could buy."

That was news to me. I wasn't aware Bentley was footing the bill for Jodi's defense. "She must be convinced of Jodi's innocence." *And so am I*, I wanted to add. But we'd already had that discussion several times over. Instead I snuggled in closer and changed the subject. "Makayla and I found a lot of interesting ideas this afternoon." I went on to tell him about the crafts we'd viewed and the ones we'd tried our hands at and how I thought they'd be a great way to personalize our wedding. "Of course, it would help if we could pick the date," I said. "It's sort of difficult to plan without even knowing the season. Have you thought any more about this spring? I know you want to wait until Christmas, but that's so far away."

I felt the muscles in his arms tense. "Do we really need to discuss all this tonight?" He moved in closer, planting little kisses on my jawline. "There's so many better things we could be doing," he mumbled playfully against my neck.

I wiggled in his arms, wedging my hands between us. "I'm serious, Sean. I really want to set the date. It's important to me." And next time I talked to Jude, I'd just love to be able to mention a date. "Really important. People would take our commitment more seriously if we had a date set." I regretted my words as soon as they came out.

He pulled back, eyeing me with a serious expression. I'd never told him about that kiss Jude and I shared a long time ago, but sometimes I wondered if he didn't suspect something. He'd never much cared for Jude. "What do you mean by that? What people?" he said, those blue eyes of his searching mine.

My cheeks burned hot under his scrutiny. Not that I had anything to feel guilty about. Nothing had happened between Jude and me, nothing at all. I tried to shrug it off. "I'm just anxious to set the date, that's all." I looked away, stammering a bit with my words. *Should I tell him what happened today? No, what good would that do? Besides, it was nothing.* "I just thought if we could narrow it down to a certain month . . . maybe June," I asked hopefully.

He sighed. "Spring just won't work for me." I lowered

my eyes and nodded, ready to agree to Christmas, when he came back with, "How about September? I think I can swing some time off then."

My head snapped up. "September?" Suddenly visions popped to mind of saying "I do" under the sweeping branches of a Live Oak tree, its shimmering leaves surrounding us with a magical sheen. My simple white sheath dress with a delicate lace that formed cap sleeves, a little satin ribbon for trim, the one I'd sighed over just this week at the expo, would stand out against the backdrop of nature's fall palette of crimson reds, deep oranges, and golden yellows. I'd carry a simple bouquet of lily of the valley tied with gold double-faced ribbon . . .

"Lila?" Sean was waiting for my answer.

"September's perfect."

He reached out and pulled me close again. "Well, now that it's settled, we can get back to more important things," he whispered against my lips.

I agreed. And for one blissful evening, I pushed aside thoughts about murder and my troubles with Trey and Mama and simply enjoyed being in the arms of the man I loved.

Chapter 15

THE STREETS WERE CLEAR ENOUGH THAT I WAS ABLE TO take the Vespa into the office first thing Friday morning. I'd planned, however, to make a midmorning trade with Trey. He was due at Machiavelli's around ten for some early kitchen prep work, at which time I'd meet him and exchange keys. I'd promised to fill his car's tank, if he'd loan it to me for my trip into Dunston. I'd then swing by and pick up Lynn at the Magnolia Bed and Breakfast around ten fifteen, which should leave plenty of time to make it to Dunston for the eleven o'clock service.

Before heading up to work, I popped into Espresso Yourself to tell Makayla the good news about our wedding date. She was just finishing up with a customer. As soon as she saw me, her mouth curved into a wide smile. "You're looking like the cat that swallowed the canary. What gives, girl?" Her musical laughter filled the room.

"Got any plans for September?" I asked.

Her brows furrowed. "September? I don't think so . . ." She squealed. "Y'all have set the date! Well, it's about time. Didn't think you'd ever pin that man down!"

I giggled. "We compromised. He wanted Christmastime and I wanted spring, so we settled on September."

She turned and started mixing my usual. "This calls for a celebration," she said, her words muffled by the whir of the espresso machine. "One caramel latte coming up. My treat."

I thanked her. "I'll need the extra caffeine jolt. I have a busy morning." I told her about plans to take Lynn to Chuck's funeral. Then I glanced around the café and commented, "Looks like you got things back in order."

Her gaze traveled around the room and she nodded. "Thankfully there wasn't anything permanently damaged. Mostly just a mess to clean up. I was able to get most of the lost supplies restocked yesterday afternoon."

My eyes were drawn to her still-barren walls. "Were you able to get hold of all the photographers yet?"

"Yes, and they've been wonderful. They not only offered to replace the damaged photos, but the frames, too. Most of them promised to bring them by today."

I remembered that Rufus hadn't heard from her yet. "What about Rufus? Were you able to reach him? He's been at the expo all week."

"Rufus? That name sounds familiar."

"Rufus Manning. The photo of the couple holding hands. The one I really liked, remember?"

She reached under her counter, retrieving the stack of photos Trey and I had removed from the broken frames, and began laying them on top of her counter. "I do remember that photo," she said. "I called everyone who had a picture in this stack, but . . ." She'd reached the bottom of the stack without finding Rufus's photo. "That's strange." She looked up at me. "Did you throw away that print?"

"I didn't. Maybe Trey did, though."

"Maybe so. It must have been severely damaged. Glad you brought it up. I'll give Rufus a call this morning."

The bells above the door jingled and another customer walked in, so I thanked her again for the coffee and headed off to work.

As soon as I opened the office door, Olive started yapping and pawing at my pants leg. Laughing, I reached down and snatched up one of the many chew toys scattered across the floor and engaged her in a friendly game of tug-of-war. "Good morning, Vicky," I said.

When Vicky didn't respond, I stopped playing with Olive and looked across the room to where she was seated at her desk, fidgeting with her desktop items: straightening the stapler and brushing away invisible specks of dirt. I abandoned my game with Olive and walked over to her. "Everything going okay, Vicky? You seem preoccupied."

She stopped fussing and clasped her hands over her desk blotter. "Yes, of course. I've already placed several queries on your desk. Ms. Duke was in earlier, but she left again in order to meet with Ms. Lambert about this afternoon's scheduled events." Vicky's eyes darted toward Olive, who'd already grown bored with her toys and moved on to sniffing around the room. Vicky continued, "Flora called earlier. She isn't feeling well this morning. She's asked if you could arrive early to the Arts Center in order to help get Pam ready for her author talk."

"Flora's not feeling well again? Nothing serious, I hope."

Vicky shook her head. "Just a virus, I believe. The stress of this week has undoubtedly made it worse."

"No problem. I'll make sure Pam is taken care of this afternoon." Today's themed events, which centered on the bridal trousseau and honeymoon, were sure to be a crowd pleaser. Ms. Lambert had arranged for several travel agents to be on hand to discuss booking the dream honeymoon, while the Dragonfly Room would be set up with displays of everything a new bride might need for her trousseau, from accessories and lingerie to bath and spa items. There would even be several cosmetologists on hand to provide mini makeovers and specialized makeup tips. And to kick it all off, Pam was going to read a couple of steamy excerpts from the latest book in her Reluctant Brides of Babylon series. Overall, it promised to be a fun afternoon.

"Has Eliot been sequestered to the break room again?" I asked, not seeing our furry orange mascot anywhere. Vicky busied herself again with straightening papers on her desk. "Are you sure everything's okay?" I asked again.

"Just fine," she replied tightly.

I shrugged and turned to head to my office. As I did, my shoulder bag swung around and slipped from my shoulder, bumping against her desk and sending a few of the papers flying to the floor. "Oh. I'm so sorry," I said, bending down to scoop up the pile. As I did, one of the papers got away from me. I'd just made a move to pick it up when Olive came out of nowhere and pounced on it.

"Hey! Let go of that!" I scolded, trying to pull it from her grip. Suddenly the paper ripped and I ended up with a slobbery half in my hand. "Uh-oh. Hope this wasn't part of someone's book proposal." For some reason a quote from one of Groucho Marx's writings popped into my head. *Outside of a dog, a book is man's best friend. Inside of a dog it's too dark to read.* I started to chuckle, but quickly stopped as my eyes skimmed the first few lines of the paper. It wasn't a book proposal but a letter to Bentley. A letter of resignation.

Vicky stood abruptly and held out her hand. "Please give me the letter, Lila. This really isn't any of your business."

"How can you say that, Vicky? Of course this is my business. I thought you were happy here. Why would you want to quit?"

Vicky plopped back down in her chair and let out a ragged sigh. "Believe me. I don't want to resign. I love this job. But I feel I have no choice."

"No choice? What do you mean?" I stared at her, wondering what had transpired to make her feel that way. Way back when, I'd started in her very position and knew that there was a certain amount of stress that came with the job, but Vicky always seemed to handle the demands of her position with a certain proficiency and perfunctory capacity. Better, I had to admit, than I felt I had. Then it struck me that maybe there was something going on, something terrible that Vicky hadn't confided. Had a sudden illness brought on this change in her demeanor? Goodness, I hoped not! I moved closer, almost afraid to ask. "Are you ill, Vicky? Because if that's the case, please know that we're all here for—"

"Ill? No. Sick. Yes." She pointed at Olive. "Sick of that dog!"

I sucked in my breath and stood straighter. "The dog? You're going to resign from a job you love because of a dog?"

"Yes. Just look at her. She's a menace."

I followed Vicky's eyes across the room to the waiting area, where Olive was once again chewing on the leg of one of the waiting room chairs. I hadn't noticed it earlier, but all the furniture did seem to be covered with little nibble marks. "Wow. She's made quick work of the furniture in there," I said, crossing the room and shooing her away.

"The problem is," Vicky continued, "Ms. Duke doesn't realize how much time a dog like Olive needs. I'm sure, with the right amount of attention and training, Olive would make someone a very fine pet. But Ms. Duke is always on the go, traveling here and there, out meeting with people or off with clients. Her lifestyle simply isn't suited to a dog like Olive."

She was right, of course. I knew Bentley truly cared for Olive, but was she the best owner for Olive? It had to be a two-way match, didn't it?

Vicky went on, "And she's dumped all the responsibility on me: walking the dog, running to the pet store for more doggie treats, watching the dog while she's at the expo . . . It goes on and on. I don't even have time to take care of my real duties."

"That *is* a problem. Have you explained all this to Bentley?"

"I tried. She didn't seem to take my complaint seriously, though. Thinks her precious Olive is no work—well, she isn't work for Ms. Duke when she's left the work for me! That's why I'm turning in my letter of resignation this afternoon. Of course, I'll give appropriate notice and be on hand to help train someone new, if that's what Ms. Duke wants. It saddens me, but I feel my talents as an office manager are being belittled by the additional tasks of pooch wrangler and poop scooping. I'm sorry, Lila, but it's obvious: I'm simply being taken advantage of, which I won't tolerate. Eliot and I must move on."

"Let me talk to Bentley before you make any rash decisions. It would be a shame for you to leave us over something like this. You're the best office administrator this place has ever had, and we'd miss you."

Two small pink circles tinged the top of her cheeks. "Thank you, Lila. But if Olive stays, I go. It's as simple as that."

* * *

THE IDEA OF Vicky leaving Novel Idea weighed heavily on my mind a couple of hours later as I maneuvered my Vespa along the cobblestone side street leading to Machiavelli's, being extra careful to avoid the leftover patches of oily slush that threatened to throw me off balance. It was good to be back on my Vespa, the cool air whipping at my cheeks and the joyful feeling of being in commune with nature—seeing, smelling, hearing things I never notice when I'm in a car.

Still, thoughts of Vicky's pending resignation invaded my bliss. Not that I could blame Vicky for wanting to leave the agency. What started out as a good idea—a companion and source of stress relief for Bentley during this difficult week— had ended up bringing nothing but stress to Vicky. We'd all overlooked how taxing Olive's rambunctious personality had been for her. Something had to be done. I tossed around several ideas in my mind, before finally deciding the best approach was to simply confront Bentley with the truth— despite all good intentions, she was not a suitable match for an active dog like Olive. I hated to see Olive go back to the pet store. The poor thing had been through so many owners already. But I didn't see any other choice. By the time I reached Machiavelli's parking lot, I was determined to set this thing straight, for Vicky's sake, if not the agency's. As soon as possible, I'd have a heart-to-heart with Bentley. In the meantime, I needed to focus on helping Lynn get through what was sure to be a difficult morning.

Even though the restaurant didn't open until eleven, I found the front door unlocked. Inside, my nose was treated to the tangy aromas of garlic and basil. No one was in the dining area, but I could hear the sound of clanking pots and pans coming from the kitchen. I moved across the room and pushed open the door leading to the kitchen area.

"Trey?" I called out.

"Back here, Mom."

Trey was bent over a long stainless steel prep table, chopping onions and peppers with a huge knife. For a second, I was mesmerized by the speed and dexterity of his movements as he expertly diced the vegetables. *When had he learned to use a knife like that?* "I'm here to trade keys," I said, my eyes roaming the expanse of the kitchen with its streamlined design and state-of-the-art appliances. Every single surface gleamed with cleanliness.

"Okay, great," he replied, barely looking up from his work. "I'm running a little behind with prep. My car keys are on the desk in the office. Would you mind getting them for me? Just leave the Vespa keys. I'll drive it home this afternoon."

"Perfect. The helmet's on the back grille," I said, heading for the office. I turned back and added, "By the way, Trey. Sean and I had some of your shrimp scampi last night. It was wonderful."

He paused and glanced up, a smile on his face. "Glad you liked it, Mom. I talked Oscar into adding a little lemon zest to the recipe. I think it freshens it up."

"It was some of the best I've had," I said. "I'm proud of you, Trey." He grinned with pride and refocused on his work, deftly coring and dicing a green pepper. I thought back to what Pam said the other day about finding and following our passions. Maybe this wasn't the life I'd choose for my son, but it really wasn't my place to make that decision. Besides, it looked like he knew what he was doing in a kitchen. And judging by the food I'd tasted last night, he was a great cook. Which was a good thing, since he'd need to keep his job in order to pay me back for his college tuition bill.

I stopped just inside the door of the office, my eyes jumping from the top of the cluttered desk to the overflowing file credenza to a bookshelf stuffed with cookbooks. Every single surface of Oscar Belmonte's office was crammed with papers, and I didn't see the set of keys anywhere. Crossing to the desk, I gingerly shuffled through stacks of invoices and bills and finally found the keys buried under a pile of inventory sheets. I also found something else. A copy of Jodi Lee's book, *The Billionaire's Bride*. The very book where the victim was murdered with a nail gun!

I picked it up with a shaky hand. I told myself I was jumping to conclusions, allowing what might be innocent facts to excuse my innate distrust of this man. Because the book didn't prove anything. Lots of people had read Jodi's book. It was a bestseller, after all. Yet I couldn't imagine *The Billionaire's Bride* would be at the top of Oscar's reading list. Unless he had it for a reason, had discovered the passage about Jodi's victim, used that as his method to—

"Lila!" Oscar's deep raspy voice caused me to jump. I dropped the book on the desk, a bit of torn napkin floating out from its pages, and I turned. He was standing in the doorway, his bulk filling the entire frame. "What brings you by?"

My mouth had gone dry, but I managed to pick up Trey's keys and give them a little jingle.

Oscar smiled. "Oh yeah, that's right. Trey said you'd be coming by for the keys. Why don't you stay awhile? Your mother will be here soon for an early lunch. I could have Trey whip up something special for you two."

"No thanks," I croaked, moving toward the door. He stepped aside, peering down with a strange look as I pressed past him.

"Everything okay?" he asked. "Been meaning to give Althea a call to see if she'd gone by the garage this morning.

Can't drive too long on a spare. Especially not this time of year with the changing weather—"

He said something else, but I gave a little half wave behind me and just kept on going, zipping through the kitchen and out the front door. Once outside, I sucked in the cold air, willing my heart to stop racing as well as my mind. That shred of napkin could have marked any passage or simply been where the man had quit reading. Or . . . it might have been at the very spot that perfectly described the method of murder used to kill Chuck Richards. For Mama's sake, and Trey's, I certainly hoped not. But, for my peace of mind, I knew what I had to do.

Chapter 16

ON THE WAY ACROSS THE LOT TO TREY'S CAR, I PULLED out my cell and dialed Sean's number. There was no answer. I stammered a bit, contemplating leaving a message about the book I'd found on Oscar's desk, but I realized that no matter how I put it, it'd sound silly. What was I going to say? *I'm calling to report a book reader?* So instead, I hung up and planned to pop by his work later and explain in person.

In the meantime, I desperately wanted to pull Trey out of that kitchen and tell Mama to ignore any attempts by Oscar to meet with her, but I knew better. If it turned out that Belmonte was no more than a closet romance reader, my overzealous reactions would spell the death of any trust they'd ever have in me again. It was bad enough that poor Mama had reacted to my concerns earlier by doubting that she deserved a romantic friendship at this stage in her life, or that Trey had been so afraid of my reactions that he'd gone behind my back with his career versus college choices.

No, I couldn't risk damaging my relationships with them, not until I knew more or my suspicions were validated by Sean in some way.

My mind still awhirl, I picked up Lynn and could think of little to say to her. As it turned out, Lynn was quiet on the way to the funeral home, too. I assumed she was nervous about confronting her past in such a direct way, so I tried to assure her that I'd be by her side to provide any support she might need, but my words failed to soothe her. Instead, she sat silently chewing her lip and wringing her hands, until I was sure one or the other was going to wear out.

Finally we reached Sunset Funeral Home, a sprawling lackluster brick building just a mile down the road from Bertram's Hotel. I'd never been inside the place—a good thing considering the services they offered—but found that despite its rather drab outward appearance, the inside was well appointed with hardwood floors, walls painted in tasteful hues of pale apricot and warm tans accented with chestnut brown trim, and comfortable, unassuming furniture. It was obvious that whoever had designed the interior knew what they were doing. The surroundings made me feel instantly at ease, like I'd just walked into an old friend's home.

An attendant greeted us at the door, taking our coats and directing us down the hall to one of the smaller rooms used for services. Lynn hesitated a second before entering, making me wonder if she'd had a change of heart. But she soldiered on, quickly choosing one of the red velvet-covered seats in the last row. I followed, taking the chair next to her, my eyes roaming instantly to the casket up front. It was closed, thank goodness! "It doesn't seem to be very crowded," I whispered. "Do you recognize anyone?"

"Just his mother. She's in the front row." I looked to the front of the room, where a woman was seated in a wheelchair.

My heart went out to this woman. A parent should never have to attend their own child's funeral.

Lynn continued, "She's a sweet woman, really, and she's been in an assisted living home for several years now. I'll say hello to her after the service, but her memory is bad. She may not even recognize me." Probably a blessing, I thought. Perhaps the grief and pain of losing her only child would be somewhat softened by her impaired mental faculties.

A prerecorded song suddenly started, melancholic strains pouring from mounted speakers on the wall. As it finished, a minister entered from the side of the room and positioned himself behind a small lectern next to the casket. As he began reading a verse, my gaze wandered. The scattering of people present didn't seem to be connected, each sitting in their own spot, segregated from the others. One of the men looked familiar, but I couldn't place him. I also noticed that no one seemed overly bereaved.

Lynn was holding up remarkably well, sitting ramrod straight, hands folded quietly in her lap, and her eyes holding steady on the minster. He was speaking of forgiveness and the power of redemption. Lynn's stoic posture along with the slight upward curve of her lips made me wonder if she was taking his words to heart, or if she was silently rejoicing in the death of her abuser, unable to evoke a spirit of forgiveness or, worse yet, believing the only redemption Chuck received was a quick nail to the head.

I shuddered. Then, catching a flash of movement out of the corner of my eye, I turned my head and saw a woman hovering in the hallway just outside the room's entrance. She was still wearing her coat, a few straggles of brown hair sticking out from under her tan woolen hat, a Burberry plaid scarf around her neck. She was dabbing at her eyes with a tissue and looking truly miserable. *Poor thing*, I thought, turning back just as the minister asked if there was anyone present who wished to add a few words about the deceased. When no one responded, he gave a signal, and a soulful rendition of "Amazing Grace" filled the room. As quickly as the service had started, and without much fanfare, it concluded. I glanced back over my shoulder, but the woman had already left.

As people started filing out of their rows, Lynn nudged me. "I'm going to pay my respects to Chuck's mother," she said. "I'll meet you out in the car in a few minutes."

I nodded and started for the coat check, taking a detour first to the restroom. There I found the crying woman, leaning over the sink and patting cool water on her tear-swollen eyes. She was youngish, maybe late twenties, plump, meek appearing, although hunched over as she was, it was hard to really say. She glanced up as I entered and quickly reached for a paper towel from a stack on the counter.

I paused, feeling like I should say something. "Are you okay?" I asked, stepping forward.

"Yes. Thank you," she choked out, but her shoulders shuddered as if she was fighting back another round of sobs. Embarrassed, she turned away and quickly finished drying her face. Then she gathered her purse and hat from the countertop and made a hasty exit before I could ask her anything else. Back outside, I saw her again, sitting alone in a parked car with a mismatched paint job and an air freshener swinging from the rearview mirror. She was talking on her cell phone and wiping her tearstained face with the end of her scarf.

I was still watching her when Lynn finally came out. "How was Chuck's mom doing?" I asked, not quite taking my eyes off the crying woman.

Lynn frowned. "Not so great. As to be expected, I guess. She did recognize me, though. I think she was glad to see me."

"I'm sure it was a comfort to her to see Chuck's friends." I pointed over to the parked car with the woman and asked Lynn if she recognized her. "I saw her inside," I explained. "She was really upset. Do you know if Chuck had a girlfriend?"

Lynn shook her head. "I've been out of touch with Chuck for so long, I really don't know if he was dating or not. But if she was his girlfriend, then she's better off with him dead." She let out a long sigh and added, "Sorry. I didn't mean that the way it sounded. It's just a relief to know that he'll never hurt me or any other woman again."

"No, he won't. His murderer made sure of that."

She shrugged, the semblance of a small smile playing on the corners of her mouth. Or was I imagining that? Nonetheless, her crassness toward Chuck's murder bothered me. But I couldn't tell if she was just relieved he was gone, a natural emotion for someone who'd endured his abuse, or if she was actually happy someone had murdered him. Then there was that little niggling doubt that still lingered in the back of my mind: Lynn's motive, her lack of an alibi, the nails so conveniently planted in Jodi's room, which just happened to be right next to hers . . .

"Would it be a problem for you to take me into Dunston?" Lynn asked as I was pulling out of the lot.

I blushed, grateful she couldn't read my thoughts. "Not at all. Why?"

"When I told Sloan I was going to Chuck's funeral, she suggested that we get together afterward. We were planning on a quick lunch, then riding together to the expo this afternoon. Would you like to join us?"

"Oh, no thank you. I should use my time to run a couple of errands before I have to be at the Arts Center." I wanted to pop by Sean's office and tell him about that book I'd discovered in Oscar's office. "But I'm happy to drop you wherever you need to go. It's good that you two are getting to know each other. Dr. Meyers seems like quite the woman."

Lynn's face brightened. "She is. You should see all the things she'd done to help women who are struggling to break away from abusive relationships. A couple of years ago, she invested her own money to buy a large house and turn it into a home for women in transition. It's really a nice place. She showed it to me the other day."

"Really. Where's it at? I don't think I've ever seen the place." We were getting close to the Dunston exit and Trey's car was handling beautifully, despite the fact that my skills with the clutch were rusty and the slush-sloppy roads weren't helping.

"In a neighborhood not far from the Dunston Shopping Plaza. It's a convenient location. Quiet, but close enough to shopping that the women can walk if they want. Many of them don't have vehicles, or much else for that matter. They've usually escaped their situations with nothing more than the clothes on their backs. Some of them with their children in tow. It's tough. Really tough."

"I really feel sorry for the children," I said, leaving the highway and struggling to downshift on the exit ramp. "How sad for them to deal with something so horrible, so young."

Lynn sighed. "I guess that's one good thing: Chuck and I never had children." She indicated for me to turn right at the next stoplight. "Sloan's office is just down this road on the left." I nodded and pulled into a small lot next to a brick office building. The sign on the outside indicated that it housed several office suites: two dentists, a financial planner, Dr. Meyers's office, and another familiar name—Rufus Manning Photography. As I put the car into gear, Lynn turned to me and added, "You know, Lila, I was just like those women that Sloan works so hard to help. Down and out, without much confidence or means to support myself. I took a job I hated just to make ends meet. I felt so alone. So lost. At night, I'd make up stories just to escape the misery I was feeling." She shrugged and offered a faint smile. "I guess writing has always been my happy place."

I nodded, understanding what she was saying. Reading was my happy place. I found comfort in books, easily getting lost in their pages. During that especially dark time of my life, after discovering Bill's affair and the ensuing bitter divorce, books were my salvation, the only thing that kept me sane. Well, that and my loving mother.

She went on. "Anyway, the happiest day of my life was when I got that phone call from you saying you wanted to represent me. Without you and Ms. Duke, I'd still be struggling to find my way. To imagine that now I might be able to make a living doing something that means so much to me . . . Well, it's just beyond my comprehension. It's like a dream. And I'm almost afraid I'm going to wake up and find out that's all it was, some sort of silly dream."

"That's not going to happen, Lynn. You've worked hard and earned your success. You're living your dream. Believe it."

She pulled open the door and started to step out, turning back at the last moment. "You're right. I *have* worked hard. And now that Chuck's gone and I can really put my past to rest, maybe I can finally start enjoying my new life."

SEAN WAS SURPRISED but happy to see me when I arrived at the Dunston Police Department. He met me in the lobby to escort me to his desk on the second floor. The police department was a three-story building located in the heart of Dunston's downtown area. It was old and dingy, and a never-ending hub of precarious activities.

When we first started dating, Sean had given me a tour, avoiding the basement. I'd never been in the "pit," as the cops referred to the lower floor of the station house where they held prisoners awaiting arraignment, but I could imagine it to be a dark, heinous dungeonlike space, full of nasty smells and vile criminals. I'd been able to pass off thoughts of that place in my mind, knowing the types of people it held. Only now my skin crawled to think that someone I knew, someone I believed was innocent, an agency's "family member," as it was, had sat in that very place for days. It was horrible that Jodi had to spend any time down there. At least now she'd been transferred to the county jail to await her trial. Sean had assured me it was a better facility and that she'd be placed in minimum security. I knew that Flora had planned to visit her yesterday. Which was probably why she missed work this morning. The stress of seeing her client and friend behind bars was probably too much for her.

When we got to his desk, Sean pulled a chair out for me and asked me to wait a second while he ducked into the printer room to make a few copies for an upcoming meeting. While I waited, I took in the activity around me; several officers were busy on their phones, others typing on their computers and paging through stacks of files. Toward the back of the room, I could see through an open door into one of the conference rooms. A group of men in suits were huddled around the table discussing something serious. Suddenly, a man in handcuffs and screaming obscenities was brought through and escorted toward one of the interview rooms. Surprisingly, his outburst didn't seem to distract anyone from their work. Most of the officers didn't even bother to look up. I did, though. I was mesmerized by the obscene tattoos that covered the top of his shaved head and wrapped around his left eye, almost like an eye patch. He caught me looking and for a second, our eyes locked and prickles of fear crawled along my skin.

I quickly glanced away, my eyes landing on Sean's desk and something else that gave me goose bumps. This time, the tingling-in-a-good-way type of goose bumps. It was a ring! And not just any ring, but an engagement ring, sitting on a bare spot on his blotter desk pad. *I've waited so long and here it is! My engagement ring!* My heart pounded double time as I reached out, its sparkling diamond calling to me.

"Lila?"

Startled, I pulled my hand back, knocking a container of paper clips over in the process. "Sorry," I said, scrambling to straighten the mess I'd made, trying to avoid looking at the ring. Did he see me looking at it? How horrible of me to ruin his surprise.

"That's not what you're thinking it is," he said, settling into his chair and picking up the ring. "I'm sorry, Lila. But this is evidence."

"Evidence?" Evidence of what? Our love for each other? What was he talking about?

He went on. "In Chuck Richards's case. It was found on his body. I've been calling around, trying to track down the place that sold it to him."

"Oh." I swallowed hard, wondering if my cheeks looked as hot as they felt. "That ring was found on Chuck's body?"

"Yes. In the pocket of his jeans. There was no box."

I nodded, ready to change the awkward subject, but something niggled at my brain. I squinted and reached out my hand. "Can I see it?" A funny feeling overcame me as I rotated the ring in my fingers. I'd seen this ring before. *Where?* I noted the center square-cut, bezel-set stone flanked by small diamonds on either side. The band itself was yellow gold, worn smooth on the bottom, as if it'd been worn for years.

"You notice that, too?" Sean said after I showed him my observation. "The ring is old. Chuck probably picked it up at one of the local pawnshops."

I thought back to the woman in the wheelchair at the funeral. "Or it was his mother's."

Sean leaned back in his chair and crossed his arms. "We checked. She said no. But the real question is, who was he going to give it to? We've checked around, but the guy was a real loner. The people who were acquainted with him didn't know much about him. Even his own mother. Her memory's bad, sure, but she didn't seem to know anything about his current situation, his friends, whether he was seeing anyone. I got the impression they weren't close. And there's nothing in his apartment that gives us any clue. We're running a check on all the calls to his cell, but so far that's also been a dead end."

I stared at the ring for a few more seconds before passing it back. *Something about the ring . . .* I just couldn't place it. But I did know who might have been its recipient. I started to explain. "I was at Chuck's funeral this morning. Lynn wanted to go."

Sean nodded.

"You knew?"

"Yup. We had a guy there."

My mind flashed back to one of the guests. I remembered a fellow across the aisle from us who looked familiar. That must have been why; he was one of Sean's coworkers. Then something dawned on me and I felt a bit better. "You're putting in a lot of time on a case that's supposedly wrapped up. I mean, Jodi's in jail, awaiting trial."

He nodded. "I can't seem to let it go. Too many loose ends. This is one of them. But my sergeant's going to be ticked off when he realizes I'm spending so much time on this case."

I smiled appreciatively. Sean was a good cop. There was no way he could ignore a loose end, no matter what his superior said. Maybe there was hope for Jodi after all. "Anyway, getting back to the funeral. I saw a woman there."

He sat up and leaned forward, his brows furrowed.

I continued, "She stayed outside the room where the service was being held, so maybe the officer didn't see her. I don't know. But afterward, I ran into her in the restroom. She was really upset. Sobbing."

"Did you get a name?"

I shook my head.

"Can you describe her?"

"Sure. And the car she was driving."

He pulled out a legal pad and took down the details. Or at least as many details as I could muster. I realized that even though I'd spoken to the woman, I couldn't recall anything particularly unique about her: brown hair, brown or maybe blue eyes, I couldn't remember. Average height, a little plump, but not too much so. About like me actually. Although I liked to refer to myself as Rubenesque, not plump. She drove a car with mismatched paint. What model? I couldn't remember, four doors, I thought.

"Okay, thanks," Sean said, putting down his pen. Although I wasn't even sure what he was thanking me for. It seemed I'd just described half the women in town, including myself.

"There's something else, too," I said, getting to the real reason I'd stopped by. He listened with interest as I proceeded to tell him about discovering the book in Oscar's office. "It just seems strange that it would be there. He doesn't seem like the type to read a romance novel," I finished.

Sean shrugged. "Maybe. Maybe it doesn't belong to him. You went in there to look for Trey's keys, right?"

I nodded.

"Could be that a lot of the employees store stuff in the office. Maybe the book belongs to one of the waitresses."

I suddenly felt silly. Of course, that was probably it. It made sense, after all, that one of the staff, maybe even Anna, his granddaughter, was reading the book on their break. They'd been selling like hotcakes at the expo. I sighed. "You're right. I guess I'm jumping to conclusions."

Sean cleared his throat and stood. I followed suit. "I've got to go to my meeting," he said. Then he placed his hand on my shoulder. "Don't worry about it, Lila. It's only natural for you to have doubts about any man your mother's dating. Trey has had his fair share of doubts about me, too."

He was right. Sean and Trey had gone through a difficult period last summer. Thankfully, all that was behind us now. Now my two men got along famously. Perhaps that was all this was. Me reading into the situation, jumping to conclusions, all because I couldn't accept my mother's interest in the man. I exhaled and nodded. "You're right. I need to get a grip on this thing with Mama. Oscar seems to really care about her. Besides, she's usually a good judge of character."

He reached across and tipped up my chin, giving me a look that made me smile. "That's better," he said. "How about a late dinner again tonight? I could get some takeout from Wild Ginger."

"Perfect," I agreed. We said good-bye, but just before I walked away, my eyes were once again drawn back to his desk and the ring. I couldn't shake the thought that I'd seen it before. But where?

OF COURSE, AS soon as I was back in Trey's car, I remembered exactly where I'd seen the ring—in Rufus Manning's photograph. The close-up shot of the couple's clasped hands.

I thought back to the photo and the way the diamond shimmered in the sun. It was the very same square setting, I was sure of it. The ring was so unique, it had to be the same. Immediately, I took out my phone and called Sean, but it was too late. He wasn't answering. Probably in that meeting he'd told me about. I was going to leave a message, then realized his meeting would take some time. By that time Rufus would likely be setting up for another day at the expo and Sean or one of his officers would have to come down there to ask about the photo—meaning one more indication to his sergeant that Sean was wasting time on a closed case. But I'd be at the expo soon after that anyway; I could at least save that much effort for Sean before I called him back. So I just hung up before leaving a message. I'd see him later at dinner anyway. I glanced at my watch. The expo was due to start in just a couple of hours. Enough time for me to swing back by the office and get a few things done before I was due at the Arts Center.

However, things didn't go quite as I'd planned. When I arrived back at the office, I found Vicky standing next to her desk with a worried look on her face. "Lila, I'm so glad you're here," she said. "All the other agents are out for a late lunch and then heading straight to the expo."

"What's going on?"

She held up Olive's leash. "Olive needs to go for a walk. If she's not taken soon, she'll have an accident. But I hate to leave the office unattended." As if on cue, Olive began whimpering. She looked like she had her paws crossed.

I reached for the leash. "I still have my coat on. How about I take her?"

Vicky exhaled. "Thank you, Lila. Besides, Olive and I could use a break from each other. It's been quite the morning." She reached in her desk and grabbed something. "And don't forget these."

I looked down and saw a plastic roll in my hand. "What's this?"

"Bags." She raised a brow at my dumbfounded expression. "For after Olive does her business. It wouldn't do to leave a mess for others to happen upon."

"No, that wouldn't do," I said with a roll of my eyes. I pocketed the bags and hooked up Olive's leash. Outside, I paused at the top of the steps, picking her up and holding her close to my chest as we navigated the stairway down to the back lot, though not too tightly for fear of an even worse accident than one on the office carpet. As soon as her little paws hit the ground, she scurried over to a set of evergreen bushes. I got a bag ready.

"Better now?" I asked, after completing cleanup detail, dangling the warm baggie of her business in my hand. She looked up at me with her big brown eyes for half a second before darting away again. With a tug of the leash, she started off in another direction, her nails scraping the pavement as she tried to pull me along. I laughed. "Okay, Olive. We'll go for a walk. Besides, we could both use the exercise."

As we passed by, I glanced wantonly toward Espresso Yourself, wishing I could take the dog inside and order a caramel latte. What I wouldn't do for a sweet caffeine jolt and one of Makayla's muffins! It'd been a long morning already and I was half starved. But instead, I barely had time to deposit the baggie in the receptacle outside the door before Olive pulled and sniffed her way through the lot and around the corner. Eventually, after several pit stops, we made our way onto High Street, where I tossed a wave at Jay Coleman at the Constant Reader. He was inside his front window dusting the books on display. Farther down the street, I ran into Ruthie Watson, my friend from Sherlock Holmes Realty. She was making her rounds to the downtown businesses, delivering the latest edition of *Valley Homes*—a real estate brochure listing local residences for sale. She oohed and aahed over Olive while we chatted awhile. Next up was All Creatures, Feathered and Furry. I stopped on the walk outside and looked down at Olive. "Shall we go inside and say hello to your old friends?" I asked. She barked her agreement.

Matt immediately stopped what he was doing and came over to greet us. "Hello, Olive! How are you, girl?" He bent down, petting her behind the ears and looking up at me. "Is she behaving?"

"Not really. You didn't tell us she was part beaver."

His face scrunched. "Huh?"

"She's chewed down all the wood in the office."

We laughed, and then Matt sobered. "I'm so sorry. Bentley can't say I didn't warn her." He stood and reached into a giant jar on his counter, taking out a dog biscuit and holding it for Olive. She snatched it from his hand, immediately chomping away. Little pieces of dog biscuit fell to the floor. "The police came by yesterday. They were looking at Chuck's handiwork. Asking all sorts of questions about the equipment he used."

"Really?" I asked, although I already knew as much. Sean had told me. I kept my attention focused on Olive, who had lapped the crumbs from the floor and was sniffing around for more. "Hey, she really likes those. Maybe I should pick up some."

"No problem. Hold on and I'll get you a box." He headed for one of the aisles. He returned a minute later with a box of dog biscuits and started ringing it up. "I can put this on Bentley's account, if you want."

I nodded. "Sounds good."

"Anyway," Matt continued. "When the cops were here, they asked to look at my nail gun. Isn't that weird?"

"They did?" I was still playing dumb, but I feared he could see guilt written all over my face. After all, the reason the cops had questioned him was that I'd told Sean about the nail gun. I quickly tried to redirect the conversation. "Have you heard that they arrested one of our authors, Jodi Lee?"

Matt rubbed his chin, his eyes rolling upward. "Jodi Lee? Why does that name sound familiar?"

"She's one of our key authors at the expo this week; there's a display of her book in the Constant Reader window. She writes romantic suspense novels," I explained, thinking Matt probably wasn't a romance reader.

"Oh, yeah. That's right. My wife's reading her latest book. She likes those sort of books." He started bagging my purchase. "She was telling me about it the other day. Something about how one of the characters was killed with a . . ." His voice trailed off.

I grabbed my bag and tugged on Olive's leash. "Thanks, Matt. Gotta run!"

Chapter 17

LADIES WERE LINED UP DOWN THE HALL WAITING TO get into the Sundance Room to hear Pam's reading. Keeping with the fun spirit of the honeymoon theme, Ms. Lambert arranged for samples of champagne to be offered during what was sure to be a steamy reading. Afterward, everyone would be directed to the Dragonfly Room, which was set up with lingerie displays and booths filled with luxurious bath and spa items—everything needed to make the bride feel beautiful on her special day. There would also be several travel talks, pitching the latest in exotic honeymoon destinations.

On my way to find Pam, I snatched a glass of champagne from a passing tray and took a couple of quick sips. The bubbly sweetness helped to calm my nerves. For some reason I couldn't figure, I'd been on edge all afternoon. Maybe it was the funeral, or the case, or Trey . . . or just plain exhaustion. Whatever it was, I was glad tomorrow's fashion show wrapped up the week's events.

Bentley caught up to me before I reached the main auditorium. "There you are, Lila. Have you spoken with Ms. Crump today?"

I paused for a half beat. I'd been dreading this conversation all day. "Yes. I spoke with her earlier."

Bentley raised a finely arched brow. "Did she mention that she planned on resigning?"

"She did."

"It's just absurd, isn't it? That she'd leave a good job over something as silly as a sweet little dog." In her typical high heels, Bentley stood a full two inches over me. That, combined with her even taller ego, made me feel like a puny kid. I was struggling with whether to accept this opening or to confront her with what was sure to become a contentious issue. Yet I'd just spent what would have been my lunchtime being pulled about by a dog that wasn't my own, picking up and pocketing its poo. There was no doubt in my mind: Vicky was right. Bentley was taking advantage of her.

"It's just that Olive is such an active little dog," I started, treading carefully on the subject. "It's a lot for Vicky to handle. Especially considering how rigorous her regular duties can be."

Bentley shifted her weight and placed a hand on her hip. "What exactly are you trying to say, Lila?"

"Just that it would be a shame to lose Vicky. She's a real asset to the agency. And . . ." I hedged. "Well, you're a busy woman and Olive needs a lot of attention and training."

Bentley raised her hand, pressing her palm outward. "That's quite enough, Lila. We'll discuss this later. Right now, I have authors that need my attention." She turned on her heel and started to walk away, only to quickly turn back again. "I know I'm busy, but Olive loves me. I can tell she does. It's easy for you to judge who should have a pet and not. You've got a dream life. A loving mother and son, and now a fiancé. You have no idea what it's like to be . . ." She caught herself before finishing. Her eyes glistened with emotion as she took a couple of shaky breaths and shook her head. But she didn't say anything else. She didn't have to. I knew what she was going to say. Bentley was lonely. I knew she didn't have a special man in her life. Probably because she was too busy building her business. She'd never really mentioned her family, either. I'd always assumed it was because she liked keeping her personal and business lives separate. Maybe it was for different reasons. Perhaps Bentley didn't have any family, or maybe she was estranged from her family. I didn't really know, but now I knew why she put so much into her agents and authors. We really *were* her family. Maybe the only family she had.

"I'm sorry. I shouldn't have snapped at you," she said, rubbing at her temples. "It's just all this stuff with Jodi and . . . Well, that blasted Ms. Lambert is on my very last nerve, now this thing with Vicky and the dog."

I wanted to say something. Something to ease the situation, put some of her worries to rest, but before I could think of anything, she excused herself and took off down the hallway. I watched her walk away, this time thinking that she didn't seem all that tall and intimidating after all. Bentley, like all of us, only really wanted one thing—to be loved.

I WEAVED THROUGH the line of fans and greeted Pam. "You're up in a few minutes."

Her eyes widened as she glanced down at her watch. "Oh my goodness. Thanks for the reminder. Time got away from me." She stood and addressed the ladies in her line. "I'm sorry, but I'm due for a reading in the Sundance Room. I'll be back at my table in about an hour." Then she turned to Mama, who was seated down a ways, hunkered over a row of tarot cards and whispering conspiratorially to a young woman. "Althea. Do you want to come along? You might enjoy my reading. It's got a few lines about the fortune-teller in it."

In response, Mama looked up and smiled. Only I noticed her smile didn't quite reach her eyes. "Sure thing, Pam. I'll be right along soon as I finish this young'un's readin'." She turned back to the gal and spoke quietly. But her usual enthusiasm was lacking. I wondered if she wasn't feeling well. Mama was strong, but it had to have been a long week for her.

Pam reached under the table and snatched up her bag. "I need to pop by the restroom real quick. I'll meet you in the Sundance Room, okay?"

"Sounds good," I replied. "I'll wait for my mother to finish and we'll join you there." While I waited, I scooted over to Rufus Manning's table. I wanted to ask him about the photo I'd seen with the ring in it. Maybe he'd remember the names of the subjects without having to check the records at his office.

"Hey, Rufus." He looked up from a book he was reading and smiled. "I have a quick question for you." I reached for the album where I'd seen the photo before and started leafing through the pages. "You know that print you had at Espresso Yourself?" I started.

He stood, setting his book aside, and came over. "Yup. Talked to Makayla on the phone about it earlier. Told her I'd make a copy this evening. Just haven't got around to it yet."

"Understandable," I said, still flipping the pages. Rufus had used actual prints to assemble his album, mounting each to black backing with silver-colored photo corners. The overall effect of blacks and whites against the stark dark background was very dramatic. "I'm sure this expo is taking a lot of time from your regular business duties."

"It is. But I've met a lot of potential customers, so it's

been worth it. Are you looking for the smaller print I have in here?" he asked, reaching for the album and looking for himself. "It's toward the back."

"Hi, Lila."

I turned to see Lynn and Dr. Meyers standing behind me. "Hi, ladies," I said. "How's it going?"

"Good," Lynn said. "We're heading to the Sundance Room. Thought we'd take a break and listen to Pam's reading."

"I'm heading that way myself," I said. "Just waiting on my mother to finish and then we'll join you. Save a couple of seats, okay?"

"Can't seem to find it offhand," Rufus interrupted, still paging through the album.

"Such gorgeous pictures," Dr. Meyers commented. "You're very talented, Mr. Manning."

Rufus dipped his chin and smiled. "Thank you."

Aware of the minutes ticking away, I glanced over my shoulder toward Mama's booth and back at Rufus, who was still paging through the album. "It's okay. I'm just wondering if you remember the ring in the picture? Or the name of the couple?" I asked, eager to make a connection between the ring and Chuck Richards.

He squinted my way. "I can't say I recall the ring, but I sort of recall the session. I believe it was sometime last month that they came by my office."

"Do you remember their names?"

Rufus absently scratched at his head, sending red curls spiraling every which way. "Sorry. Can't say that I do. I have a part-time secretary who does my bookings, so she deals with all the details. Plus I'm really bad with names and with all the couples that have been in and out lately, it's hard to keep track. But I can pop into the office sometime tomorrow morning and see if I can find it in my records."

Lynn spoke up. "Sorry to interrupt, but we'd better get going and reserve those seats in the Sundance Room." Dr. Meyers agreed and assured me that she'd save Mama and me a seat.

I told them we'd be right along. Glancing Mama's way, I saw that she had finished her reading and was sitting forward, elbows on the table, resting her chin in her palms. "Are you ready to go, Mama?"

"Sure thing, sugar." She rose slowly from the table and started my way.

"Excuse me," I said to Rufus, scurrying over to give Mama a hand. "Are you feeling ill?"

"Just a bit tired, that's all it is. And a little stomach trouble. Been eatin' too much of Trey's good cookin', I'm 'fraid." She rubbed at her stomach. "Lawd, my guts rollin'. But I'll be fine, hon. Don't you worry. Besides, a little nightcap with Jim later will put me right as rain."

Mama considered Jim Beam the cure-all for every ailment. "Do you want to head out now? I can give you a lift home."

She straightened her shoulders and waved off my suggestion. "And not hear Pam's readin'? No way. I've been wantin' to read her book myself, just haven't had the chance. I'm curious to see what the fuss is all about. Must be really good stuff, considerin' all the fans she's got."

"You still haven't read one of her books?"

Mama shook her head. "Nope. Not had the chance."

I took a deep breath and released it slowly. If Mama's stomach was upset now, I'd hate to think how she was going to feel after she heard Pam's reading. My mama's forays into romance reading consisted mostly of an occasional sweet paperback romance she got from the library; she preferred instead to read science fiction novels. Which always surprised me, as one would think she'd be into the fantasy genre, especially books about the paranormal. But no, she'd always preferred science fiction. "I like readin' about how technology could make things possible, things we could never imagine," she'd once told me when I asked about her reading habits. "Fantasy is more about the impossible, don't y'all think? Wizards and talking ghosts . . . who in their right mind would want to read all that cock-and-bull?"

Go figure.

We made it to the Sundance Room with a little time to spare. Dr. Meyers and Lynn had saved us seats toward the back. I settled in next to Dr. Meyers, Mama on my other side. Jude and Zach were seated a couple of rows in front of us. My stomach lurched at the sight of Jude. I hadn't seen him since our little encounter at the author's table.

"Everything okay?" Dr. Meyers wanted to know.

"Yeah. Just a lot on my mind this week."

"Jodi?"

"Yeah, that. And just a lot of unanswered questions." I sighed. "Ever feel like you're spinning your wheels? Missing something important, but you just can't figure it out?"

She nodded. "All the time. Especially in my business."

"I bet. Lynn was telling me about all the good work you've done. I mean, the home for women in transition. What a wonderful thing!"

Dr. Meyers smiled and leaned forward, her eyes gleaming. "Thank you, Lila. I'd love to show it to you sometime. I feel the more people that are aware of the plight these women face, the more willing they will be to help. We're in need of all the community support we can get."

"What do you mean?"

"Well, most of our staff is volunteer, counselors who give their time, and we receive a few grants, of course. And the women, the ones who can, work and contribute what they're able, but many of them are between jobs, or they have young children . . ." She sat back and shook her head. "I'm sorry. I promised myself I would quit doing this."

I squinted. "Doing what?"

"My sales pitch, that's what. Friends have told me that all I talk about is the home and the women there." She shrugged. "Guess I'm just passionate about what I do."

There it was again. Passion. Dr. Meyers's passion for her work was evident in everything she did, as was Bentley's passion for her agents and authors, her family, as she put it. And, of course, Trey's passion for cooking. Perhaps if we didn't follow our passions, we'd never achieve our purpose in life. I hated to think where all these women would be if Dr. Meyers hadn't followed her passion. "Please don't apologize," I said. "I think it's wonderful what you're doing. I'd be happy to help in any way I can."

"Welcome, everyone." Pam's voice cut into our conversation. Dr. Meyers shot me a smile before leaning back and focusing her attention forward. Pam was on the stage, leaning against the lectern, looking poised and beautiful. She'd chosen to wear a deep burgundy blouse today, which really offset her brown skin tone and dark hair. She must have applied a little extra makeup during her restroom break, because her dark eyes were sparkling. "Are you ladies ready to turn up the heat?"

A chorus of whoops rang out. I glanced around, a little surprised by the outburst, and wondered if perhaps Ms. Lambert's idea of serving champagne samples to this already rambunctious crowd might not have been the best idea after all.

Pam slowly opened her book, the wicked little smirk on her face playing right into the crowd's feisty mood. I dared a glance Mama's way, wondering what she was thinking.

To my dismay, she looked positively green. "Mama," I whispered. "Are you okay? Is this upsetting you?"

"Is what upsettin' me?" she asked, regarding me with a strange look.

Pam continued, "I'm going to start with a scene that unfolds between my two main characters: Joseph, the dark sultan, and the object of his desire, the innocent Sasha whom he's abducted from a foreign village and is about to ravage. Let me warn you, ladies. This is some spicy stuff."

"Bring it on," someone cried out. Another round of whoops and giggles ensued.

I peeked at Zach and Jude, noticing that Zach was more focused than I'd ever seen him. So focused that his mouth practically hung open. I was surprised he wasn't drooling. Jude must have sensed me staring, because he suddenly turned around and shot me one of his irritating winks.

Next to me, Dr. Meyers was covering her mouth to keep in the giggles. On my other side, Mama was also covering her mouth. Not to keep in the giggles, though, but out of shock. At least that was what I thought until she bolted from her chair and ran from the room. I went after her, following her down the hall to the restroom.

A few minutes later, I asked, "Mama? You okay in there?" She'd holed herself up in a stall and had been vomiting. I'd run some paper towels under cold water and waited for her to come out. "What can I do to help you, Mama?"

She finally finished, opening the door and crossing straight to the sink. While she splashed her face with cool water, I held the damp paper towels against the back of her neck. "I'm so sorry you're sick. Let me drive you out to my place. I've got Trey's car here and we can get yours tomorrow. Just stay the night with me."

She wiped her face with a towel, a little color returning

to her cheeks. "No need, sugar, I'll just head home. I'm feeling a little better already. But I'll take ya up on your offer of a ride. 'Fraid I'm not in much shape to be drivin'."

Suddenly the restroom door flew open and Bentley came charging in. "Althea. I heard you're not feeling well." She came right over and placed her arm around my mother's shoulders. "Do you need to see a doctor? I can get you to the best physician in town."

"Thank ya, Ms. Duke. No need for a doc. Just a little too much rich food, that's all. I'll be all right with a little rest."

I smiled at Bentley, grateful for her offer of help. "I'm going to run Mama home," I told her. "She needs to get into bed."

"Of course." She turned to my mother. "And if you need anything, don't hesitate to ask me, Althea. Okay? And, Lila, I know tomorrow is Saturday, but I've informed everyone that there will be a status meeting at ten o'clock sharp. There's a lot on the table for discussion."

I nodded dutifully, wondering if she meant Jodi's case or the issue with Vicky and Olive or the roundup of the expo week. Or maybe all three. But for now, the status meeting was the furthest thing from my mind. I placed my hand under Mama's elbow and gently coaxed her to the door. "Come on, Mama. Let's get you home."

Chapter 18

BY EIGHT O'CLOCK SATURDAY MORNING I WAS IN LINE at Espresso Yourself, anticipating my caramel latte. I'd been up late taking care of Mama, so I was eager for my morning caffeine hit. Especially since today was sure to be the busiest day at the expo. Not only was the weather cooperating— sunny, crisp, and most importantly dry—but Ms. Lambert and her crew from Southern Belles Bridal had planned an event that was sure to draw a crowd—a bridal fashion show! And without any author presentations scheduled, I'd be able to just sit back and enjoy. I thought back to the dress I'd seen just this week, the simple white sheath, timeless and so classy, and hoped they'd chosen it for the fashion show.

A baby's cry drew my attention to the young mother in front of me, who jostled a fussy toddler on her hip as she waited for her coffee order. Makayla returned to the counter with what looked like a double shot of espresso. "Did Jackson have another rough night?" she asked, taking and swiping the woman's credit card. It always amazed me that Makayla knew so much about her customers. She made everyone who walked through the door feel special.

The woman shook her head. "I'd say. Can't wait until this tooth comes in." The baby was sucking his fist and whimpering, big tears running down his pudgy cheeks.

Makayla reached over and tickled the baby's arm, clucking and making little goo-goo sounds. She was rewarded with a brief but toothy grin. "Now, don't be complaining too much, Mama. Just look how precious that smile is!" And just like that, the child jammed his fingers back into his mouth and started fussing again.

The mother chuckled and took her coffee cup from the counter. "Are you volunteering to babysit tonight?"

Makayla threw up her hands. "No way, girl. I'm just here to provide your morning cuppa joe, not babysitting services."

We all laughed as the woman hugged her precious little bundle and made her way out the door.

"Boy, do I remember those days," I said, moving up to the counter.

Makayla turned to steam my milk, speaking louder so I could hear her over the whirring of the machine. "And it only got easier from there, right?"

I rolled my eyes. "Ha, ha." Makayla finished steaming and started mixing. "Did that missing photo ever turn up?" I asked her.

"Photo?"

"The one Rufus Manning took." I'd tossed and turned throughout the night, the whereabouts of that photo bugging me. With my agent duties and Mama getting sick and everything, I hadn't much time to question Rufus about it the day before.

Makayla scrunched her face. "No, it never did show up. And Jay says he didn't throw anything away."

I'd asked Trey about it over breakfast, too, and he'd said the same thing. Which led me to believe that the break-in at Makayla's shop was less about vandalism and more about eliminating that photo. The killer must have wanted to make it difficult for the police to trace the ring. But who and why? *Chuck's fiancée*, I thought. After all, the ring would link directly to her. Was the woman I'd met at the funeral, spoken with, even tried to comfort . . . I shivered. Had I really been that close to a vicious killer—a desperate woman, fallen victim to Chuck's abuse, who decided to stand up for herself . . .

"Hello, Lila?" I snapped back to focus to hear Makayla say, "I was saying that I missed you last night." I must have looked confused. She raised a brow and clarified, "At the lingerie show?"

"Oh, I'm sorry!" I'd forgotten that I told Makayla that I'd meet her at the Dragonfly Room. We'd planned to try out the spa items and maybe even get a mini makeover. "Mama got sick and I had to take her home."

She stopped mixing and turned her full focus my way. "Althea? Is she okay?"

"Just a little stomach bug, or maybe something she ate. I took her home and got her settled into bed. By the time I left, she was doing much better."

Makayla let out a relieved sigh and went back to mixing. "Oh good. Well, you missed out on my big purchase."

"Your purchase?"

"Uh-huh." She finished my latte and capped it off. After handing it over, she reached under the counter and brought out a small shopping bag. Then she glanced around, just to make sure the place was empty, before pulling out a daring lace teddy. "What do you think?"

My hand flew to my mouth. "Makayla!"

She stepped back and held it up to herself. It was a gorgeous, deep green satin with black lace and dainty straps.

"It's beautiful!" I said. And I meant it, too. The color was almost a perfect match for her mysterious fern green eyes.

Jokingly, she began sashaying back and forth, flaunting her stuff. "Watch out, Jay. Here I come!" Just then, the door jingled open and in came an older gentleman. He immediately lifted his eyes and hand to greet Makayla before stopping short with a jaw-popping expression. His face reddened instantly, and he turned and fled, the door slamming behind him with a chorus of jostling bells.

I burst out laughing when I saw the mortified look on Makayla's face. "Oh my Lawd!" she cried. "That was Mr. Goldman. He's one of my best customers."

I placed a bill on the counter and tipped my cup her way. "Don't worry. Once he gets over the shock, he'll be back." I gave her a wink. "I guarantee it."

I WAS STILL laughing as I made my way into the office and found Vicky sitting at her desk. "I didn't expect to see you in so early today," I said. It was Saturday, and no one was technically required to be at work until the ten o'clock status meeting, which was still almost two hours from now.

"Just trying to get caught up on some work. I've already placed several queries on your desk."

"Thank you." I walked over to the waiting room chair, where Eliot was contently curled up, and stroked his spine, eliciting a soft purr. "Bentley and I spoke yesterday about

Olive. I told her that I support your position. We both agreed that it would be horrible to lose you."

She looked up from her computer screen. "Thank you, Lila. But when I spoke to Ms. Duke yesterday, she seemed intent on bringing Olive into the office. I even went as far as finding a suitable doggie day care nearby, but Ms. Duke said she prefers to keep Olive with her during the day. I've already given her my notice. I'll inform the other agents of my decision at the status meeting."

My heart fell, but what could I do? I'd already spoken to Bentley, and that didn't get me anywhere. But perhaps once the other agents were aware of the situation, we could team up and persuade Vicky to stay. Or persuade Bentley to come up with a compromise. Like the dog care service Vicky suggested for daytime hours. Anything besides burdening Vicky with Olive's care.

Vicky had turned back to her computer screen, her chin elevated as she peered through the blue-rimmed reading glasses perched on the end of her nose. I hovered for a while, not knowing what else to say, before heading back to my own office.

The queries she'd mentioned were in the middle of my desk, but I pushed them aside for a second, fired up my computer, and opened up a browser window, anxious to find out if Rufus had been able to look at his records yet. I typed in *Rufus Manning Photography* and called the phone number listed on their website. My call was sent directly to an answering service. I glanced at my watch. It was early yet; I'd try back later. Next, I went back to the browser and typed in Chuck's name with several key words that might link to some sort of engagement announcement, but nothing popped up. Then I went directly to the online edition of our local paper and searched engagement announcements, still not finding any mention of the name Chuck Richards.

My mind wandered back to that very first day I'd met Chuck at the Magnolia Bed and Breakfast. I remembered him saying he couldn't reschedule the work on Cora's kitchen because he had a trip planned. To see his fiancée, perhaps? But why would the ring be in his pocket? Obviously, she'd already worn the ring for the photograph. I shrugged to myself. Probably something as simple as needing repair work, especially since it looked like an older ring. But if he needed to travel to see her, that would mean she wasn't a local gal. She could live anywhere.

I sighed and sank back into my chair. How frustrating. It felt as if I were grasping for something just out of my reach. Something big, something key to this whole mystery and, more importantly, something that would exonerate Jodi and prove without a doubt that my client Lynn had nothing to do with Chuck's murder.

I leaned forward again, my eyes scanning the piles of work waiting for me. Any further sleuthing would have to wait for a while. Maybe Sean would have some luck tracing the ring's owner, but for now, I needed to get some work done. I clicked over to my inbox and did a quick check, and an email from Makayla's editor practically jumped off the screen: "The Barista Diaries Cover Art," the subject line read. I opened the attachment, my breath catching. The artist had created what looked like an Impressionist painting of the inside of a busy café. Soft hues of gray and blue and shifts in shades captured the essence of patrons grouped around tables as they enjoyed both coffee and conversation. I could almost imagine the smells, the whirring machines, the laughter and din of constant chatter . . . Makayla was going to love this!

Normally I simply forwarded cover attachments to my clients, but with Makayla, I wanted to be there to see the look on her face when she saw her cover for the first time. So instead of forwarding the email, I copied the image and made a color print. I'd take it down to her later as a surprise.

The next email I opened was the manuscript I'd requested from the author of *Death of a Dame*, the Roaring Twenties mystery query I'd read a few days ago. I opened it right away and was immediately disappointed. The manuscript was over a hundred thousand words, way too long for the typical cozy mystery of seventy-five thousand words. I skimmed the first chapter, realizing the author used a lot of unnecessary narrative about the characters' backgrounds, facts that could be condensed and easily woven throughout subsequent chapters. Overall, the writing wasn't bad; he just needed to rework and polish the manuscript. And I did like the premise of the mystery, which was set in the 1920s. I hesitated . . . Did I want to take the time to make a few notes, see if he would be willing to rewrite and resubmit, or should I simply reject the proposal?

Undecided, I kept reading until the end of the third chapter and found that despite a few rambling scenes, the storyline was solid. I knew this author had a good book in him, maybe even this one if he made a few changes, so I decided to take a chance. I composed a note with a few suggestions and requested a rewrite and resubmission. But as soon as I clicked send, I regretted my decision. Taking a chance on this author was a long shot and nine times out of ten, this type of scenario never panned out well. Either the author was offended by my suggestions or they simply hadn't developed the skill set needed to write a marketable book. But it was already done. Only time would tell if my initial instinct was correct.

My thoughts turned back to Pam, an author who had more
than enough skill and a ready-made fan base, and I wished I'd
thought to ask her more about her mystery. Was it cozy, or hard-
boiled? Chock-full of romance or more Agatha-like? Whatever
it was, I knew it would be a vivid, enthralling story. It gave me
a thrill to think that I'd be reading it soon. Piggybacked to that
thrill, however, was a bit of trepidation. How would Flora react?
Certainly it was an author's choice to change genres, but it meant
cutting Flora out of one of her strong authors. Plus I'd be put to
the task of convincing the publisher to switch genre horses as
well. Or find another publisher. Not that any publisher would
usually hesitate to take on an author with an established fan
base who was branching into a new genre, but still . . . suddenly
I wondered if this might be part of the reason for the ten o'clock
meeting.

A knock sounded on my office door and Jude stepped
inside, shutting the door behind him. "I was hoping I'd find
you here early." Without being asked, he seated himself in
one of my guest chairs. He'd worn a casual outfit this morning: blue jeans with leather boots and a dark blue button-
down shirt that hugged his torso in all the right places. I
averted my eyes, irritated that I'd noticed that last detail.

"Don't worry," he started. "I'm not here to talk about this
thing between us."

This thing between us? The muscles in my neck tensed,
a dull ache suddenly rising at my temples. "There is no *thing*
between us, Jude. And for your information, Sean and I have
set a date. Next September."

He raised a brow. "September what?"

"Uh . . . just September. We haven't set the *exact* day yet."

"I see." He smirked. "Well, like I was saying, I'm here
about something entirely different. It has to do with Zach."

"Zach? What about him?" It occurred to me that I had

seen him last night but I hadn't really talked to him much in the last couple of days. "Is he okay?"

"Yeah, yeah. He's fine. It's just that he took that stuff Bentley said at Monday's status meeting seriously."

"About keeping our eyes and ears open at the expo?" I remembered Zach wanting to make some sort of bet over who could solve Chuck's murder first. Suddenly, my stomach rolled with dread. Or maybe I was catching what Mama had. I hoped not. "Did he find something?"

Jude chuckled. "He thinks so. In fact, he says he's nailed down the killer." Jude paused, noticed my grimace, and offered a quick apology for his poor choice of words. "The good news is he believes Jodi is innocent."

"That is good news," I said.

I was about to add my own theories when he snapped back with, "But the bad news is that he's convinced your client, Lynn, is the killer."

"Oh no." I collapsed my head into my palms and closed my eyes for a second.

"Yup. Apparently, he's been asking around town about Chuck and has come up with some interesting facts. And he says they all point to Lynn."

I squeezed my eyes even tighter. Without opening them, I asked, "And what facts might those be?"

I heard Jude stand and opened my eyes to see him heading toward the door. "Heck if I know," he said over his shoulder. "Just thought I'd warn you before the meeting." He reached for the door handle and paused, turning his wrist to see his watch. "Which, by the way, starts in just a few minutes."

THE TENSION IN the conference room was almost palpable. Gone was the usual chatter and good-natured ribbing that usually occurred when we gathered. Instead, all the agents, except Flora, who was still out sick, sat in their prospective seats, staring straight ahead with rigid expressions. Well, all except Zach, who looked like he was about to burst with excitement.

At precisely ten o'clock, Bentley made her grand appearance, breezing through the conference room door with Olive tucked under her arm. She gently set the pooch in the new pale pink doggie bed in the corner before she turned to face us with a determined look. "Good morning, team. I'm glad to see we're all here. We have a lot of ground to cover this morning, so let's look alive, shall we?"

Franklin cleared his throat and sat a little straighter. Jude shifted forward and ran a finger under the collar of his shirt and stretched his neck. Then there was Zach, who was already looking alive. So much so that he was practically bouncing out of his seat. Only Vicky remained quiet and somewhat disengaged.

Bentley regarded her, pursing her lips before putting on her reading glasses and moving toward the whiteboard. Pointing up to the timeline we'd sketched earlier in the week, she started, "First item on the agenda is—"

Zach's hand shot up. "I've solved the case! It wasn't Jodi. It was Lynn. Lynn Werner. Lila's client. I'm sure of it." He shot me a smug look. "You really are a murder magnet."

"Zach!" Bentley tore off her glasses and regarded Zach with disdain. "Have you uncovered some sort of *irrefutable* proof against Lynn? Because if I'm not mistaken, our goal this week was to keep our eyes and ears open for anyone, *other* than one of our clients, who could have committed this murder."

Zach's eyes went googly. "It's not my fault the clues point to Lynn as the killer."

"Lynn's not the killer," I fervently maintained. Although I'd been doubting Lynn all along, I was now certain, not to mention measurably relieved, to have a more likely suspect—Chuck's fiancée, the mysterious out-of-town woman.

I was about to mention my conclusions when Franklin asserted himself. "Why don't you tell us about these facts first, Zach, and then we'll all decide if they really do point to Lynn's culpability."

"Okay," Zach started, sitting up a little straighter. "Well, I've been doing a lot of checking around the last couple of days, asking everybody I know about Chuck Richards. And I mean everybody."

Jude sighed. "And what did you discover?"

"For starters"—he hesitated and shifted a few times, obviously trying to prolong his moment in the spotlight—"that lady who owns the Magnolia Bed and Breakfast . . ."

"Cora Scott," Vicky inserted.

"Yeah, that's her name. She said that she'd overheard Chuck talking on his cell phone several times to some woman."

His fiancée, I concluded in my mind. The woman at the funeral.

"Did she know who the woman was?" Bentley wanted to know.

"Naw, but it's not hard to figure out." That comment stumped me, but before I could ask what he meant, he tapped his head and said, "Then I got to thinking, Chuck's a working man and where do working men hang out?"

By now, everyone was getting a little annoyed. Jude sighed yet again. "We don't know, Zach. Perhaps you could enlighten us?"

"The Pub, that's where," Zach said as if it were the most brilliant thing ever. "So, while everyone was heading home after last night's event, I headed over to the James Joyce to

mingle with the Friday night crowd. Asked almost everyone
there about Chuck. And as it turns out, he was in there a
couple of nights before he met his demise."

I was leaning forward, all ears. Zach continued. "And get
this. He was flashing a ring. Said he and his girl had picked
it out at that secondhand store, Beyond and Back."

Beyond and Back. Of course! I blinked double time, surprised that Zach had come up with something substantial.
Beyond and Back, a charming consignment shop, had just
opened last summer. I hadn't even thought about the store
when Sean mentioned calling around to local pawnshops. I
made a mental note to try to get hold of him and tell him
where Chuck had purchased the ring. Maybe one of the clerks
would remember the woman's name.

"A terrific store," Franklin was going on. He looked
across the table at me. "Do you remember all those wonderful items we found there for our last event?" I nodded and
offered dear, sweet Franklin a smile. Last summer, Franklin
and I were in charge of planning a gala for a local television
celebrity and budding author. We'd created the most beautiful table decorations from repurposed items purchased at
Beyond and Back. The event didn't go quite as planned,
something I'm afraid Franklin blamed himself for . . . but
that was a whole other story. "Such good deals," Franklin
added, his voice tinged with regret as he reminisced.

Zach pointed his finger and clucked his tongue. "Righto,
Franklin. But getting back to our current murder." He
emphasized the *current* with a solicitous glance my way.
"The bartender told me that Chuck was going on about how
he and this girl had split up, she'd returned the ring, but now
she'd seen the light and was begging for him to come back.
He was getting ready to meet up with her."

"Did the bartender know the name of the woman Chuck was talking about?" I eagerly asked.

Zach rolled his eyes and sighed. "Well, duh. Isn't it obvious that he was talking about Lynn? But just to make sure, I stopped by Beyond and Back this morning and had a little chat with the owner. He'd only sold one engagement ring lately and he remembered the couple—well, not their names, but what they looked like. And yes, I asked about a sales receipt, but they paid cash."

My heart fell as my hopes for a solid lead were dashed. Still, maybe Sean would have more luck ferreting information from Beyond and Back's owners.

"But here's the big clincher," Zach was saying. He paused for drama. "The woman had brown hair."

The room went silent. Finally Bentley asked, "That's the clincher?" She glanced around the room with an incredulous look. "Both Lila and I have brown hair."

"Half the women in town have brown hair," Vicky added, patting her own silky white mane.

Zach blinked a couple of extra times. "Well, when you put it all together, it's obvious the killer was Lynn." He held up his hand and used his fingers to tick off the points. "The brown hair; Lynn has brown hair. The bartender said they'd broken up; Lynn and Chuck are divorced, right? And . . . well, I guess that's it." He quickly put down his hand, glancing around sheepishly.

"It couldn't have been Lynn with Chuck at Beyond and Back picking out the ring. She hasn't been back to the area for several years," I pointed out.

"That's what she wants you to think," Zach said. "You only have her word for that. And, really, how well do you know Lynn?"

He had a point. I really didn't know Lynn all that well. Still, there were a lot of holes in his theory. And Sean thought *I* easily jumped to conclusions.

Bentley had moved to the whiteboard and readjusted her glasses, and was making a few notes. "I don't agree with your assessment, Zach. But you have made a few valid points and revealed a few facts about Chuck that we didn't know before. First of all, he was in a relationship of some sort. Perhaps engaged or not." She wrote the word *girlfriend* on the board and followed it with a giant question mark. "And I believe this mysterious woman may hold the key to this entire case," she said. "We need to find her."

"I may have met her," I admitted. All eyes turned to me, curious and expectant. I explained about the funeral and the woman I'd met in the restroom. "I didn't get her name, but I saw her drive away," I finished. "She had a sedan with mismatched paint, gray on the front passenger side, like she'd been in a wreck and hadn't had time to have the car repainted."

"Did you tail her?" Zach wanted to know.

I shook my head. "No, I didn't. And I have no idea how to find her again."

The room grew silent as everyone contemplated this new information. No one seemed to have anything to add. Of course, I knew of a couple of other things, like the fact that the ring was found on Chuck's body and that it was the same ring displayed in the missing photo from Makayla's café, the very same photo that had been stolen, but I wasn't sure if Sean would want me to divulge that type of information yet.

Bentley started in again. "Our next step, then, is to see if we can find this woman. Remember, people, one of our own is sitting in jail for a crime she didn't commit. It's up to us to find a way to prove her innocence." She paused for a second before changing topics. "As for today's agenda. There aren't any authors scheduled for presentations this afternoon, but at the conclusion of today's fashion show, each and every one of you is expected to dismantle your authors' booths. Ms. Lambert has made it clear that this responsibility is not to be left for her people at Southern Belles Bridal Company." She turned to Jude. "Do you have an up-to-date sales record for us?"

Jude opened his portfolio, extracted a sales sheet, and began reading the numbers. So far, it seemed nearly every author had sold twice as many books as expected. "A smashing success!" Bentley concluded. We continued to talk about the expo and then moved on to new business for a while, each of us giving a brief status on new proposals and prospective new clients before Bentley started wrapping up the meeting. "Before we adjourn, there's one more item on the list." She took a deep breath and exhaled slowly. "I believe Vicky has something she'd like to announce."

All eyes turned to Vicky, who slowly rose from her chair, brushed the creases from her skirt, and moved to the front of the room. My eyes slid toward the pup in question, who, ironically, had behaved perfectly during the whole meeting: no barking, scratching, not even a whimper. Vicky removed a tissue from the front pocket of her sweater, dabbed at her top lip and began with a shaky voice, "I regret announcing that I've turned in my resignation. Next Friday will be my last day. Thank you."

"What!" The room exploded in protest as she made her way back to her chair. Everyone wanted to know the reason for her resignation and began pelting her with questions. I'd expected as much, of course. What I was curious about was Bentley's reaction. To my amazement, she appeared stoic, almost immune to the buzz around her. I couldn't fathom what must be going through her mind. I knew she cared for Vicky, just as much as the rest of us. And the business side of her certainly realized what an asset Vicky was to our literary team. Why, just last fall, Vicky was out sick for three days with a terrible cold and the place about fell apart! But Bentley remained silent, watching and listening, her face empty of any expression that might reveal her true emotions.

For the next few minutes, everyone continued to fire questions at Vicky, who remained tight-lipped about her reason for resigning. I was only half listening, though. Instead, I tilted my head and let my eyes wander to where Olive slept peacefully, curled in a brown and white lump in the corner of the room. As I watched, she shifted in her sleep, yawned, and licked her muzzle with a lazy swipe of her tongue. I sighed and wondered how something so little and so sweet-looking could cause so much trouble. I thought back to the chewed furniture, the scratched-up door, the constant barking and begging for attention. It was almost as if Olive needed a team of owners to take care of her. *A team of owners?* I sat up a little straighter. *Maybe, just maybe it might work* . . . My eyes darted between Vicky and Bentley, the beginning of an idea forming in my mind.

Chapter 19

I'D BARELY SETTLED BEHIND MY DESK BEFORE I HEARD my cell phone buzzing. I opened my drawer and dug into my bag, only the moment my fingertips connected to the phone, it quit ringing. I checked the display, expecting to see that Rufus had called with the name of the couple. Instead, I was surprised to see several missed calls from Trey, apparently coming in while I was in the meeting. I was about to call him back when Vicky burst into my office. Trey was on her heels, his work apron hanging below his winter jacket. What could have prompted him to leave in the middle of work? "Trey. What is it?"

"It's Nana. I was at work when Oscar called. He's was getting ready to take her to the hospital. Said she was real sick."

Mama is sick again? "But she was doing fine last night. I was at her place until almost midnight." I blinked, a dread crawling up my neck as I realized I hadn't checked on her this morning. I'd been too busy, my mind on the case, and hadn't even thought about . . . "Really, she was much better when I left." My last statement sounded pathetic, neglectful, even to my own ears as an image of Mama in a hospital bed shot shivers up my back.

"You get going with Trey and check on her." Vicky shooed me with her hands, her voice of reason cutting through the haze of confusion and guilt clogging my mind.

I nodded, snatching my purse and motioning for Trey to follow me out. "I'll inform Ms. Duke immediately," Vicky called after us. "But please call and let us know how Althea is doing. We'll all be worried."

WE MADE THE normally half-hour drive to Dunston in a mere twenty minutes. The lady managing the front desk took one look at our frazzled expressions and immediately directed us through the double sliding doors that led to the emergency room area, where we were about creamed by a gurney zipping past with a bloodied man.

"Everything's going to be fine with Nana," I tried to reassure a wide-eyed Trey. But my voice, which sounded thin and frantic, betrayed my own anxiety as I approached the nurses' station to inquire about Mama's room. She pointed us down the hall, where we found Mama propped up in bed, holding Oscar's hand. An IV line trailed from her arm to a stand with a large fluid bag.

"Mama!" I crossed over, stepped between her and Oscar, and clumsily took hold of her shoulders, giving her a little squeeze. "Are you okay? What's going on?" I took in her dry lips and shallow complexion as she nodded with a little sigh.

Trey had moved to her other side and was nervously hovering. Mama smiled his way and reached for his hand, grasping it weakly. "Wipe that worried look right off your face, boy. No need to fret about your Nana. I'll be just fine. Just needed a little fluid, that's all." She nodded toward her IV bag. "Told them to mix in some Jim Beam, but they didn't take kindly to the notion." She chuckled and waved me closer so she could whisper in my ear. "The sooner you can spring me from this place, the better. I'm 'bout to go nuts in here."

"Nurse said there's a possibility of an early release for good behavior," Oscar teased, his slight accent more pronounced than usual. "But seriously, Althea's going to be just fine. Just got a little dehydrated, didn't ya, sweetheart?" He reached around me and patted her arm. "They said she'd probably get to go home later today."

"I'm glad you're okay, Nana," Trey said, now perched on the side of her bed, holding her hand.

"What happened?" I wanted to know as I stood beside her, still perplexed. "You seemed better when I left last night."

"Thought I was," Mama said. "But the darn stuff snuck up on me again in the middle of the night." She scrunched up her face. "Lawd, but I was sick."

Oscar nodded. "Yeah. Lucky for you I stopped by this morning." He looked my way. "I went by her place around nine or so, just to see how she was. When she didn't answer the door, I got worried. I looked through one of the windows and saw her on the floor."

I clasped a hand over my mouth. Mama on the floor! And I hadn't even called her this morning . . . She could have—

"Oh, honey, I was fine," she reassured me. "I just got up too fast or somethin'. I heard him knockin' and was just trying to get to the door," Mama explained. "Just got a bit dizzy. Nothin' major."

Oscar went on. "Scared me, seeing her like that, ya know? Had to kick in her front door to get to her. Anyway, she seemed weak, a little confused. Couldn't even recall what day it was."

"Aw shoot!" Mama looked around. "Y'all know I can never keep track of days. That's nothin' new."

I patted her hand and smiled Oscar's way. "I'm so glad you were there for her. Thank you." My voice caught as I spoke. I looked down at Mama. She seemed so vulnerable lying in bed with tubes coming out of her arm. What would have happened if Oscar hadn't come along at the right moment? Dehydration, especially in someone Mama's age, could be so dangerous. Guilt swept over me. I should have been the one checking on her.

I felt a hand on my shoulder and looked back at Oscar, who was studying me with concern. "I know what's going through your mind, Lila. Don't go beating yourself up over this. You couldn't have known."

He was right; still, it did little to assuage the guilt I felt. I turned back to Mama. "Well, I'm here for you now. And I'm not going to leave your side until you're better."

"Oh yes, you are!" Her cheeks suddenly glowed pink. "There's no need for you to be hangin' out here all day. Neither one of you." She looked between Trey and me. "You both have plenty to do without wastin' your day here."

"There's nothing more important than you, Mama," I insisted.

"Nonsense." She waved her hand through the air, shaking her IV line and causing a little ripple in the bandage holding it in place on her arm. "Ouch!"

I grabbed her hand and placed it back at her side, then smoothed out the bandage. "See, that's why I need to be here. To keep an eye on things."

"Really, sugar. I don't want y'all here fussin' all day. Especially with this bein' the last day of the expo."

Oscar spoke up. "I'd be happy to stay, if you don't mind,

Lila." He nodded toward Trey. "I'm sure Trey and the rest of my crew can cover for me at the restaurant."

Trey shifted. "Yeah. A couple of the other guys are taking care of the prep work. But the lunch crowd's due soon."

"You go on, then, Trey," Mama said. "And don't worry none about me. I'm just fine." She looked my way. "You, too, hon. Head on back with Trey and take care of your business."

"I'd be happy to take her home later," Oscar offered.

"Not to her home. Bring her by my place," I insisted. "You'll stay with me tonight, okay, Mama?"

"That's a good idea," Oscar agreed. "It'll give me a chance to get the front door replaced at your place, Althea."

Mama shook her head. "Listen to you two! There's no need for—"

"Either you let Oscar bring you to my house, or I stay here the rest of the afternoon and wait for your discharge, so I can take you there myself," I said.

She sighed and shook her head. "Well, then. Guess I'll be stayin' at your place tonight."

"I'M SURE GLAD Nana's okay," Trey said, keeping his eyes on the road as we made our way back to the Valley.

"That's for sure," I said. I'd just called Vicky, letting her know I was on my way back and that Mama was doing fine.

"I sure was scared when I heard she'd gone to the hospital."

I peered across the seat, resisting the urge to reach over and ruffle his hair. "Me, too," I admitted. "I guess I'm glad Oscar was there to help her."

"I know you don't like him, but you should probably try to give him a chance."

"What do you mean by that? I like him."

"Come on, Mom. It's really obvious. I get it. I didn't like Sean at first, either. Now I think he's great. And Oscar's a really good guy. You'll see. Eventually."

I sat back against the seat and looked out the window. I was pretty sure now that Oscar had nothing to do with Chuck Richards's murder. Sean was right. I'd let my emotions cloud my judgment. Honestly, I wanted to like Oscar. I really did. Maybe once I got to know him better . . . Suddenly my gaze caught on something. "Hey, turn around up here and head back to Bertram's, would you?" We'd just passed by the hotel and I'd noticed a sedan with mismatched paint out front. As we pulled into the lot, I got a closer look. It was the car that the crying woman at the funeral had been driving! I pointed it out to Trey, my heart kicking it up a notch. She hadn't left town yet! "Pull up there. Next to that car with the two-tone paint job."

As soon as we parked, one of the hotel's room doors opened and the woman from the funeral home came out dragging a large suitcase. "That's her," I said, reaching for the door handle.

"Who?" Trey groaned. "I gotta get to work, Mom. It's lunch hour and—"

"Just hold on, okay? This is important." I hopped out and approached the woman. "Hey, there, how are you?"

She looked up, her lips pressing into a thin white slash.

"We met yesterday at Chuck's funeral." I reminded her.

"I remember." She opened her car trunk and loaded her suitcase before moving around to the driver's side of her car without another word.

I hurried after her. "You were engaged to Chuck Richards."

She stopped short.

"He had your engagement ring in his pocket when he died," I added.

She turned and slumped against the car, folding her arms across her chest. "In his pocket? How do you know that?"

"I'm the one who found him . . . after he was . . . murdered." I tried to gulp away the tightness in my throat as I thought of this woman driving a nail through someone's skull.

She clasped her arms tighter around her midsection and rolled her eyes skyward, blinking several times. Each time her lashes closed, another tear rolled out until thin black lines ran down both cheeks. I was surprised at her sudden show of emotions. Certainly someone who'd committed such a brutal murder wouldn't be moved to tears like this.

"Where's the ring now?" she asked. "I want it."

"The police have it."

She pushed off the car and started for the driver's door again. "Fine. I'm outta here."

"Wait!" I reached out, snagging her arm.

"Let go of me!" She ripped out of my grip and started opening her car door.

"What's your name? Where are you going?" I called out, trying to get some information, any information, but she ignored me and slammed the car door in my face.

I took note of her license plate number as she sped off and ran back to Trey's car to get my phone. "Who was that anyway?" Trey asked, backing the car out.

"The murdered man's fiancée," I explained quickly as I dialed Sean's cell phone.

He answered on the second ring. "Lila? Everything okay?"

I quickly relayed my discovery and gave him her license plate number.

"Did you get a name?" he asked.

"No. She wouldn't tell me. But I now know she was Chuck's fiancée." I quickly relayed my conversation with the woman. I also explained my thoughts about the break-in at Makayla's shop and how I was sure it was the fiancée trying to cover her crime. Then I filled him in on Zach's discoveries, including how he found out that Chuck and an unnamed woman purchased an engagement ring from Beyond and Back. "Zach said the people at the store didn't recall the woman's name. Only that she had brown hair. But maybe one of your guys could question the manager and find out a little more."

I heard some paper shuffling in the background. "Uh . . . sure. I'll put in a call to the owner at Beyond and Back and see if he remembers anything."

"Did you have a chance to check with Rufus Manning about that photo he took?" I pressed. "He was supposed to look up the names of the couple."

"Hold for a sec," he said, covering the phone as he spoke to someone in the background. I waited patiently, watching out the car window, until he came back online, his voice much lower than before. "Sorry. What were you asking me?"

"About Rufus. Have you been able to contact him?"

"No one's been able to reach him by phone yet, but I'll keep trying. I'd send a guy over, but truth is, my sergeant caught wind of how much time I've been putting into this case and he's not happy."

Uh-oh. "Are you in trouble?"

"Yeah. But he'll get over it. Eventually."

"But you'll still try to track down the fiancée, right? I mean, it's got to be her, Sean. You can find her with the license number, right?"

"I'll do what I can to locate her and bring her in for questioning. You know that. Right now, though, I've gotta run.

It's nuts around here today and I just got called out on another case. I'll call you later and let you know if we find out anything."

If they find out anything, I thought. It didn't sound very promising, but I could understand Sean's dilemma. According to his superiors, this case was already wrapped up. Unfortunately, there was never a shortage of crime and Sean's desk was always overflowing with cases, so it was only natural that this would fall to the bottom of his priority list. If only I could have been able to find out the woman's name. Still, I did confirm that she was Chuck's fiancée, so that was something. I flipped over my phone and checked the display again. Still no call from Rufus. That was strange. I did a quick Google search on my phone and found his office number again. But once again, my call went straight to an answering service. I kicked myself for not getting his cell number. I hated to wait until the expo to find out the fiancée's name. Who knew how important the information might be to Jodi's case. I glanced at my watch. I still had a few hours before I was due at the Arts Center—plenty of time to run by the photography studio and see if I could connect with Rufus. That way, I could save Sean the extra manpower—and any more trouble with his sergeant.

"Trey, would you mind if I used your car to run a couple of errands? I could get it back to you this afternoon." Certainly one of the other agents would follow me back to the restaurant later so I could return Trey's car.

Trey glanced at his dash. "Sure, but I'm getting a little low on gas." He downshifted and turned off High Street, headed toward Machiavelli's.

"Again? I just put gas in yesterday." I chuckled and this time didn't refrain from reaching over and ruffling his hair. "Okay, buddy. I get it. I'll top off the tank for you, okay?"

I'd sure been putting a lot of money into his tank lately. "But don't you be forgetting about that tuition money you owe me," I added, thinking I'd better keep reminding him or I might never see that money again.

"Don't worry, Mom. I'll pay you back. You have my word." His chin jutted out with determination. "I'm doing well at work. Oscar says I show promise."

Promise? Promise was a solid four-year degree and a distinct career path . . . I stopped myself, thinking back to what Pam had said about following her passion to write mysteries and how I'd followed my own passion and become a literary agent, how Dr. Meyers's passion had led to a career of helping desperate women and families. Certainly Trey deserved the same opportunity. He'd either sink or swim. Besides, he was young yet, so if he was going to try something like this, it was better now than down the line when he had a family to support. "I'm sure you do show promise," I started, trying to be positive. "You've always been a good cook. You get that from your nana."

He pulled up to Machiavelli's and put the car in gear. "Yeah. I hear stuff like that always skips a generation." He grinned and hopped out, waving over his shoulder as he sauntered into the restaurant.

I EASILY REMEMBERED the location of the Dunston Office Plaza from the other day when I dropped Lynn at Dr. Meyers's office. Only today, the place looked deserted and except for a couple of vehicles, the lot was completely empty. Hopefully, one of the cars belonged to Rufus. I couldn't shake the fact that Chuck's fiancée knew more than she was telling me. Whatever she was hiding could be the key to the whole case and the evidence that cleared Jodi. If I could only find out her name, Sean would be able to easily track her down.

A blast of hot air hit me as I entered the main doors of the office plaza. I scanned the directory on the entryway wall and found that Rufus Manning Photography was on the second floor, suite 201. My footsteps echoed on the tile as I headed for the staircase. On the way, I saw a sign marking the entrance for Dr. Meyers's office. I noticed it was tucked toward the rear of the building and near the back entrance, making it easy, I supposed, for clients to come and go discreetly without walking past the other offices.

Upstairs, I found the main door to Rufus's studio open. A good sign. Maybe I'd get that information after all. "Rufus," I called out. The reception area was empty, so I ventured down the hall toward what looked like a couple of smaller rooms. Offices probably. "Rufus. It's me, Lila."

"Hello?" I called out, knocking on the first door. No one answered, but I heard some shuffling noises. I pushed the door open. "Rufus?"

It wasn't Rufus in the office, but Dr. Meyers. She was standing near a desk, a manila file in her hands. "Dr. Meyers?" My eyes took in her startled expression, the clutched file. "What are you doing here?" I asked.

She gripped the file tighter, her eyes darting to the door behind me. "Just stopped by to pick up some pictures Rufus took for me. He told me I could just come in and get them." She started to push by me. "But I better get going. I have a client coming in for an appointment. See you this afternoon, Lila."

I maneuvered to block her way, stealing a quick glance at the folder. The label read *Richards*. "Why do you have Chuck Richards's file?"

She tried to sidestep me. "Just let me by, Lila."

I strengthened my stance. "Did you know Chuck?"

She started to push past me, but I stood firm. "Let me by, Lila," she hissed. "I'm going to be late for my appointment."

"Not until you answer a couple of my questions." I reached for the file, my fingertips gripping the edge. "Why are you stealing *this* file? What's in it that you're trying to hide?"

She pulled back, but I gripped tighter and yanked on the file, tearing part of it out of her hand. A piece of paper fluttered to the carpet. I bent down and snatched it up, squinting at the print. It was a receipt for a photography package for Chuck Richards and Amanda Meyers. *Amanda Meyers?* "Amanda Meyers?" I asked out loud. An image of Chuck's fiancée popped into my mind—her eyes, the way her nose tipped at the end. Now that I thought about it, there was a resemblance. "Your daughter," I concluded.

Dr. Meyers took a couple of steps backward, her back pressing against the desk and her head shaking slowly. "Yes. My daughter. Can you believe it? It's been my life's passion to empower women to fight against the atrocities of domestic violence and here my own daughter was going to marry a man who"—her face twisted with hate and scorn—"a man who hit her."

Something slowly came back to me: The day of the murder, when I needed someone to give me a break, I flagged down Franklin. He'd mentioned that he was looking for Dr. Meyers. Why was he looking for her? She should have been at her booth . . . "You killed Chuck." The words slid out of my mouth, more of a realization than an accusation.

"I had to. Can't you see that?" Her eyes took on a wild look, her normally cool, controlled expression gone as her face flushed. "She wouldn't stay away from him. It was sick. He'd hit her and then come back all apologetic and everything and she'd forgive him. Take him back. I see it all the time with the women I counsel, but my own daughter . . . It made me sick. Then she came home one day, all happy and gushing over some piece of junk engagement ring he bought her. She was sure he'd changed. She kept telling me how happy they'd be. Then it happened again. This time he beat her so badly she ended up in the hospital. I was able to get to her then. I convinced her to give the ring back and leave him. Even set her up in another state, helped her find a job . . . I did everything I could to try to help her."

"But she went back to him."

Dr. Meyers nodded slowly. "He found her. Hunted her down like a wounded animal. Wouldn't leave her alone. Eventually she started talking to him again. Again, he convinced her that he'd changed. But I knew better. Men like him never change."

I remembered that first day at the Magnolia Bed and Breakfast, when Chuck told Cora he needed to finish the job because he was getting ready to go on a trip. "He was getting ready to meet Amanda somewhere, wasn't he?" I asked. "He was taking the ring back to her."

Dr. Meyers nodded. "They were going to meet in Raleigh and elope. So, you see, I had no choice. Certainly as a mother, you can understand." Her voice was level, her expression calm again as if the logic of it excused her actions.

There was no way I could stand by and let someone hurt Trey, so I could almost understand Dr. Meyers's being pushed to murder, except for one thing. "But you didn't just kill Chuck; you set up someone else for your crime."

"I know. I know. But I'm not going to let Jodi stay in jail. I just need to divert the police long enough until I can leave the country. I plan to go to Indonesia. There's a clinic down there offering me a position on staff. After I'm settled and sure I can't be extradited, I'm going to call and confess. Make sure Jodi is freed from prison. Once Amanda gets over Chuck, she'll join me. We can both start over together."

Her use of present tense gave me shivers—how could she still think she could get away with this? Did she really think that since we were both mothers, I'd simply understand and excuse her actions? I had to keep her talking. Maybe convince her to turn herself in to the authorities. "What about the nail gun? How did you—"

"That was the easy part," she said, interrupting me, her mood lighter, as if pleased with the plan she'd laid and sure that I was going to stand by and go along with it. "Smuggling it in was easy. I just carried it in my bag."

"Does Amanda know you killed her fiancé?"

"No. Of course not." Now she wiped a bead of sweat from her top lip, her mood vacillating yet again. "Maybe she suspects it. I don't know. I haven't been able to reach her since Tuesday."

"She was here this week. I met her at the funeral."

"Here? In Dunston?" Her face paled.

"Yes. She was staying at Bertram's. I saw her again this morning, right before she left town."

Dr. Meyers gripped the side of the desk to steady herself. "I didn't know. She . . . must not want to see me."

I noticed her fortitude wavering, her eyes growing wide with . . . ? What? Regret? I stepped a little closer, reaching toward her. "Why don't we go together to the police station? You could explain—"

The sound of merry whistling drew both of our gazes toward the office door. Suddenly, Rufus appeared, his arms laden with a couple of brown bags stuffed full of office supplies. "Dr. Meyers? Lila? What are you two doing here?"

"Your door was open and—" I automatically started to

explain, then stopped abruptly as the reality of the situation hit me: I came in to question him about a photo to help solve a murder case and found Dr. Meyers stealing one of his files. And confessing to that murder.

"That's fine. Glad you caught me. I just ran across the street to pick up a few . . ." His voice trailed off as his eyes focused on the torn file in Dr. Meyers's arms. He stepped forward, until he was just inches away from us, his ruddy complexion growing redder by the second. "Hey. What's going on here?"

Dr. Meyers suddenly shoved me in the back, the force of the impact sending me sprawling against Rufus. We both landed against the far wall with a thud, office supplies flying everywhere. I looked up but Dr. Meyers was nowhere to be seen. I recovered and started after her, flying down the steps and racing to the front door. Outside, I stopped and scanned the lot, but she wasn't anywhere. *How'd she get away so . . . The back door!* I turned, ran back through the office building, and burst through the back door just in time to see Dr. Meyers's sedan peeling out of the lot.

I pulled out my cell. I knew Sean said he was heading out on a case, so I wouldn't be able to reach him in person. Instead, I dialed 911. "This is Lila Wilkins," I told the operator. "I have important information about a murder the police are investigating."

Chapter 20

AFTER SPENDING ALMOST AN HOUR FIELDING POLICE questions, and then answering even more questions from Sean after he arrived on the scene, I drove straight to Machiavelli's to give Trey back his car. I was in a hurry and no one was available to give me a lift, so I ended up walking back to the agency to pick up my Vespa in order to get to the expo. In the meantime, it had started snowing again, so I was wet and cold and just a wee bit cranky when I swung open the door to the Arts Center.

"You're over an hour late," Bentley said, catching me as soon as I entered the building.

I started to tell Bentley about Dr. Meyers and why I was late, but she cut me off, pointing to a pale pink dress draped over her arm. "We've got a problem," she said. "Ms. Lambert is out with some sort of stomach virus. Half her crew has it, too."

Dread crept over me as I eyed the dress. If Bentley had

a problem, I was going to have a problem. She was a master of problem delegation. "What type of a problem?"

"Well, thank goodness the auditorium is already set up. Franklin and Jude really came through for me there. They organized our agents and the rest of Ms. Lambert's crew, prepared the stage, and got the seating situated. Flora and Vicky already took care of taking down the author booths."

Uh-oh. She was building up to something big.

She continued, "And I got all the authors situated, except for Dr. Meyers. No one can find her anywhere."

Again, I started to tell her why, but she shoved the dress my way. "So, it's your turn. See if this fits."

"This dress? Why?"

"We need a bridesmaid."

"Oh, no." I started shaking my head. "Not me. Can't you get someone else? Besides, I look horrible in pink."

"It's not pink. It's called light blush. And it's supposed to complement any skin tone." She pointed me toward the auditorium. "The models are changing in the small room off the back of the stage. There's an entrance down the hall from the main auditorium doors. You can't miss it. Someone will be there to do your makeup and hair. Vicky's in there, taking care of the lineup. Just find her and she'll tell you what to do."

"Vicky's here? Did you leave Olive alone at the office?" Visions of shredded furniture and chewed documents snapped to mind.

"Are you serious? Of course not. Olive's here, tucked safely in the Potter's Room. Zach has offered to keep an eye on her for me. Oh, here comes Lynn." She motioned her over. "Be a dear, won't you? Show Lila where the dressing room is in back of the stage area. Would you mind?" Without waiting for a reply, she pointed a bejeweled finger in the general direction. "Now go on, Lila!" she said. "There's not a second to spare."

I took off with Lynn to find the dressing room, thinking perhaps it was better I didn't get a chance to tell Bentley about Dr. Meyers. It had been enough for her to see one of our writers arrested for murder. Clearing Jodi as a result of a confession of yet *another* of our authors would not please my boss one bit. That bad news could wait until the show was over.

"Lila? Are you okay?" Lynn was asking. "You seem upset. I heard about your mother. Is everything okay with her?"

"Yes, she's fine. It's just . . ." I thought about how close Lynn was to Dr. Meyers. Certainly the news that she'd confessed to Chuck's murder and would soon be arrested would be upsetting to her, too. I hesitated, deciding that as soon as this fashion show crisis was over, I'd call a meeting and tell everyone at once. The news could wait another hour. "It was just upsetting to see Mama in the hospital today. She's doing fine. But I wish I could have stayed with her, though." Guilt pricked at my conscience. With everything going on, I hadn't called to check up on Mama.

We were standing in front of the dressing room. I jostled the slippery peachy fluff of the dress hanging on one arm and my shoulder bag on other arm and started shrugging out of my coat. "I hate to ask this of you, Lynn, but would you mind watching my purse for me? I don't want leave it unattended in the dressing room. And could you check my coat for me?"

"Of course. Would it be helpful if I gave your mother a quick call? I could explain that you've been called to duty, but that you wanted me to check on her."

Oh, how sweet. I breathed a sigh of relief. "You wouldn't mind? It would make me feel a little better."

"Absolutely not. Anything to help," she added, gathering

my coat and shouldering my purse. "Consider it done. What's her number?"

I anxiously glanced over my shoulder as I entered the dressing room. "Oh, just use my phone. It's in my purse. I listed her under *Mama* in my contacts."

Lynn chuckled. "Sounds good. I'll give *Mama* a call." She offered a quick smile. "You're going to do great. Good luck."

ONCE IN THE dressing room, it wasn't difficult to find Vicky. Her A-line skirt, wool stockings, and sensible shoes stood out like a sore thumb in the room of flowing taffeta and high heels. "I'm supposed to try this on," I told her.

She turned a harried look my way, reading glasses teetering on the edge of her nose, and then she stole a quick glance at her clipboard. "Let's hope it fits. There's no time for me to find anyone else, and each bride is supposed to be preceded down the catwalk by a bridesmaid. It simply won't do to have an unaccompanied bride." She pointed toward a bank of stalls with curtains. "Go slip it on and come out here so I can see how it looks. And hurry."

I scurried to the dressing room. As quickly as possible, I slipped out of my clothes and stepped into the dress, tugging and shimmying until I maneuvered the bodice past my hips. Lucky for me, the skirt flowed softly from a high empire waist that actually minimized what I liked to think of as my pleasantly plump hips. And it camouflaged the bit of tummy I preferred not to think about at all. I breathed a sigh of relief. It looked okay. Good, actually.

"Lila!"

I turned from the mirror and stepped out. Instantly, I was snatched to the side by a woman wielding a comb and a can of hair spray. She plunked me in a chair by a lit mirror, raised a hand to start her magic, and squeaked, "What have you done to your hair? It's matted against your head. I'd have to be a miracle worker to do something with this."

Talk about the pot calling the kettle black, I thought, daring a glance at her own closely shaven style that sported multicolored streaks. At least I had an excuse. My snowy walk to the agency from the police station had thoroughly soaked my hair, and then slapping on my helmet to get to the Arts Center had form-fitted my chestnut tresses flat to my skull. But all I said was, "It was snowing outside, and I was wearing a helmet."

"A helmet? Cool." Her eyes lit up. "Harley?"

"Vespa."

"A what?" She scrunched her nose at me.

"Vespa. It's a scooter."

"Oh." She quit talking then and started torturing me with the comb, pulling, backcombing, and pulling more, intermittently dousing me with hair spray. Then she started spinning me in the chair, examining me from every angle.

"How's it going over there?" Vicky wanted to know.

"I need a little more time," my torturer claimed. Then she said to me, "You need color. You look as pale as a ghost." She turned to dig through a bag on the counter. She whipped back around with a tube of lipstick in hand. "Pucker."

I did, and she swiped color on my lips. Then, tossing me a tissue, she ordered, "Blot." She turned back to her bag again and started rooting for something else. "Darn! Thought I packed brown eyeliner. I've got every other color in my tool bag." She sighed. "Guess black will have to do. Look up."

Tool bag, I thought as she started penciling around my eyes. Funny she should call it that. But I guess for a cosmetologist, a makeup bag did hold the tools of her trade. *Tools*. I thought back to something Dr. Meyers had said earlier.

"Smuggling in the nail gun was easy. I just carried it in my book bag." But how'd she know Chuck would be here? More precisely, how'd she know the refrigerator would break down at that particular time? The good news was that Sean would probably get all those answers soon. He'd reached me on my cell earlier on my walk back to the Arts Center and told me that the state police had already apprehended Dr. Meyers on the freeway to Raleigh and they were transporting her to his department for questioning. He promised to shoot me a text later with an update . . . and to let me know if we were still on for dinner. Which I hoped we were. After a day, heck, a week, like this, I was craving some downtime and a chance to pick his brain about the case. There were still so many unanswered questions.

"Done!" the cosmetologist declared, turning me for a quick glance in the mirror. My face reflected back the shock I felt. I'd never worn this much makeup in my life and my hair poofed out like a poodle's! But there was no time for adjustments. As if on cue, the first notes of the string orchestra filled the air, signaling the start of the show. Vicky began sending the first of the models out to the catwalk.

"There's nothing to it," she told me, once I found my place in line. Of course, it was just my luck to get paired with a tall, lithe bride, in an ever so slinky mermaid-styled shimmery satin wedding gown. Together we looked like a mismatched pair of bookends. "Listen for your cue and when it's your turn, walk to the end of the catwalk and step to the left side. That's your *left* side. Your bride will be right behind you, with a groom meeting her halfway. When they reach the end of the catwalk, she'll stop and both of you will turn a couple of times to let the audience view the dresses from all angles."

All angles? The very thought of it sent shocks of fear

through me. Instinctively, I pulled my tummy in against my backbone.

The hair and makeup woman butted in with a pair of strappy sandals in her hand. "Size eight?" she asked.

"That'll work." I dropped them on the floor and slid into them, bending to fix the strap around my ankle.

Vicky continued, "After you've turned a couple of times, follow your bride off the catwalk and onto the floor. You'll be mixing with the audience, so the ladies can get a close-up look at the dress."

I smiled and bobbed my head as if I were happy about all this, when in reality, I wanted to turn and flee. "You'll do great," Vicky promised, before hurrying off for a few last-second adjustments to one of the brides' veils.

While my bride and I waited for our stage cue, my mind wandered back to my earlier quandary. If Dr. Meyers had brought the nail gun to the Arts Center, she must have known Chuck would be here at that precise time. How'd she know? Unless . . . was it possible that she'd sabotaged the kitchen refrigerator? Workmen had been in and out to set up the expo, using both entrances; it was plausible that she'd managed to sneak in at some point. But how'd she know Chuck would be called for the repair? Bentley could have called any other repairman in town. Something niggled at my mind, but before I could think it through, the music shifted and the announcer started the program.

"Okay, we're on," Vicky proclaimed, her cheeks flushed with excitement. Organizing and multitasking was Vicky's strong point, and she was definitely in her element. It was good to see that her normal enthusiasm had returned, if only for one evening.

Ahead of me, ladies started shuffling forward, stepping

up the back stairs, which led to the stage area. With every inch we moved forward, my heart beat faster. Soon, I felt my palms grow moist; my legs felt heavy. I tried to swallow down my nerves but my mouth was so dry, everything seemed to stick in my throat. Then, before I knew it, we were up. As our ensemble was announced, I tentatively stepped out from behind the curtain and moved toward center stage, my every step tracked by a blinding spotlight.

At first, my movements felt stiff, and probably looked stiff, but as I made my way down the catwalk something overcame me. My breathing eased and my grip suddenly loosened on the bouquet I was carrying. I began to imagine my own wedding, all eyes on me as I walked to the altar and Sean's waiting arms. At the end, I stepped to the left and waited. When the bride and groom arrived at the end of the platform, we all effortlessly turned, receiving a large round of applause. How exhilarating!

Stepping off the stage, I started weaving my way through the crowd, turning this way and that, showing the dress to its best advantage. After I'd worked my way around the room a couple of times, Bentley waved me over to where she and the other agents were seated at the back of the room. Well, all except Zach, who I imagined was regretting his decision to watch over Olive. "Lovely," Bentley commented as I approached. "Didn't I say that color would suit you?"

"It sure does," Jude chimed in with an appraising up and down.

"Our Lila always looks good," Franklin offered.

I smiled at my friends, happy to notice that Flora was seated next to Franklin. "Flora, you made it! I'm so glad you're feeling better."

Touching a finger to her cheek, she replied, "Yes, but what

a terrible virus. I heard it put Althea in the hospital. We're all so very grateful to hear she's doing better."

The mention of Mama reminded me that Lynn was going to give her a call. "Where's Lynn?" I asked, not seeing her seated with the others.

"I think she left," Pam said. "I saw her just a short while ago. We were with her out in the hall when she . . ." She shrugged. "Actually, I'm not sure what happened. She might have gotten a call or something."

My heart stopped. I leaned forward, palms on the table. "I'd loaned her my phone to make a call to my mother for me. But you think she *got* a call? Was it something about my mother? Is something wrong?"

"I don't think so." Pam furrowed her brow. "She didn't actually talk to anyone. Now that I'm thinking about it, I believe she saw a text come in on the phone . . . something that upset her. But certainly if it was about your mother, she would have told you right away."

A text? My mother didn't text. Heck, I wasn't even sure she knew how to use the cell phone I'd given her a couple of Christmases ago. Most of the time, she didn't even have it turned on. Could the text have been from Trey? Car trouble? But why would that upset Lynn? Then I remembered Sean saying he'd text me with updates. Had she seen his text and found out that Dr. Meyers had been arrested? I knew they were friends. Would that have upset her enough to leave?

Then, suddenly, all those niggling doubts came flooding back to me: Lynn's lack of an alibi, the nails planted in Jodi's room, Lynn's incessant bitterness toward Chuck, and something else, too. I'd thought all along it was strange how she'd become chummy with Dr. Meyers so quickly. Lunches out, drinks together, private therapy sessions, and she'd even started calling her Sloan. Nobody else called Dr. Meyers by her first name. Almost as if they'd been friends much longer than they pretended. Then there was the one thing that brought it all together. That day at the Magnolia, when Chuck said he'd just taken a job as part-time maintenance man at the Arts Center. Well, Dr. Meyers wasn't there, but Lynn was. She was also there to plant the nails in Jodi's room. And she was missing right before the time they estimated Chuck was killed. Was *she* the one who'd sabotaged the refrigerator? Zach was right! Lynn was guilty of murder. And so was Dr. Meyers. They were in on it together.

"Lila?" Bentley's voice cut through my thoughts. She nodded toward the other models, who were heading toward the stage for the final encore. "Aren't you supposed to be onstage right now?"

I ignored the question and asked a couple of my own. "How did Lynn leave? She doesn't have a car here. Did someone give her a ride?" But as I asked, the answer came to me: my Vespa!

In the hall, I broke into a wobbly high-heeled jog and burst through the double front doors and out into the cold air, nearly wiping out on the slick asphalt lot. It was gone. My Vespa was gone. And not only did she have my Vespa; she had my purse with my phone, my ID and credit cards, and . . . and my house keys. A desperate, cold-blooded murderer had my house keys!

Fear overcame me as I turned to run back inside for help, each ragged breath of cold air stinging my lungs. What if she was at my home right now? Had Oscar already dropped off Mama? Was she there alone? Or maybe Trey was home from work and watching his favorite television show?

"Lila!" Zach's voice came out of nowhere. His gloved

hands struggled to control Olive's leash as she pulled him down the walk. "Is everything okay?"

"No. No, it's not." I hurriedly explained about Lynn. "She's got my Vespa, my house keys, everything. I need to get home *now*."

Zach reached into his pocket and pulled out his own set of keys. "No problemo. I can get you there in no time. Come on, let's go." He picked up Olive, leash and all, and started sprinting toward Bentley's rental SUV, with me right behind him, wobbling in the strappy sandaled heels to keep up.

He reached the car before me and pushed the key fob to pop the locks. "Get in," he yelled, sliding open his driver's door and placing Olive inside.

A couple of seconds later, we were peeling out of the lot. Olive jumped onto my lap with a startled yelp as we accelerated. I gripped the dash with one hand and wrapped my arms protectively around the little dog. Not a moment too soon, either. We hit a speed bump that about took out the bottom half of the car.

"Do you have a cell phone?" I needed to call the police. Get someone over to my house.

Zach loosened his grip on the wheel and made a move for his back pocket. The car suddenly veered too far to the right, nearly sideswiping a parked car.

"Never mind!" I yelled. "Just get me to my house."

"So, I was right," Zach said, gripping the steering wheel tighter and hunching forward as he accelerated. "Lynn's the killer. I knew I'd solve the case!"

"Stop worrying about the case and just focus on the road, would you?" Suddenly he cranked on the wheel, taking a corner at breakneck speed. My arms tightened around Olive, poor thing. She'd buried her head in the crook of my arm and her tiny body was trembling with fear. I thought of telling him to slow down, for Olive's sake, but I was sick with fear over Mama and Trey. If Lynn had been heading for my house, she could already be there by now.

"You just don't want to admit that I solved the case before you," Zach was saying.

"That's not it," I said, sliding the other way as he turned again. "I just want to live through this car ride. Besides, you're only half right."

"Half right? What do you mean by half right? Did Lynn kill him or not?"

"Dr. Meyers killed Chuck. Lynn just helped her set it up."

"What? Dr. Meyers?"

"Never mind about all that right now. Just drive." I began a silent plea inside my head, repeating over and over, *Oh, please don't let them be at home! Please don't let them be home.*

Up ahead, I saw the turnoff for Walden Woods Circle. I squeezed my eyes shut and braced myself. Suddenly, we came to a screeching halt.

I opened my eyes and looked around. We'd made it, but I didn't see the Vespa anywhere. "Hold on." I handed over Olive and ran up the walk to try the front door. Locked. Plus all the lights were off and everything looked quiet. Thank goodness. No one was home.

"She didn't come here," I told Zach, climbing back in and shutting the door. I asked for his cell phone again, planning to call Sean with this new information, when another idea came to me. "I don't think she could get far on the Vespa in this weather," I commented, glancing out window at the falling snow. The roads were already coated with a slippery sheen, making it hazardous for even cars. Navigating the Vespa, especially for someone inexperienced, would be difficult. She'd want to get as far from here as possible, but where would she go? The airport in Dunston? I just couldn't see her navigating the mountain roads in the snow on a scooter. Maybe the train station. But I knew the last train out of the Valley had left over an hour ago. She'd probably go after a car. But where would she . . . "Go to the Magnolia Bed and Breakfast," I told Zach. "Hurry!"

As we sped off, I started punching Sean's number into the cell phone, only to find that Zach's phone was out of charge. "It's dead," I said, waving the phone his way. "Do you have a phone charger in here?"

Zach reached his hand across the seat toward the car's glove department. "Yup. Right in—"

"I've got it," I said, batting his hand away and rummaging through the cubbyhole until I located the charger. I immediately plugged it in and waited impatiently for the phone to gain enough charge for a call. In the meantime, we'd pulled onto Sweet Pea Road. After a few more hair-raising curves and one near wipeout, we screeched to a halt in front of "The Grand Lady."

DURING THE DAY, the Magnolia Bed and Breakfast was breathtakingly beautiful. The light pink exterior always brought to mind lazy summer days under the shady branches of a fully blossomed magnolia tree. But tonight, with darkness fallen and snow swirling around the turret, it looked brittle and spooky. "There aren't any lights on inside," Zach commented. "Maybe she didn't come here, either."

"She's here," I said, pointing to the side yard, where a single tire track in the fresh coating of snow betrayed her presence. "Those tracks belong to my Vespa. She must have driven it around the side of the house. Probably to hide it."

Zach reached for the car door. "Let's go get her, then."

"Wait!" I said, pointing to the phone. "There's almost enough charge to make a call. You get hold of the police. Tell them to send someone right away. Then follow me."

I cranked the car handle and hopped out, not waiting for his reply. On the porch, a loose board screeched under my weight, the sound magnified by the stillness of the cold night air. I stopped and collected myself, breathing deeply. Slowly I opened the storm door, cringing as its rusty hinges screamed out my arrival. After another deep breath, I tried the knob on the main door. It turned easily. The door was unlocked.

"Cora? Lynn?" I called out, groping the wall until I found a switch. Light flooded the entryway, casting shadows across the hall and into the still-darkened parlor. "Cora, are you home? It's me, Lila."

The only answer was the rhythmic ticking of the parlor's grandfather clock. Suddenly all of Cora's beautiful antiques, lovingly collected over the years, seemed menacing. "Lynn?" I called again. An abrupt movement made me startle. I whipped around to find Zach standing behind me, holding Olive. "Why'd you bring the dog in here?"

"Yeah, right. Leave her in the car so she can chew up the leather seats? Or worse, freeze to death. You think I want to get fired?" He put her down on the floor and attached the leash to her collar. Then he handed it to me as he removed a brass-headed antique cane from the umbrella stand in the corner. He gripped it like a baseball bat.

"I don't think that's necessary," I told him, although my eyes slid over to the remaining cane, one with an ornately carved eagle on the handle. I shook it off. No, Lynn might have helped kill Chuck, the man who'd tormented her for years, but she'd never hurt me. I was sure of it. "You called the police, right?"

"Yup. They're on the way. Think she's in here?"

"Yes. I do." I couldn't explain how, but I could sense Lynn's presence. Maybe I had a little of Mama in me after all. "But I've called her name a few times and she hasn't answered. We should wait on the police."

"Yeah, but Cora might be here. And she might need help."

Zach was right. If Lynn came to get Cora's car, she might have . . . No, I just couldn't believe that Lynn would hurt anyone. Would she? But she *had* been a party to murder.

"I'm going to check upstairs," he said.

"No, really, Zach, we should wait. It might be dangerous."

Zach dropped the leash and swung the cane like a bat. "Listen. I'll go upstairs and you stay here. Hey, I'm the one who figured out she was the murderer, right? And I play on the summer softball league."

"Huh?"

He swung the cane again. "Yup. A .420 batting average."

I didn't know beans about batting averages, but I did know about Zach's overzealous, impulsive tendencies and I didn't want him knocking Lynn's head off with the cane. "I don't think that's a good idea, Zach. I'll go."

He looked at me like I had a third eye. "Do I really have to remind you of what happened the last few times you took on murderers?"

I sighed. He was right. I didn't exactly have the best batting average when it came to confronting murder suspects. Not to mention I thought the idea of going up there was a poor one anyway. Olive's leash started slithering away from us, and I pounced on the end of it, then reached down to pull her back. "Stay here, girl." When I glanced up again, Zach was already on the staircase.

"Besides," Zach continued, moving up the steps. "You're

engaged to a cop. He'd be really ticked if I let you get killed. Like I need to have a cop mad at me. No thanks."

He ascended the steps, hunched slightly forward, the cane clenched in his hands. He called out Lynn's name a couple of times, but still no answer. When he reached the landing, which was just large enough for a small wing chair and side table, he paused for a second, tilting his head to one side as if he'd heard something. He took a couple of practice swings with the cane and then continued up the second flight of stairs.

I shuffled my feet nervously and listened hopefully for the sound of approaching sirens. I was actually starting to worry about Lynn's safety. Especially now that Babe Ruth was on the case.

Then suddenly I heard a large crashing sound overhead, followed by pounding footsteps that seemed to echo throughout the house. "Zach!" I yelled, quickly tying the end of Olive's leash around the leg of an antique hall table. I snatched the remaining cane from the umbrella stand and started for the stairs, but I stopped on the second step when I heard another noise coming from behind me. Backtracking, I inched my way toward the parlor. Again, I heard the noise and it sounded like someone moaning.

The light from the entryway only illuminated a few feet into the parlor, leaving the rest in shadows. "Cora? Lynn?" I called before finally locating the light switch. As soon as the light flooded the room, I saw Cora, gagged and bound on the sofa. I went to her. "Cora! Are you okay?" I asked as I struggled to undo her gag. In the hall, Olive started protesting her confinement. Her high-pitched yelps echoed throughout the house.

As soon as I'd loosened the gag enough, Cora spit out, "It's Lynn. She did this to me. She's here. Upstairs. We have to get out of here."

I noticed dried blood on her head. Looking closer, I saw

a small gash. "It's okay, Cora. The police are on their way."
I hurried to undo the ties from her raw wrists. "Can you
make it over to the neighbor's house?" I had to speak up,
just to be heard over the racket Olive was making.

She started to sit up, and then her eyes grew wide as she
reached out to steady herself. "I don't think so. I'm too weak."

"Then you'll have to wait here while I—"

"No! Don't leave me. She's still here. Somewhere in this
house. Please, just get me out of here."

"Listen, Cora. You're going to have to be brave. I need
to check on my friend. He's upstairs. He may be hurt."

Suddenly, Olive's barking stopped and I heard the clicking of nails against the hardwood floors. I also heard something else. Footsteps. "Where's that coming from?" I asked
Cora. "It sounds like footsteps in the wall."

"It's someone on the back stairs. Probably Lynn!"

I gripped her arms and leaned in close. "Calm down,
Cora! Where do the steps lead to?"

"From the top floor to the kitchen, on the other side of
the pantry. By the mudroom."

"And the back door?" When she nodded, I took off in
that direction, her protests following me through the house.
But I didn't hesitate. I knew it had to be Lynn, making her
getaway. I wasn't going to let that happen.

As I ran through the front hall, I almost tripped over
Olive's leash lying slack on the floor, her empty collar still
attached. But I kept running, hoping I'd beat Lynn to the
back door. When I got to the kitchen, I found her standing
at the counter, her bag slung over her shoulder as she rifled
through Cora's purse. "Are you looking for Cora's car keys?"

She wheeled, her eyes wide and wild. "Let me go, Lila. I
didn't kill him, Dr. Meyers did. But you already know that.
So just let me go."

"Where's Zach? Did you hurt him?"

"He'll be fine. Crap! Where did that woman put her keys?" I inched closer as she lifted the purse and dumped the contents. The keys fell out, landing with a jingle on the granite countertop. I pounced forward, my fingers connecting with them first.

"Give me the keys, Lila." Her voice was tight, her teeth clenched as she spoke. "I need those keys."

"You must have seen a text from Detective Griffiths on my phone," I surmised. She didn't reply but simply bobbed her head, her eyes still locked on the keys. "So you know it's only a matter of time before your part in all this comes out."

"Just give me the keys." She was begging now.

I was hoping to stall her, just until the police arrived. *Where are they anyway?* I dangled the keys. "Just answer a couple of questions first. How long have you really known Dr. Meyers?"

"Awhile," she answered, every muscle in her body tense and coiled like a snake ready to strike. "She contacted me last spring. Her daughter, Amanda, was dating Chuck. She was worried about her and looked into his background and found our divorce records."

"And she asked you to help her plan Chuck's murder?"

Lynn's expression loosened a bit. She shook her head. "No, it wasn't like that. At first we just talked. I told her about my writing and I found out she was a writer, too. Can you believe that?"

I nodded.

"And she thought my book was good. She helped me do some editing and then convinced me to submit it to you."

"*She* told you about our agency?" Had Dr. Meyers actually set this plan in place that long ago? Found just the right person to help her? Someone who could easily be convinced to follow along with her twisted plan? After all, Lynn was used to being bullied; it wouldn't be difficult to manipulate her. And Dr. Meyers, of all people, knew the techniques that bullies used, techniques she clearly exposed in her books to help women out of abusive relationships.

Lynn was still talking. "It was good, you know, to talk to someone who understood what I went through. She helped me. She really did."

"You mean she was like your counselor?" I'd heard of this type of thing. Counselors who convince their clients to perform illegal acts. "I don't understand. How exactly did Dr. Meyers talk you into helping her?"

Lynn's jaw clenched. "I knew exactly what her daughter, Amanda, was going through. Sloan helped me see the truth—that my own abuse wasn't over just because I'd left him, wouldn't be, as long as others like Amanda suffered that way, too. Amanda was making the same mistakes I did. Chuck would beat her and she just kept going back to him. Eventually, he'd kill her. I knew he would have. He almost killed me."

"You really trusted Dr. Meyers, didn't you?" I heard the slight sound of movement outside the back kitchen window. I hoped it was the police.

"Of course. She's helped me through so much. I . . . I probably wouldn't be here, if it weren't for Sloan." She lowered her eyes and spoke softly. "I'm ashamed to admit this, but I was thinking of . . . Well, I'd lost all my will to live. Even though I'd divorced Chuck, something inside me had died in the process. Until Sloan came into my life. She saved me, Lila. I know what you must think of her, but you're wrong. She's really an amazing person. All the good she does to help women like me. And, well . . ." She looked up, her eyes bright and intense. "All she wanted to do was protect her daughter. You can understand that, can't you?"

Yes, any mother could understand that instinct, but murder? "So she decided the best way to protect Amanda was to kill Chuck?"

"She'd tried everything else. She even sent Amanda away, but Chuck found her. They were going to get married. Sloan was beside herself with worry. She told me she just needed my help for a couple of little things. How could I say no? She'd helped me with so much."

"What little things, Lynn? The refrigerator system? Did you sabotage it?"

"No. That was Sloan's idea. She was going to kill Chuck here, in the pantry, but when I told her about Chuck working part time at the Arts Center, she came up with a different idea. A better idea, she said, because there would be so many people at the Arts Center. More suspects to throw the police off our trail."

"So she sabotaged the refrigeration system?"

"Yes. She just snuck through the back door. A lot of vendors were using it to set up their booths in the culinary wing. Then she snuck back out and came around the front of the building."

"And brought the nail gun with her."

Lynn didn't answer that question. For a second she seemed almost remorseful. Then her face hardened again and she said, "Chuck deserved what he got. The world is better off without him."

"No, Lynn. What Chuck did was absolutely wrong. He deserved to rot in jail for it. But no one deserves to be murdered. Maybe he would have changed one day. With the right help . . . I don't know. Maybe not. But we'll never know, because he was robbed of the choice. He was robbed of his chance to reform his life. And how ironic that you and Dr. Meyers chose to answer violence with violence."

Lynn's eyes grew wide and I noticed tiny beads of sweat gathering around her hairline. "But I didn't kill Chuck. Sloan did," she whispered.

"You helped her. And to make it worse, you planted the nails in Jodi's room to make an innocent woman look guilty." I remembered Cora saying she saw Chuck leaving Jodi's room that morning. "Why was Chuck in Jodi's room that morning? Did you have something to do with that?"

She slowly nodded, her eyes wide with worry now. "Yes," she admitted. "We just needed it to look like Jodi and Chuck knew each other. So, I told him Amanda would probably love a signed copy of Jodi's book. Chuck was always big on gifts. After a particularly bad fight, he always brought me something: flowers, chocolates, even a necklace once. It would work, too. I'd melt right back into his arms, the same cruel arms that . . ." She squeezed her eyes shut and then opened them again and continued, "Anyway, I told him how crazy women were for Jodi's books. And a signed copy? Well, that would really be something. I even saved him the money and effort by giving him my copy."

"The same copy you and Dr. Meyers used to plot his murder?"

The corners of her lips tipped upward. "Ironic, huh?" Then she caught herself, her face softening again. She reached out. "Give me the keys, Lila. Please."

"I'm not going to do that, Lynn. I want you to go with me to the police. Tell them your side of the story. Dr. Meyers was your therapist; she used you. Manipulated you into going along with her plan. Into helping her commit murder."

Lynn pulled her hand back, her features sinking and eyes narrowing into tiny slits. "That's not true. Sloan was my friend."

"No, Lynn. She wasn't. She used you. You need help."

Without warning, Lynn lunged at me, knocking me back

against the counter. The keys flew from my hand and landed on the floor. Before I could react, she pounced on them and made a break for it. But just as she reached the back door, it flew open, revealing a police officer with his gun drawn. "Stop!" he ordered.

Then another officer stepped around him and grabbed Lynn, turning her hand, putting cuffs on her wrists. Right behind him came Sean, bypassing both officers and coming straight to me.

"Zach's upstairs," I immediately told him. "He might be hurt." I started for the back staircase. "And Cora's in the living room. She needs help," I said over my shoulder.

Sean raced up the steps after me, shouting for another officer to see to Cora and then barking orders for medical assistance into his radio. At the top of the steps, I hesitated. I was facing a long hall, doors on either side. "Zach!" I called.

Olive started barking from down the hall. I ran toward the sound, finding Zach inside one of the bedrooms, sitting on the floor, a dazed look on his face and feathers floating all around his head. *Feathers?*

"Zach. Are you okay?" I asked, kneeling down next to him. My movement sent more feathers flying into the air.

Above me, Sean was still talking into his radio, explaining our location. "Help's coming, buddy," he said, bending down. "What happened, do you know?"

Zach's eyes rolled around a bit. He finally answered, "She hit me with something. Completely blindsided me." He waved his hand in front of his face and blew a raspberry. "What in the world?"

I glanced around. Olive had managed to pull the comforter off the bed and was busy shredding it to pieces. Feathers were flying everywhere. "Stop that!" I scolded.

Zach moaned and covered his ears. "Not so loud. Man, my head hurts."

"You don't know what she hit you with?" Sean asked.

"No idea," Zach said, rubbing a spot on his forehead. "Whatever it was, it came out of nowhere."

As if to answer our question, Olive began nudging her nose at something under the comforter, finally revealing a billiard ball. She sat back, tongue out and panting. Her tail twitching expectantly. I picked up the ball and held it up to Zach's forehead. "I think we found her weapon." The shape of the ball was a perfect match for the round welt between his eyes. Apparently Pam was right when she said Lynn was a pool shark. A grin tugged at my lips as I took in Zach's dubious expression. "Looks like you need to work on that batting average of yours," I told him.

I laughed. And Sean laughed, too. Poor Zach just moaned.

AMBULANCES SOON ARRIVED to transport both Zach and Cora to the hospital. They seemed fine, but the extra precaution seemed prudent in both cases. Olive was also being transported. By police cruiser, that was, straight to Bentley's residence. I was the one to think of the idea. After all, the back of a police cruiser was designed to transport violent, hardened criminals to justice. It might just survive transporting Olive across town to Bentley's condo. I'd recovered my purse and phone and called ahead to give Bentley a quick rundown on the events that had transpired. After hearing that not one, but two of her clients were murderers . . . well, let's just say, if Franklin was right and dogs did lower blood pressure, then Bentley would be needing as much comfort as Olive could provide.

"I hope Cora won't mind me parking my Vespa in here,"

I told Sean, who was helping me push my scooter into the carriage house behind the inn. He'd given me a police-issue jacket from his vehicle to cover my bare arms. I plodded behind him, the high heels of my sandals catching in the cracks of the snow-covered cobblestone path that ran between the main house and the carriage house.

"I'm sure she won't mind," Sean replied. He reached up and pulled open the large wooden door and pushed my scooter inside. "It'll at least stay dry in here. I'll bring you back by tomorrow to pick it up." Despite what must have been a rough ride over snow-covered roads, it didn't seem to have sustained any damage. Thank goodness. Between saving for the wedding, and the extra demand on my grocery bill since Trey was home, there wasn't much wiggle room in my budget for scooter repairs.

"I almost feel sorry for Lynn," I said, as he lowered the kickstand. "It's almost like she was under Dr. Meyers's spell. You should have heard her tell about it. Dr. Meyers had convinced Lynn that she'd never be free of Chuck until she'd helped get rid of him. Like it was part of a therapy to get out of her depression. She was so in awe of the woman."

"Still, she participated in murder. Premeditated murder. We have a full confession from Dr. Meyers."

"But what a waste. She'd already broken away from Chuck's abuse. Found a way to make her life count for something. She'd found her passion . . . writing. But now she'll never get a chance to know where it could have taken her." I shook my head again. "Such a terrible waste of talent. Of a life."

We were back outside. Sean reached up and pulled the garage door shut. "Don't worry, Lila. She'll have a full psych workup. Her lawyer will make sure of it. Maybe she'll finally get the help she needs."

"I know; it's just that—"

He had stopped and placed his hand under my chin, forcing me to look into his eyes. Those intense blue eyes that never ceased to mesmerize me. He put his finger to my lips. "We can talk all about the case another time. I'm just glad you're safe." A snowflake landed on my nose and he brushed it away, and then his eyes rolled skyward. I followed his gaze to the full winter moon, which hung in the sky like a luminous pearl. "Beautiful, isn't it?" he said.

I nodded. It was breathtakingly beautiful. The way the silver moonlight cast a bluish tinge to the sky, making the snowy white branches of a nearby tree seem to almost glow in the dark. All around us, big fluffy snowflakes fell, like glittery confetti. Cold, but beautiful. I shivered.

"Cold?" he asked.

"Well, this dress wasn't exactly designed as outdoor wear." I pulled the jacket he'd given me tighter around my body.

"Did I mention that you look beautiful in it?"

I shook my head and felt a grin tug at my lips. "No. You didn't."

His eyes crinkled. "I'm a lucky man. You're both beautiful and smart, Lila. You never cease to amaze me."

"Are you complimenting my sleuthing abilities, Detective?"

A slight shadow overcame his expression and he dropped his hand. But after pausing a half beat, he shrugged and smiled again. "I guess I am. Maybe there's something to all that mystery reading you do, after all."

I tilted my head back and laughed, really laughed. And it felt good. For the first time that week, I let go. I let go of my worries about Trey, work stress, the case, Mama, and . . . "Oh my goodness," I said, snapping forward and looking into Sean's amused expression. "My mother! I should go and give her a call."

Sean reached out, placing his hands on my shoulders. "She's fine. I just talked to her a little while ago."

"You did?"

"Yes. Bentley became concerned when you left the Arts Center so quickly. She assumed it was something with Althea, so she called me. I called the hospital and just barely caught her before she checked out. She was doing fine, but of course my call put her on edge. So when she got to your house she did what she always does when she's on edge."

"Reach for a glass of Jim Beam?"

He chuckled. "Well, probably that, too. But I meant she consulted her tarot cards. She must've seen something, because she called me twenty minutes later, all hysterical like, going on about this card and that . . . Heck, I have no idea what she was saying except that you were in trouble."

"Didn't you already know that? I mean, didn't Zach call 911?"

Sean nodded. "He did. But all he said was something about how he'd solved Chuck Richards's murder and how he had the killer cornered and we needed to come right away. Then he hung up."

"He didn't say where?"

"Nope. We were in the process of trying to track the cell signal when Althea called."

"I don't understand. How did Mama know where I was just from her tarot cards?"

"She didn't."

"Then how—?"

He grinned. "All those cards she was talking about . . . the Queen of Cups, the King of Swords, the Knight of this and that . . . Well, I got to thinking maybe her intuition was trying to tell her you were in a castle."

"A castle?"

He pointed up at the turret, snow swirling around its spire. "A castle."

I shook my head in wonder. "Amazing."

He pulled me close, the warmth of his body enveloping me. "Yes. Amazing." He bent down, his lips covering mine, warm, comforting with the snowflakes falling against our face. When we finally parted, he pulled back, reached in his pocket, and pulled out a small velvet box. "I was going to give this to you at dinner, but . . ."

"YOU'VE BEEN LOOKING at that thing for the last ten minutes," Bentley chided. We were riding in her Lexus, headed toward Dunston. Olive was in the backseat, strapped in with a canine seat belt and riding contently. The rest of the car was loaded to the brim with every sort of doggie apparatus and toy imaginable.

"I can't help it." I turned my finger this way and that, admiring the filigree engraving and the way the diamond sparkled against the vintage art deco setting. "It's exactly what I dreamed about."

Bentley glanced across the seat. "I'm happy for you, Lila. I really am."

"Thank you." I folded my hands and added in a more serious tone, "For everything. Especially for helping Lynn." It had been a couple of weeks since Dr. Meyers's and Lynn's arrests. Bentley had retained one of the best lawyers in the area to defend Lynn. We were all hoping for a lenient sentence. As for Dr. Meyers, she'd fully confessed to everything. Even manipulating Lynn into becoming her co-conspirator. Personally, I wouldn't have cared if they locked Dr. Meyers up and threw away the key. She'd connived such a twisted, evil plot. Someone like that should never be set free into society again. Not ever.

On a positive note, Jodi was released from jail and her record completely expunged. Due to some clever write-ups, Bentley was able to turn the whole fiasco into a grand publicity campaign. Jodi's sales had more than doubled in the past two weeks and propelled her to the top spot on the bestseller lists. There was no doubt she'd have a long and successful career ahead of her.

Speaking of careers. I'd talked to both Bentley and Flora about Pam's wish to switch genres. While they were both shocked by the news, and a little concerned how it would affect the agency's bottom line, they showed Pam an amazing amount of support. I was glad. Because I'd read her mystery manuscript and it was terrific. I could hardly wait to introduce her work to the world of mystery readers. Knowing that I had even the smallest part in bringing intriguing stories to eager, discerning readers fueled my passion for the written word. I felt so fortunate to be able to live my dream and help others achieve theirs. Including my best friend, Makayla, who was overjoyed when I finally presented her with the cover artwork for *The Barista Diaries*. With the publication of her first novel and her upcoming nuptials, my friend was on cloud nine.

As for Trey. Well, he was still working at Machiavelli's. And I was still concerned about his career choice. But he was happy and as long as he continued to pay back the money he owed me, I could be happy, too. And as it turned out, Oscar had proven to be a good boss. He'd taken Trey under his wing and shown him the business. He'd assured me that Trey was blossoming into a great chef.

Trey's cooking skills weren't the only thing blossoming.

So was the relationship between Oscar and Mama. And I didn't mind a bit. I'd never seen my mama so happy.

"Well, here we are," Bentley said. She parked in front of a large Craftsman-style home, located on a tree-lined avenue in one of Dunston's older neighborhoods. The weather had finally started to turn, and if I squinted, I could almost make out tiny buds lying in wait along the tree branches, ready to burst with color as soon as spring gave the official nod.

"It's a lovely place, isn't it?" I said.

Bentley nodded.

"Are you still okay with this?"

She looked over her shoulder at Olive, then back at me, her eyes glistening with rare emotion. "Yes. I think it's probably the best thing for everyone concerned." By that, she meant Vicky. And thank goodness Bentley had come to that conclusion, because no one at Novel Idea could imagine not having Vicky on staff. "Besides," Bentley continued. "Olive needs a lot of attention, maybe kids to play with her, and I . . . well, I live a pretty sterile life, if you haven't noticed. Business, business, and more business. Not exactly a nurturing, loving environment."

I hesitated. Not sure what to say. Over the past week, I'd come to know a different facet of Bentley. A caring, sensitive side. In many ways, it was easier before when I only knew the cutthroat business side of her. I wasn't quite sure how to relate to the new Bentley.

"But," she concluded. "This time with Olive has opened my eyes to something I believe is very important and given birth to a new and lucrative venture for our agency."

Aw . . . the old Bentley was back. "Oh, and what might that be?"

Her eyes took on that old familiar gleam, the one that sparkled with dollar signs. "A benefit for dogs like Olive, rescue animals. We'll combine it with a campaign for that author Franklin's always talking about, the one who wrote *Get a New Leash on Life*. And what's that new mystery series you just signed last summer?"

"The Trendy Tails Mysteries?"

"That's the one. Catchy title, by the way." She swept her hand through the air as she imagined all the possibilities. "We'll call our event something like . . . like . . . Oh, I don't know. I'm putting you in charge, so you can come up with the event name. But make it good. We're going big. Think . . . uh, what's that big dog show that's always on television?"

"The Westminster Kennel Club Dog Show?"

"Exactly!" Bentley enthused. "But it doesn't just have to be show dogs; we could incorporate something for working dogs, service dogs . . ."

"Police dogs?" I threw out. Although I don't know why I was encouraging her. This event was getting bigger by the second.

"Now you're thinking. And we'll donate part of our proceeds to help benefit dogs like Olive."

I reached across and placed my hand over hers, giving it a quick squeeze. "Another brilliant idea," I told her. "Come on, let's go introduce Olive to her new home."

As soon as we stepped out of the car, the front door of the home flew open and several children came running out—their faces lit up with excitement. Right behind the children came Ms. Jensen, the new director of the Home for Women in Transition. She reached out and grasped Bentley's hand. "Ms. Duke. We can't thank you enough for your generosity. Your donation means so much to us."

My head snapped to Bentley. Donation? I shook my head in wonderment. My boss never ceased to surprise me.

The woman continued, "And this . . ." She waved her hand

to where the children were huddled around Olive, giggling and laughing with joy. "What a wonderful idea. I wish I had thought of it. A dog. Just the thing these children need to distract them from the troubles they've faced. A spot of joy in their lives."

Bentley nodded, her gaze fixed on the children as they took turns holding and nuzzling Olive. I moved closer and whispered in her ear. "Look at Olive. She seems happy."

Bentley nodded, a lone tear falling down her cheek. "Yes. It looks like Olive has found a happy ending for her story."

I nodded. Bentley's comment reminded me that we all have our own stories, each and every one of us. And if we're lucky, we have a host of supporting characters to see us through the many plot twists in our lives. I was truly blessed to have a wonderful fiancé and many good friends to fill that role. And who could ask for a better sidekick than the Amazing Althea? With them by my side, I was ready to turn the page on a new chapter in my life. One that would include bringing more captivating stories to readers and promising careers to budding authors, as well as supporting my own loving family—Mama and Trey and my work family, too—no matter what story they'd choose to write for themselves. I looked down at the ring on my hand, its glimmer almost matching the lightness I felt in my heart. Best of all, I'd have Sean by my side to see me through each new scene and every new event.

I could hardly wait to see what the rest of my story would bring.

Turn the page for a preview

of the newest book in

Susan Furlong's

Georgia Peach mystery series

REST IN
PEACH

Coming soon from
Berkley Prime Crime

Any woman who's had the privilege of growing up below the Mason-Dixon Line understands the history and tradition of a debutante ball. My mother was no exception. From the time I could walk, she started grooming me for my debut to polite society. I can still remember her little bits of advice to this day—tips she called her Debutante Rules. Of course, some of them were a little offbeat; but they did encourage me to become the best woman I could be. You see, my mama's advice taught me that being a debutante is less about the long white gloves, the pageantry, and the curtsey, and more about a code of conduct that develops inner beauty, a sense of neighborly charity, and unshakable strength in character that sees us women through the good times and the bad. Later, as I traveled the world, I came to learn these rules of hers transcended borders, cultures, and economic status. In essence my mama's Debutante Rules taught me that no matter where you're from or who your people are, becoming the best person you can be is key to a happy life.

Debutante Rule #032: Like a magnolia tree, a debutante's outward beauty reflects her strong inner roots . . . and that's why we never leave the house without our makeup on.

FRANCES SIMMS'S BEADY EYES WERE ENOUGH TO MAKE
my skin crawl on any given day, but at that particular moment
the presence of the incessantly determined owner and editor
of our town's one and only newspaper was enough to frazzle
my last nerve.

"Can't this wait, Frances? I'm right in the middle of something." I turned my focus back to my project. Truth was, I
could have used a break; my arm was about to fall off from
all the scrubbing I'd been doing in my soon-to-be-new storefront. Still, I'd suffer through more scrubbing any day if it
meant I could avoid dealing with the bothersome woman.
And today, of all days, I didn't need her pestering presence.

Frances persisted. "Wait? I'm on a deadline. Especially if
you want the ad to run in Tuesday's issue." *The Cays Mill
Reporter*, the area's source of breaking news—or rather,
reputation-breaking gossip—faithfully hit the hot Georgia
pavement every Tuesday and Saturday. Since I was a new
business owner, Frances was hoping to sign me on as a con-
tributing advertiser. For a mere twenty-four ninety-nine a
month, I could reserve a one-by-one-inch square on the paper's
back page, sure to bring in hordes of eager, peach-lovin' customers to my soon-to-open shop, Peachy Keen.

"This offer isn't going to be on the table forever," she continued. "I'm giving you a ten percent discount off my normal
rate, you know."

"Oh, don't go getting all bent out of shape, Frances," my
friend Ginny spoke up. Having a slow moment at the diner
next door, which she owned with her husband, Sam, Ginny
had popped over to check my renovation progress. "This is
only Saturday," she went on. "Besides, Peachy Keen doesn't
officially open for another few weeks."

Over the past nine months since my return to Cays Mill,
what started as a little sideline business to help supplement

my family's failing peach farm had grown into a successful venture. From that first jar of peach preserves sold at the local Peach Harvest Festival to a booming online business, Harper's Peach Products had been selling like crazy. Unable to keep up with the demand, I had struck a deal with Ginny and Sam: For a reasonable percentage of profits, I'd get full use of their industrial-sized, fully licensed kitchen after the diner closed each day, plus a couple hours daily of Ginny's time and expertise in cooking. Since the diner was only open for breakfast and lunch, we could easily be in the kitchen and cooking by late afternoon, allowing Ginny enough time to be home for supper with her family. Then Ginny offered to rent me their small storage area, right next to the diner, for a storefront—a perfect location—which now stored much of my stock until we could open. The deal worked for both of us: I needed the extra manpower and Ginny needed the extra money. Especially with one child in college and her youngest, Emily, finishing her senior year in high school.

Frances was pacing the floor and stating her case. "That may be true, but space fills up quickly. My paper's the leading news source for the entire area."

"Oh, for Pete's sake, Frances," Ginny bantered, "it's the *only* news source in the area. Besides, that quote you gave Nola is five bucks higher than what I pay for the diner's monthly ad."

I quit scrubbing and quirked an eyebrow Frances's way. "Is that so?"

"Well, I've got expenses and—" she started to explain but was cut off mid-sentence when the back door flew open and Emily burst inside.

"Mom!" Emily cried, her freckled face beaming with excitement. She held out Ginny's purse. "The delivery truck just pulled in front of the boutique. The dresses are in!"

Ginny let out a little squeal, cast a quick glance toward the window and reached into her bag. "Okay, okay. Just give me a minute to freshen up." She pulled a compact out and started touching up her lipstick, a shocking red color that looked surprisingly fabulous with her ginger-colored hair. "Oh, I can hardly wait! Emily's cotillion dress. Can you imagine!" she gushed and glanced my way. "Come on, Nola. You said you'd come with us, right? You've just gotta see the gown we ordered."

I peered anxiously at the stacks of wood for the unfinished shelving, the loose plaster, and the wood floors that were still only half-refinished. Knowing the renovation was too much for me to handle alone, I'd hired my friend, Cade McKenna, who owned a local contracting business, to help me transform the storage area into a quaint shop. One of the interior walls sported exposed red brick and would add the perfect touch to the country-chic look I wanted. But my vision versus reality didn't mesh easily; I'd been scrubbing loose mortar from that wall for hours already. Cade said the loose stuff really needed to be removed before he could seal the rest. I sighed and glanced out the window. I'd already known my work would be interrupted later today when the delivery truck arrived; I'd been dragged into my dear friend and her daughter's excitement since the get-go. But truth be told, I almost preferred flaking mortar to facing up to the debutante issues I knew would soon erupt into a community-wide frenzy. "I'd love to go," I said. "But I really should keep at it."

Ginny waved off my worry. "You've been at it all morning. You need a break."

"Hey!" Frances turned her palms upward in protest. "I wasn't done discussing the ad."

"Oh, shush up, Frances," Ginny shut her down. She reached back into her bag, this time pulling out a small bottle of cologne and giving herself a couple quick spritzes behind the ears.

"You're fine, Mama," Emily interrupted. "Let's get going. I'm dying to try on my dress."

Ginny finished primping and shouldered her bag. "All right, sweetie. Let's go." Her eyes glistened as she squeezed her daughter's arm. "I just know you're going to be the most beautiful debutante at the cotillion!" Then, turning to me, she added with a mischievous grin. "Are ya coming with us, or do you want to stay here and discuss the ad with Frances?"

Since she put it that way, I decided I could use a little break and proceeded to rip off my apron and remove the bandana covering my cropped hair. I ran my hand through the short strands, trying to give it a little lift, the extent of my personal primping routine, as I made my way to the back door. Opening it wide, I shrugged toward Frances, who was still standing in the middle of my would-be shop, a befuddled look on her face. "Sorry, Frances. Guess we'll have to talk about the ad some other time."

She opened and shut her mouth a few times but all that came out was a loud huff. Finally relenting, she threw up her hands and stormed out the door. I couldn't help but stare after her with a grin on my face. Usually I didn't take so much delight in being rude, but ever since Frances's paper ran a smear campaign on my brother-in-law last August, I'd had a hard time being civil toward her. Who could blame me? At the time, she'd relentlessly pursued, harassed and tried to intimidate information from not only me, but my then-very-pregnant sister, Ida. And when Frances found she couldn't coerce information from us, she printed libelous half-truths about Hollis—on the front page, nonetheless!— that all but landed him a lifetime prison sentence. Thank goodness all that misery was behind us now. What a relief knowing the only thing Frances could hound me about these days was a silly display ad for the back page of the paper.

EMILY WAS RIGHT; Hattie's Boutique was already teeming with a small but enthusiastic pack of giggling debutantes and their equally excited mothers. They were pressing against the main counter like a horde of frenzied Black Friday shoppers while Hattie pulled billows of white satin and lace from long brown boxes. Carefully, she hung each dress on a rack behind the counter. "Ladies, please!" she pleaded. "Take a seat in the waiting area. I just need a few minutes to sort out the orders."

One of the mothers, Maggie Jones, the preacher's wife, was at the head of the pack sticking out her elbows like a linebacker in hopes of deterring the other gals from skirting around her in line. "Did the dress we ordered come in? Belle would like to try it on."

Hattie smiled through gritted teeth, once again pointing across the room toward a grouping of furniture. "I'm sure it did, Mrs. Jones. If y'all would just take a seat, please, I'll be right with you." She lifted her chin and kept her finger pointing across the room, making it clear she would not unpack one more dress until we complied.

With a collective sigh, the group, including Ginny, Emily, and me, sulked to the waiting area. The mothers politely settled themselves on the flower-patterned furniture while the girls huddled off to the side to discuss the latest debutante news. It was a wonder they never tired of the topic. I, for one, could hardly take much more. For months, I'd been hearing constant chatter about our town's spin on a high society debut: the presentation, what would be served at the formal dinner and, of course, all about how elegantly Congressman Wheeler's plantation would be decorated for the Peach Cotillion.

Usually the whole shindig was held up north at some ritzy country club, but this year, thanks to the generosity of Congressman Jeb Wheeler, who just happened to be up for reelection, the cotillion was staying local with the ball taking place at his family home, the historic Wheeler Plantation.

"She's awful pushy for a preacher's wife, don't you think?" Ginny whispered.

I looked over to where the other women were seated. "Maggie Jones?"

Ginny's shoulders waggled. "Uh-huh."

Leaning back against the cushion, I inwardly moaned. That was why I hadn't wanted to come; Ginny was taking this cotillion stuff way too seriously. As a matter of fact, the impending cotillion and its accompanying affairs seemed to be bringing out the worst in all the town's ladies. Like the well-dressed woman across from us who sported an expensive-looking beige leather handbag and an all-too-serious attitude. She was seated with ramrod straight posture and legs folded primly to one side, a proud tilt to her chin as she impatiently—and imperiously—glanced around the room.

"Who's Miss Proper over there?" I quietly asked Ginny.

She glanced over and quickly turned back, her face screwed with disgust. "That's Vivien Crenshaw. You know, Ms. Peach Queen's mama." She nodded toward the group of girls, where a tall blonde with dazzling white teeth stood in the center. She was gushing dramatically about her date for the dance while the rest of the girls looked on in awe. "Her name's Tara," Ginny continued. "Emily says she's the most popular girl in high school. Top in everything: lead in the school play, class president, and head cheerleader . . . You know the type."

Yeah, I knew the type. A picture of my own sister's face formed in my mind. Ida, the star of the Harper clan, always exceeded everyone's expectations; whereas I always did the unexpected, keeping my family in a continuous state of quandary. Even to this day, there were things I just couldn't bear to tell my parents, for fear it would put them over the edge. I shook my head, telling myself not to think about all that right now.

Luckily, a movement outside distracted me from my downward spiral. Adjusting my position to get a better look, I gazed curiously at the young girl washing Hattie's windows. She was dressed in sagging jeans and a too-tight T-shirt topped off with shocking black hair that shadowed her features. This must have been the girl Hattie mentioned hiring for odd jobs. She was nothing like the other girls in town. I felt an instant connection to her. As I continued to look on, the girl paused, reached into the pocket of her jeans and extracted a hair band. She pulled back her hair, exposing several silver hooped earrings running along the rim of her ear and topped off with a long silver arrow that pierced straight through to the inner cartilage. Ew. That must have hurt! I felt no connection now. But still, it was fascinating. It reminded me of some of the extreme piercings I'd observed in remote African tribes during my days as a humanitarian aid worker.

I was about to ask Ginny if she knew the girl when Hattie called out from the other side of the room. "Okay, ladies. I think I've got everything straightened out. Now one at a time . . ." She held up the first dress. "Belle Jones." The preacher's wife and her daughter scrambled to grab the dress before heading off toward the dressing rooms. "And, this one's for Sophie Bearden," Hattie continued, handing out the next dress to a squealing brown-haired girl.

Just as Hattie was reaching for the next gown, jingling bells announced the arrival of a short, stout woman dressed in sensible polyester slacks and a scoop-neck top. She removed her sunglasses and unwrapped a colorful scarf from her head. "Lawdy! Can y'all believe this humidity today?" She patted down her tight black curls before using the scarf to dab at her décolletage.

Hattie's face lit up. "Mrs. Busby, thanks so much for coming in early."

The woman waved off the thanks with, "So how many girls spied that early delivery truck?"

"Just a few, but if you could pin them up, it'd save having to make extra appointments."

"Sure enough. Just send them back to my station."

In the back corner of the shop, Hattie had utilized a lovely folding screen with an inlaid floral motif to partition an area for alterations. Behind the partition, a large corner table held an industrial sewing machine, racks of thread spools, a myriad of scissors and a divided box of pins, buttons and clasps. To the side of the workstation, a carpeted platform rested in front of an antique white cheval mirror.

Hattie disappeared behind the counter again, where she continued opening boxes and checking order slips while the rest of the girls waited impatiently. The first girls were coming out of the dressing room, proud mamas trailing after them and holding up their gowns as they made their way to Mrs. Busby for alterations. After a couple more girls disappeared into the dressing rooms, the Peach Queen's mother heaved a sigh and glanced disgustedly at her watch. "How much longer is this going to take? I have an appointment at the salon in about ten minutes."

Hattie was still behind the counter, tearing through packing material, her expression panicked. "Of course, Mrs. Crenshaw. I'll be right with you," she answered with a strained voice.

Next to me, Ginny shifted and rolled her eyes, quietly

mimicking the woman under her breath. "Can you believe how demanding that woman is?"

Ginny's usually good-natured demeanor was being stretched thin by the overbearing woman. At the moment, she reminded me of a spark getting ready to ignite and explode. I patted her hand and mumbled under my breath, "Remember why you're here. To show your daughter the importance of social grace, right?" I shot her a sly grin and stood. "I think I'll just go over and see if Hattie needs a hand." Hattie had seemed cool and controlled before but she looked like maybe she could use a bit of help now.

Just as I reached the counter to offer my assistance, the bells above the door jingled again. This time it was a model-thin woman wearing crisp linen pants and a matching jacket. Her silky silver hair was cut at a precise angle to accentuate her strong jawline and graceful neck. Upon seeing her, Hattie stopped her work, straightened her shoulders and plastered on a huge smile. So did everyone else in the room. It was as if they were all marionettes and the puppet master had just pulled their strings.

"Mrs. Wheeler! Uh . . . you must be here to pick up your alterations." Hattie's voice was thinning even more and her eyes darted nervously between her waiting customers and a rack of clothing lining her back wall. She took a little shuffle step as if she wasn't sure which way to go first.

Mrs. Wheeler glanced over the crowded waiting area and sensing Hattie's stress, put on a gracious smile and said, "I didn't realize you were so busy. Please don't bother with my order right this minute. I've got business at the flower shop down the street. How about I stop by when I'm done there? Perhaps things will have settled down by then."

Hattie let out her breath and nodded gratefully, promising to have the order ready when she returned. But as soon as the

woman left, Hattie turned back to me with an even more panicked expression. "There's a problem," she whispered.

"A problem? What?"

She nodded toward the box on the floor. "There's only
one dress left."

I shrugged.

"You're not getting it," she hissed, discreetly pointing
across the room. "One dress, but two girls."

My eyes grew wide. "Oh."

Joining her behind the counter, I squatted down and
started ripping through the mounds of packing paper. "Are
you sure?" She slid down next to me. My mind flashed back
to a competitive game of hide-and-seek we once played as
kids. Hattie and I crouched together behind the peach crates
in my daddy's barn, suppressing giggles as her big brother,
Cade, searched and searched in vain. Only this situation
wasn't fun and games at all.

She chewed her lip and nodded. "I'm sure."

"Well, whose dress is it?"

"Any chance you can hurry things up a bit?" Vivien Crenshaw called out from across the room. "Like I said, I'm on
a tight schedule."

Hattie raised up and peered over the counter. "Be right with
ya!" Then, popping back down, she started to fall apart. "I just
don't know what's happened . . . Neither of the numbers on
the order forms match the one on the dress, but I think it's
Emily's. It's just been so crazy here . . . Maybe I messed up
when I placed the order. What am I going to do? Of all the
dresses to be missing."

"Relax. Just tell Mrs. Crenshaw there was a mistake. The
cotillion is still a couple weeks away. There's plenty of time
to get Tara's dress shipped and altered. Mistakes happen,
right?"

She nodded, drew in a deep breath and stood up. "Mrs. Crenshaw, would you mind coming over here, please?"

I busied myself behind the counter, folding up the packing materials, revealing more of the dress that was left in the box. I couldn't help but smooth my hand over the shimmery satin of the gown. Actually, it gave me a little thrill to finally see the dress Emily had been talking about for so long. But seeing it up close also gave me a little prickle of regret. Due to a tragic, youthful mistake I didn't really want to think about at that moment, I'd missed my own cotillion, something my mama had never quite forgiven me for. Actually, thinking back on it, I was always a bit of a tomboy and never put much stock in the debutante craze anyway. Charm classes, dance lessons . . . all that was never really my thing. Of course, being raised by a mama who prided herself in her southern heritage, I understood the reasoning behind such formalities. Like many things southern, it was a ritual passed down since the days before Mr. Lincoln's war. And, we southerners lived and died by our traditions, whether it was sweet tea, SEC football, or fancy cotillions.

I ran my hand over the fine lace accents on the bodice of Emily's dress. Still, it would have been fun to wear something so elegant. . . .

"What do you mean her dress isn't in yet? That's it right there."

My head snapped up. Vivien Crenshaw was pointing at the dress I was caressing. Her daughter, Tara, stood next to her, nodding enthusiastically as they both peered over the counter.

"Oh, no. I don't think so. I believe this is Emily Wiggin's dress," Hattie responded.

At the mention of her name, Emily started for the counter. Ginny was right behind her. Guessing by the wild look in Ginny's eye and the slight flush of her cheeks, her hackles were up. I sucked in my breath.

"Let me see that," Ginny demanded. I stood and held it upright. She took a quick look and turned to Vivien. "I'm sorry, Vivien, but you're mistaken. That's the dress Emily ordered. I'd know it anywhere." And she would, too. She and Emily had spent days scouring over the catalogs at Hattie's Boutique, searching for Emily's dream cotillion dress—special ordered all the way from Atlanta—which I'd heard described a thousand times as an off-shoulder, satin sheath that would look all so beautiful on Emily's slim figure. Why, she was going to look just like a princess in it!

"No, you're the one who's mistaken," Vivien countered. She reached across the counter and snatched the dress from my hands. "Go try it on, Tara. And hurry. We're pressed for time."

"Now wait just a minute," Ginny intercepted her, placing a hand on Vivien's arm. "That's my daughter's dress and—"

"Ladies, please!" Hattie interrupted. "There's an easier way to resolve this. Just give me a few minutes and I'll call the dress company and get this straightened out." She already had the phone in her hand and was dialing the number as she walked toward the back room for privacy.

In the meantime, a crowd was gathering. Mrs. Busby, pin-cushion in hand, came tooling over to see about the ruckus. Right behind her shuffled one of the debs, dragging the hem of her too-long gown. Out of one of the dressing rooms came Belle Jones and her mother, Maggie, their eyes gleaming with anticipation. Even the dark-haired, window-washing girl stopped working and came inside to gawk. I swear, the whole scene reminded me of school kids gathering on the play-ground to witness a smackdown.

Emily spoke up, her eyes full of concern. "That's my dress, Mrs. Crenshaw. I'm sure of it."

Vivien's eyes shifted from Ginny and homed in on Emily. "This isn't your dress, young lady, and you know it."

Ginny recoiled then sprang forward, her eyes full of venom. "Are you calling my girl a liar?"

"Just calm down, Ginny," I pleaded, dashing out from behind the counter and grabbing ahold of my friend. "We'll get this figured out."

Under my grip, I could feel Ginny's muscles tensing. She was ready to fight for this dress. Thank goodness Hattie finally came out of the back room. She was carrying a large binder, her hands trembling as she flipped through the pages. "I'm afraid I've made a horrible mistake," she started to confess.

Vivien raised a brow. "A mistake?"

Hattie nodded. "Yes, you see, I would never order two of the same style dress for a cotillion. Y'all know how embarrassing it would be for two girls have the same one." She choked out a nervous little laugh before continuing. "But it seems both Tara and Emily picked the same dress from the catalog but I somehow got the numbers on one of them mixed up, so I didn't know there were two of the same. So when I ordered it, the company called for clarification on a number, and . . . well, the right catalog number was already ordered, even in the right size . . . so I thought I had everyone covered . . ." She swallowed hard, unable to dredge up her usual shopkeeper's smile.

Ginny lifted her chin. "Well, it's simple enough. Which one of us placed the order first?"

Hattie turned back a couple pages in the binder. "It looks like Emily did."

Vivien clutched the dress tighter. "Why does it matter who ordered first? We picked it up first. Besides, I'm sure Emily can find something else to suit her."

Two bright crimson circles suddenly appeared on Ginny's cheeks. "No way! You heard Hattie. That's our dress."

"I don't think so," Vivien countered.

Ginny reached for the gown, but Emily stopped her. "Don't, Mama. Please. It's all right. I'll pick out another." Tears welled in her eyes and her cheeks flushed with embarrassment as she scanned the room, taking in the reactions of the other girls.

Ginny wheeled and glared at her daughter. "Why should you? They're just trying to bully us."

Emily didn't respond. Instead, she pleaded silently with the most heartbreaking expression I'd ever witnessed. I knew exactly how she was feeling. If Tara Crenshaw was the most popular girl in school, crossing her would mean social suicide. The same thing must have dawned on Ginny too, because instantly her expression softened and she backed away from Vivien and the coveted dress.

Taking the change in Ginny's demeanor as a sign of surrender, Vivien triumphantly marched over to Mrs. Busby and shoved the dress into her hands. "Like I said, Tara and I are on a tight schedule. I'm afraid we won't be able to be fitted for alterations until later this evening. Let's say, six thirty."

Mrs. Busby looked shell-shocked. "Six thirty?"

Hattie piped up. "I'm afraid we close at six tonight, Mrs. Crenshaw. You'll have to—"

Mrs. Busby held up her hand. "It's all right. I don't mind staying a little longer."

"But, Mama!" Vivien's daughter cut in. "I'm supposed to meet my friends at the library. We won't be done by six thirty."

"Don't interrupt," Vivien admonished, then turned back to Mrs. Busby with a slight nod. "It's all settled, then." She turned on her heel and headed for the door, Tara following behind and whining all the way about the appointment messing up her plans.

As soon as the door shut behind them, Ginny's hands shot to her hips and her chest heaved as she drew in a deep breath.

Emily tried to intercept her. "It's okay, Mama. Let's just go. We'll come back tomorrow and look for another dress."

But my fiery friend was never one to simply back down from a fight. With an exaggerated harrumph and a waggle of her shoulders, she started in with, "Well, I never . . . !" and continued on describing Vivien Crenshaw with a list of colorful adjectives that would threaten anyone's good standing with the local Baptists, finally finishing the tirade with something like, " . . . I sure hope that nasty, dress-stealing, backstabbing snob gets hers one day!"

A collective gasp sounded around the room followed by a moment of stunned silence. Emily looked like she wanted to crawl under a rock. This was definitely not social grace. "It's okay, everyone!" I assured the ladies, while trying to pull Ginny aside for a little chill time. "She's just been under a lot of pressure, that's all."

But Ginny shook me off and stomped toward the door, turning back at the last minute. "I meant what I said," she spat. Then she lifted her chin and announced with a murderous gleam in her eye, "That witch stole my girl's cotillion dress. And don't y'all think for one second that I'm going to stand for it, neither. You mark my words, I'll make sure that woman gets her due!"